PEACE IN MY HEART

The war is over, and Evie Talbert eagerly awaits the return of her three children from their evacuated homes. But her carefree daughters and son are barely recognisable — their education has been disrupted, the siblings split up, and the effect on them has been life-changing. Her son has developed serious behavioural problems, and with her daughters, there's jealousy and a nervous disorder that cannot be explained . . .

Evie's husband also has problems. Having returned from being in action, he suffers nightmares and fits of rage. He's no longer the gentle, quiet man Evie married. Peace may finally be here, but Evie's family is in shreds. Now she must rebuild a loving home to achieve the happiness she's always dreamed of . . .

FREDA LIGHTFOOT

◆

PEACE IN
MY HEART

Complete and Unabridged

MAGNA
Leicester

First published in Great Britain in 2017 by
HQ
An imprint of HarperCollins*Publishers* Ltd
London

First Ulverscroft Edition
published 2020
by arrangement with
HarperCollins*Publishers* Ltd
London

A catalogue record for this book is available
from the British Library.

ISBN 978–0–7505–4828–1

Published by
Ulverscroft Limited
Anstey, Leicestershire

Set by Words & Graphics Ltd.
Anstey, Leicestershire
Printed and bound in Great Britain by
T. J. International Ltd., Padstow, Cornwall

This book is printed on acid-free paper

1

May 1945

The celebrations for the end of the war had gone wild, the streets on VE Day packed with jubilant revellers all singing, dancing and laughing, much to Joanne's delight. There were rosettes, flags and bunting all around; lights on everywhere and a band playing. Her gaze shifted to the lilting waves as they lapped below the North Pier. She felt quite familiar with all the moods of the sea from gentle and benign, as it was today, to fiercely destructive when towering waves would fly over the promenade and small boats could be battered. Having adopted HMS *Penelope*, a ship the locals supported, they were devastated when it was tragically hit by a torpedo near Italy in 1944 and sank, killing 400 men. There had been a dreadful plane crash on Central Station and an air disaster in nearby Freckleton when a B-24 Liberator had crashed into the village school and houses killing over fifty people and dozens of children. The many airports had endured some problems throughout the war but the town had still welcomed holidaymakers in need of a little fun, and had generously provided accommodation to thousands of evacuees, including herself and her younger sister. Fortunately, Blackpool had suffered fewer disasters than many other places, certainly much less than Joanne's

1

hometown of Manchester. Life seemed to be rather like the sea, one moment calm and benevolent, the next cruel and harsh because of the horrors of war. But they'd found it a great place to live.

Thankfully the war was at last over, so hopefully things would improve. Looking out across the calm blue Irish Sea, the sandy beach was smooth and golden, stretching for some distance. Joanne had brought some sandwiches and cakes to contribute to the party they would all enjoy later. She'd even seen someone bring along a stack of odd-looking yellow pieces of fruit, which were apparently bananas, not something she'd ever tasted, and she greatly looked forward to savouring them.

'God save the King,' somebody called out. Cheers of joy met this cry, turning it into the national song.

Joanne glanced at her watch. Half past three. Her afternoon break would generally be almost over at this point. Lunchtime at the boarding house where they lived, the two landladies having cared for them this last three years, had been busy as usual with many wives having come to visit their RAF husbands. Joanne always looked forward to an hour or two of freedom in the middle of the afternoon when she could refresh herself in the sea air and sunshine. Those two dear sisters, Aunt Annie and Aunt Sadie, readily encouraged her to take a break, and today being one of celebration, there was no demand for her to rush back to work. No doubt they too were around somewhere enjoying this celebration. From where she stood on the promenade close to the Tower and the North Pier, Joanne watched her sister Megan happily dancing with Bernie, their landladies' nephew. He'd first asked Joanne but she'd politely declined, anxious to sit and wait for Teddy to come, knowing in her heart that she could love no man but this GI.

Oh, but why hadn't he arrived when he'd promised that he would, knowing she so enjoyed dancing with him? He was a most dapper and exciting GI, billeted in Garstang. Joanne did once visit him there to attend a dance at the village hall. She'd been shown around the camp, tripping along duckboards in her heeled shoes to view the Nissen huts, cookhouse and officers' mess. It was a bit of a dump, packed with gallon drums, jeeps, fuel; wet clothing hanging on hedges or trees to dry that didn't look at all proper. He'd taken her to see the tent where he and his mates were accommodated and had given her a cuddle and a kiss. She took care that he did no more than that, not wishing to be taken advantage of. Many girls were happy to lose their virginity with a man who could be killed in the war, something they felt they should not object to. Joanne was far more cautious being only seventeen, very young and innocent.

Oh, but how she loved him. These GIs were most attractive men and happy to come into Blackpool to visit one of the many pubs on the promenade, or enjoy the dancing at the Tower Ballroom, sometimes dressed as a civvie instead of in their uniform.

After the dance she and Teddy would often take a drink in a pub and she would sit on his lap for him to kiss and caress her, sending her senses skittering at the thrill of his touch. More often than not there were other girls hovering close by. Joanne paid them no heed, accustomed to the fact that these guys were never short of admirers, being popular men. And she was perfectly certain that Teddy viewed her as his favourite girl. Hadn't he told her so a million times?

So why wasn't he here on this special day? There was so much she felt the need to say to him now the war was over. Joanne gave a sigh and stood up, brushing away the sand that had blown onto her skirt.

When a hand lightly touched her shoulder she felt a frisson of recognition. He'd arrived at last. Instantly filled with pleasure and excitement, Joanne quickly turned to give him a hug, eager to welcome him while inside she felt in complete turmoil. Did she dare to tell this man how much she dreamed of a happy future together? 'Oh, Teddy, it's so wonderful to see you. This day of celebration is such a thrill. I've missed seeing you this last couple of weeks,' she softly told him.

He gave her a wink. 'I've missed you too, honey. All my mates are revelling in VE Day, so why wouldn't I do that too?' he blithely responded. 'It's a great cause for us guys who've worked hard for you Brits during the war.'

'Thankfully you've been spared the trauma that many have suffered. I'm so thrilled you are still fit and willing to join us.' Joanne felt utterly breathless. His face was mere inches from her own, so irresistibly close that her heart pummelled with anticipation. His sculpted mouth curled into an entrancing smile and she ached to taste it and stroke his soft cheeks. This handsome GI was so intoxicating, such a wonderful and fun man and no doubt a hero as many American troopers were.

As he stroked away a curl of her fair hair, his blue eyes gleaming with admiration, Joanne twinkled her gaze provocatively up at him, desperately hoping the sight of her in this new blue dress that hugged her figure in a most becoming way would captivate him. She'd clipped some of her blonde hair up on top of her head into rolled bangs and the rest fell neatly over her shoulder. She'd also patted her pale face with a little powder and wore a bright red lipstick, eager to look as attractive as possible.

As if recognizing this emotion in her he gave a wicked smile and kissed the tip of her nose. 'You're such a pretty girl, honey.' Then licking the soft curve of her upper lip, he slid his hand over her cheek and neck.

Blushing with delight at this compliment, Joanne found her breathing quicken under the thrill of his caresses. Seconds later she was held in his arms where she'd most longed to be during all these endless days of waiting to see him again. How fortunate she was to receive the attention he was giving her. His hands rested possessively around her back, his cheek lay against hers and he was pressing her hard against his tall, strong body to give her a passionate kiss. Her heart raced and she felt slightly giddy at the quiver of his tongue as it probed her mouth, the enticing warmth of him running through her like fire. Oh, how she adored him.

It was then that she became aware of a young woman standing close by. Doe-eyed and attractive, she was clinging fast to his arm. Shrugging her casually off, he whispered in Joanne's ear, 'Not too impressed with this festivity. Don't we usually slip away somewhere quiet on our own, which is far more entertaining, huh? Let's take a walk along the beach, honey.'

Joanne had always loved the time they'd spent walking barefoot on the beach together, holding hands and enjoying the comforting sounds of the sea. He would talk about his dreams for a new career once the war was over and she would happily listen, hoping to be a part of his plan. He'd also succeeded on numerous occasions to persuade her to join him in some quiet Nissen hut near Squire's Gate airport, or in his jeep, where they would hug and kiss. She felt completely smitten by his attention to her.

Today the promenade was packed with hundreds of folk having fun, plus horse-drawn carriages and GI jeeps scuttling around. Glancing across at her sister, who was now dancing with a young boy, she hesitated. Megan was still quite young, about to turn eleven come September. Being only five at the start of the war she had at first badly missed their mother and suffered much in the way of trauma. Mam had used to write to them quite regularly, but then there came a time that whenever she or Megan wrote to her they failed to receive a reply. They'd entirely lost contact with their mother, perhaps because she'd moved or was dead. Megan being something of a shy, awkward girl, greatly in need of care, was convinced their mother had lost interest in them. How could they know? Not certain they would ever find her again, Joanne thought of herself as a surrogate mother, so felt entirely responsible for looking after her sister.

Bearing all this in mind she should maybe stay close to her right now, but the loud sound of music playing was destroying all hope of her speaking to Teddy, which Joanne felt desperate to do. Walking along the beach would be much more private. Noting his admiring gaze fixed upon her, Joanne found the prospect of spending time alone with him far too irresistible to refuse. Giving him a nod, she said, 'I am looking forward to dancing with you but we could take a short walk first, although not too far.'

''Course not, honey.'

Giving the other young woman's furious expression a charming smile of apology, Joanne linked her arm with his and let him lead her away from the promenade down the steps to the beach. Would she now have the opportunity to ask the question she longed for an answer to? How to go about that was not easy to decide.

They walked for some distance along the beach close to the sea, feeling the coolness of tiny waves splashing against their feet, causing them to jump and giggle. Once they reached the quiet area below the North Pier, he leaned his back against a pillar and pulled her tightly into his arms. Joanne eagerly welcomed more of his

7

passionate kisses, giving a little sigh of pleasure as he slid his hands over her breasts and stomach. When he pushed her down onto the sand, tugged up her skirt to caress her thighs and pressed hard against her private parts, she squealed. Whether that was his hand or another part of him pressing into her she felt too naive to understand. A sense of panic overwhelmed her and, pushing him away, she gave him a frown, lightened with a small, fetching smile.

'Don't be naughty, Teddy, we aren't married. Although were you to ask me to go home with you to America to become your darling wife I might well say yes, having spent so many happy months with you and absolutely adoring you.'

Leaning back, he gave her a rueful smile. 'Oh my, how irresistible you are, sweet, shy and prudish little Joanne. I adore you too. Wish that could be possible.'

'Why would it not be?' It surprised her that he was accusing her of being prudish, considering what she'd just allowed him to do. Had she said the wrong thing by having finally admitted what she dreamed of and how much she loved him?

'We guys have to go through quite a long process to receive the necessary permission for that,' he said, giving a sparkling smile before he kissed her again, proving how the glory of his desire had lit a certainty within her that he was in love with her.

'Oh, I see. I should make it clear that when you manage to arrange our future together my young sister must also accompany me to America and remain a part of my life. You need

8

to understand how very much she depends upon me. I'm sure you will accept that as you have no wish to lose me,' she coyly remarked, giving him an enchanting smile. 'Will you write and let me know when you wish us to join you?'

'Hey, sure thing, honey. I'll give that some attention once I get back home, find a job and sort my life out.'

Excitedly waiting for more details of where he lived and when he was leaving, she was startled when a tribe of his pals suddenly appeared by his side and they started to punch and laugh at each other. The expression in his blue eyes now looked much more obsessed with these other Yanks than with her. He lifted her up in his arms, gave her a warm hug and one more kiss, smoothing his lips over hers, his tongue again dipping into her mouth. Then he whispered in her ear, 'Sorry, can't hang around any longer. We gotta go now!'

What he seemed to be saying did not fully register in the fuzz of emotion that clouded her brain. 'Oh, no, please don't go back to the camp yet. I want you to stay and dance with me on this day of celebration.'

After giving a burst of laughter, he said, 'I'm aware of your fondness for dancing, honey. It's been great to spend time with you. Have fun and enjoy life, now this blasted war is over.' He released her and flung his arms around his mates. Joanne felt a cold wind blow over her as she watched them race away then up the steps to the prom- enade, jump into a jeep and, giving her a wave, they drove away. It came to her in that terrifying moment that these GIs were not simply returning to the camp in Garstang or Warton Military Site where some of them were stationed, but heading back to the United States of America. And she had no notion of where Teddy lived in that far away country, since he'd been interrupted by his mates before getting round to giving her such detail.

Oh, what anguish Joanne felt at losing him. She could but hope he would write to her, knowing she lived with those dear landladies in Jubilee House, once he'd sorted his life out as promised. Or might he forget all about her? What a dreadful prospect. And having lost contact with her mother, as well as their dear brother Danny, uncertain whether either of them was alive or dead, Joanne worried that she might never find any love in her life ever again.

2

Evie, her niece Cathie and friend Brenda had together enjoyed the VE celebration for the end of the war. Many local merchant seamen had delivered food for the party, including non-rationed pork, which they'd happily roasted for everyone. What a treat that had been. Now the three of them were sitting in Campfield Market, each savouring a delicious custard tart. The outside market was bustling with people as always, today all chatting and laughing, singing and joking. Here, in the inside market at their favourite café, it was quiet and more relaxed, happily surrounded by smiling faces. Evie watched as a pretty young girl tried on a red felt wide-brimmed hat at Higginson's millinery stall, turning her head this way and that to admire herself in the mirror, perhaps her way of celebrating.

An ache punctuated her heart as Evie recalled how she'd seen very little of her son and even less of her daughters, Joanne and Megan, since they'd been evacuated. They had spent a brief spell at home back in 1940, when it had initially appeared to be a phoney war, but once the bombing started they were again evacuated.

At first they'd remained easily in touch and she'd gone to help her girls when concerned about the way they were being treated by one family they'd been billeted with. A short time

11

later she'd received no further letters from them to say where they were living, probably because they'd been moved around quite a bit. Evie had too, sadly losing their first home and had rented many other single rooms since. During the Christmas Blitz when one of the grain elevators had been bombed, buildings had collapsed and burned for days afterwards. Many mills and warehouses, including the one she'd worked for, had also suffered fires. How tragic that had been. It had turned into a nasty war, not least to lose touch with her daughters. She'd had to endure severe rationing, hard work at a different mill and the anguish of not knowing whether her missing husband was dead or alive. At times Evie's strong resilience had faded because of this heart-rending pain and exhaustion. Even now she felt a slur of anguish within her as she longed to have her family back. Would they too be enjoying this celebration?

'I'm aware this bloody war is still going on in the East, but I live in hope my son and daughters will all be home soon,' she stoutly announced. 'They've been gone over five years and I've missed them so much.'

'Haven't you seen them at all?' Cathie asked, looking stunned.

'My son Danny is in Cumberland where he's lived throughout the war. I've written to him regularly and did once pay a visit. It took twenty-four hours or more to get so far north with the train constantly halting. And the cost of the journey was considerable, not to mention finding local accommodation. Not an experience

I could afford to repeat. He was then moved out to a camp for some reason or other.'

'Oh, poor you. I've every sympathy with that, Aunty. And didn't you once tell me that you have to pay six shillings a week for their care?'

'Indeed I do, whenever I can afford to, although thankfully the Government has helped with that cost. Frustratingly, I've not received details for some years of exactly where my daughters are. I've spoken to our local billeting officer to ask him to investigate where they might have been moved to, presumably somewhere in Cumberland or Westmorland. He's agreed to look into that for me by contacting the volunteers who do this job in rural areas without pay,' she said, showing a slight tension in her smile of approval.

Reaching forward, her niece gave her hand a little squeeze. 'I'm sure they'll be located and soon be back in your care. Little Heather here is safe too, although as you know we've recently lost her mum, my beloved sister,' she said, tears suddenly flooding her eyes and rolling down her cheeks.

Evie gave a sad smile. 'I know, dearie. Such a tragedy that Sally should be killed in a road accident having survived this dratted war. Thanks to you this baby is indeed safe and well loved. And, as you know, I'm happy to help child-mind whenever necessary. Oh, it is a bit nerve-wracking when I think the last view of my children was when they too were still young. Now they are so much older I worry about how they'll react once they do come home. Will I even recognize them?'

Cathie's friend Brenda gave a little nod. 'I can understand your concern, Evie. When I was working in France with the *Oeuvre de Secours aux Enfants*, known as the OSE, many children who had lost touch with their parents developed problems and some had no wish to return home. They might have grown very fond of the family they'd been living with throughout the war, some suffered the loss of memory of their real parents, or their father could be dead and they'd no idea where their mother might be.' Brenda fell silent, making no mention of what she had suffered in France.

'Are you saying mine could accuse me of abandoning them?' Evie asked, filled with a burst of anxiety.

Brenda firmly shook her head. 'I'm sure yours were much safer than was the case in occupied France. Some suffered a heart-rending and difficult time there. Not at all easy for them. I'm sure your son and daughters will be eager to come home and see you, their beloved mother.'

'I do hope you're right.'

'Why would they not be when you're such a loving, caring person?' Cathie said. 'Your family has been much more fortunate than mine, despite the war. I wish you'd been my mum, instead of my own selfish mother who is always more interested in her string of lovers. Not to mention my absentee father, your brother, whom I haven't seen in years as he's apparently living somewhere abroad. But have you heard any news about dear Uncle Donald, your darling husband?

14

Could he be safe and well?'

A crease marred Evie's brow as she recalled the years of silence she'd endured after he'd been declared missing, constantly worrying over whether he would ever be found or presumed dead. Eventually she was informed that he'd been captured and was being held as a prisoner of war. Now she unfolded a letter and handed it over to her niece with a warm smile. 'I've recently had word that as an ex-PoW he's now in rehabilitation being cared for by the Civil Settlement Service. They are checking his health and helping him to recover. He's apparently a bit thin and worn out, but alive and will hopefully be home soon. How wonderful that will be. I can't wait to see him,' she said, her face a picture of joy. 'My dream is to have all my family together again. I do hope you're right, Brenda, and my son and daughters will be eager to come back home. I will pay attention to any possible problems they might have. Having no idea where they are, I shall go and speak to the billeting officer again, to see if he's found them.'

★   ★   ★

'I'm goin' to fall, sir. One more move and this mountain and I will part company,' Danny yelled. He was attempting to climb a mountain and a piece of rock had broken off somewhere below his right foot. He could feel his legs weakening, control oozing out of them.

'You're doing fine, Danny. Pull back. Your stomach is too close to the rock face. Look for a

15

hold. You're fourteen, not four. As you are so fond of telling us.'

'If I lean back I'll be into a skydive without a parachute.' Panic swelled and bubbled in his stomach. 'I daren't move me eyes let alone me 'ead.'

A chuckle came from below. 'There's a jug handle up there. Get your hand round that and you'll feel safe and secure again.' This advice came from the camp leader who was supposedly a gifted mountain instructor if dismissive of this climb, treating it as a small practice.

Danny, however, had a very different view. He could hardly believe this death-defying feat he was involved with, probably his last movement in this world. How could a mountain have a jug handle? He did know, of course, that this name was simply a label for a particular type of hold. But he'd give anything right now to be safely back in his tent enjoying a glass of milk, his mouth having gone dry with fear. In all the time he'd spent at this camp he'd made no attempt to learn how to climb. But he'd been bullied into taking part in this event. Now he clung on, shivering, knowing that if he was to stand any chance of being chosen as a team leader on the next walking expedition he had to make an extra-special effort. His fingers stretched out and curled around the jug handle, which did feel better, and he let out a sigh of relief.

'Now put your right foot where your left hand is and make ready to swing round and go backwards up the chimney.'

These instructions would have set him

laughing if he hadn't been too nervous of the results of such a foolish act.

'This rope is too slack. I'm jiggered, so take it up,' he yelled. 'Who is belaying me?' When the answer came from above he wished he hadn't asked.

'It's me-ee. Yet again I have you in my power.' This comment was followed by a much-exaggerated imitation of a wolf howling.

Danny saw a smirk of satisfaction on Willie's face. Why had he stupidly agreed to come on this climb, which made him feel a complete and utter fool? He could never trust this alleged old friend who'd become so domineering and bad-tempered due to a disagreement and row they'd had some years ago. He'd been a pain ever since because of what he'd done back then. At first Danny had been billeted on a farm, which he'd loved. It had been hard work with one or two problems but he'd enjoyed roaming around the countryside, milking cows and feeding chickens. Willie had lived nearby and when charged with some petty crime of nicking fruit and veg, he'd insisted that he was only helping Danny look for stuff to eat and sell. They'd both been sent to this camp, classed as problem boys.

Since then this nasty liar frequently ordered him to do all manner of jobs or stupid tasks that Willie had no wish to be involved in, demands Danny had to accept to avoid being beaten. Or else he'd find his food messed up by Willie spitting in it. Now he'd got him into this mess, a climb he was making far worse than it should be. It felt as if this bully was wielding the power of life or death over him. Holding a knife in his hand and chortling with laughter, he looked as if he might cut the rope upon which Danny was hanging then drop him off the mountain.

The voice of the camp leader penetrated into his head, again giving him careful instructions. 'Concentrate on what you are doing, laddie. Keep your weight on your feet. Don't reach too high with your hand or you'll lose your balance. Then move one foot at a time.'

Giving a tug, Danny pulled himself up through the so-called chimney but then came the last part — a nasty overhang. He felt his stomach heave into a dark hole of terror. If this practice pitch of fifty feet was so difficult, how did anyone ever have the nerve to climb a big mountain such as Scafell? And how could he be sure he'd survive? He strived not to assume he would suffer a possible disaster, telling himself that he must prove he had the courage to do whatever was required of him. Searching for a hold without the help of his stomach, let alone the unreliable strength of his limbs, he jammed every toe and finger into the minute cracks he could find and hung on to them, silently praying. He'd be so much happier on level ground, or preferably no higher than the bottom rung of a very wide ladder. But he had no intention of being beaten by this rocky crag. Gritting his teeth, Danny swung up his right foot and stuck it on a wide fissure of rock, rather like a long split in a bread roll. Now he just had to get his bottom round, his left foot up and — aah! His feet jerked and slipped off the ledge. The view of the countryside tilted around and a cold sweat broke out over him. Was this the moment he'd die?

'Help!' he yelled.

The jerk of the rope tied to his climbing belt felt almost worse than the slip. Knowing how a person could fall twenty feet in one second, he felt deeply grateful for this safety rope that the camp leader always attached in these practice climbs, in addition to the belay. Fortunately, Danny had fallen less than two feet, his nails managing to find contact with a crack in the rock face. Tearing himself up in a fury of panic, he dived over the top as if the devil himself was on his backside. Once he'd recovered from the initial effects of the shock, unhooked himself from the rope and pulled off his safety helmet, he flung himself at Willie to start belting him.

'Yer a nasty wiry worm! Stop bloody attacking me the whole damn time.'

Within seconds they were fighting. Willie thumped Danny much harder and more brutally, being fatter, taller, stronger and nastier than him. 'Do as I flamin' well tell you,' he roared.

Growing taller and stronger, Danny felt the need to defend himself more, following years of bullying. It was only when they saw the camp leader reach the top of the climb that they pulled away from each other. Danny gasped for breath; all too aware he'd probably collected yet more bruises, as had happened to him so often in the past.

'It was just a joke, what I did. I'll make sure you regret having hammered me,' Willie snarled as he stalked off, leaving Danny spitting with fury. How could he believe he'd done the wrong thing when this bastard was constantly harassing him? Willie Mullins had made his life a thousand times more difficult and painful throughout this dratted war. How he longed to be rid of him and ached to be back home with his mam, whom he sorely missed, as well as his sisters. According to the camp leader that wasn't going to happen until the war in the East also ended, the Government having no wish to risk danger for evacuees.

Unfortunately, Willie too lived in Castlefield, both of them having attended the same school even though he was two years older than him, so when that did happen Danny could but hope he'd manage to stay well clear of him, now he too was almost grown up.

3

When Joanne and Megan returned to the boarding house where they happily lived, they found it packed with soldiers. These comprised Polish aircrew, as well as many of their wives and children who had come to visit their husbands, always welcome thanks to these kind landladies. On this occasion everyone was happily engaged in watching a performance of brightly lit puppets before a curtain strung across part of the dining room, the children in particular excitedly laughing and enjoying the show. Joanne guessed the man creating this show would be Tomasz, a dapper young Polish man with fuzzy dark brown hair. He would often sing, play music or perform a mime, acting out a story with no speech but lots of clever movement. He was most gifted and great fun. Soon, he and his Polish colleagues would all be gone, and Joanne could see by the joy in this group how they were all looking forward to returning home. Not something she could expect to happen for herself and her sister.

Striving to block out the fears for their uncertain future, Joanne grabbed an empty tray of plates and carried it briskly to the kitchen. Aunt Annie was busily boiling kettles on the stove to make tea. Aunt Sadie stood at the table, slicing bread to make more sandwiches. This younger sister, in her mid-fifties was a small, round-faced lady with a plump nose, her piercing dark eyes guarded by tiny spectacles, her black hair firmly clipped up. As always, she was tidily dressed in a long dark skirt, a white blouse and a huge apron, her stockinged feet held in a neat pair of strapped flat shoes.

Joanne dashed to help by starting to chop Spam and lay slices onto the bread 'We've had a lovely time today on the promenade and, of course, have enjoyed living here in Blackpool these last few years.'

Giving her a warm smile, Sadie said, 'I remember the happy day we met you in that centre on Whitegate Drive early in 1942. You were such lovely little girls, if looking rather tired and sad, poor little Megan constantly weeping. How could we resist taking you in?'

'We greatly appreciated that. Now I can't get my mind round to leaving here and moving back to Manchester. I would sorely miss this town and you two caring ladies.'

'Don't fret, dear. We'll miss you too when you leave but once that happens you can come and visit us any time you wish. Our work will thankfully calm down soon, although I shall miss spending each afternoon knitting scarves and rugs, soldiers no longer being in need of them, the war now over.'

Quietly piling the sandwiches onto the tray, having little appetite for food herself right now, Joanne gave a tremor of a smile. She was highly appreciative that Aunt Sadie's efforts to support the troops had been a most important part of this lovely lady's life, as it was for her sister, Aunt Annie. They were also most supportive and

22

kindly towards herself and Megan, as this conversation highlighted. But she had no wish to reveal the anguish she'd just gone through by losing the GI she adored. 'My mam always loved knitting too, plus sewing and lacemaking. Not that I've seen anything she's made in years, let alone any sight of her. Who knows if I ever will again.'

'I'm sure you will, dear.'

Joanne met her sympathetic gaze with speculation in her own. It was then that Megan burst through the kitchen door in a cloud of steam, her cheeks scarlet because of the heat of her surroundings as well as her fury. 'If that RAF chap won't keep his hands off tapping my bottom, I'll land him a smack on his ear.'

Aunt Annie, older and taller with similar coloured hair, eyes and spectacles to her sister, let out a heavy sigh, clearly realizing who she was referring to. 'He's probably just a bit drunk on this day of celebration and was only teasing you, lass. Not all men are a problem, although the odd one can sometimes enjoy marlicking about on occasion. Ideally, I should mebbe chuck that fellow out and be in possession of a vacant room come dinnertime. However, he's a man very much in charge, visiting some of the troops and paid to stay here by the Government so there's nowt I can do about that.'

'He's no right to touch me,' Megan tartly remarked. 'I don't like men at all.'

'Quite right, love. Go and have a rest up in your room and keep well away from all these drunken chaps. That would be wise. I'll have a quiet word with that Wing Commander Ramsbotham, silly fool that he is.'

Excusing herself with a spirited smile, Aunt Annie pushed up her sleeves and marched off to the dining room, a fierce look in her eyes as she prepared to do battle with this offender. What a character she was, and very meticulous. She had no intention of waiting hand, foot and finger on other folk's whims and peccadilloes, appreciating the fruitlessness of such behaviour. Folk in this boarding house had to behave themselves or they were dispatched elsewhere, in spite of these landladies' care and concern. Joanne knew that this dear lady was of the opinion that the amount the Government paid for the soldiers and other military personnel who occupied rooms here, which didn't match the amount of money they earned from tourists, at times left them a bit short of cash.

Joanne gave Megan a quick cuddle, aware that she hadn't found it easy being an evacuee with no mother present to comfort her, and having been constantly moved around because of ill treatment they'd suffered at times. At least they'd been fortunate to happily live here in Blackpool these last three years. She watched with a smile as her sister stamped off upstairs, knowing that she was not required to do any work, being far too young. She'd no doubt happily go and read or draw, as she so loved to do. Joanne didn't at all mind working for these lovely ladies, really quite enjoying it, but she felt that their lives were in complete turmoil. What on earth would happen to them now?

The next morning, having suffered a sleepless night quietly weeping over her loss, Joanne anxiously worried that Teddy might never write and arrange for her to join him. She felt herself engaged in a world she no longer wished to be a part of. Not that life throughout the war had been at all easy, with bombs falling and sirens screaming and wailing. Now, wiping the tears from her eyes, she got out of bed and found that she'd tossed that new blue dress she'd bought for the special VE Day celebration onto the floor the previous evening. She gazed in dismay at the creased fabric, parts of it torn and marked with brown stains, perhaps because Teddy had pushed her down on the wet sand under the pier. What exactly had he done to her? A part of her shook with fear; not at all clear about that. Could her life be ruined as well as this frock?

'What's troubling you, sis? I heard you crying last night. Do tell me what's wrong,' Megan whispered, looking deeply distressed.

'I've just damaged my new frock,' Joanne remarked, not wishing to discuss the truth of her distress. She'd never spoken about her feelings for Teddy, preferring to keep their relationship private.

'Oh no, what a nuisance and we had such a fun time yesterday.'

How dare she deny that? Panic pulsated through her, making Joanne feel badly in need of Megan's comfort. Should she tell her more or keep what happened a secret? All possibility of making that decision vanished when Aunt Annie politely opened the door to ask Joanne if she would please start serving breakfast to their guests.

'Of course,' she said. After quickly dressing, she tossed the dress aside and dashed off downstairs to take part in her usual morning chores.

Later that afternoon, Annie handed the dress back to her, suitably repaired. 'Megan told me of your problem. You looked such a pretty girl wearing this frock yesterday, I've cleaned and mended it for you, dear.'

'Oh, thank you, Aunt Annie,' Joanne said. 'What a wonderfully kind and helpful lady you are.' Tears spurted and ran down her cheeks, making her feel desolate and low. She feared that her heart could break having lost the man she loved. He'd told her how pretty she was, making no mention of what he felt for her, something she hadn't noticed at the time. 'I do so appreciate your care for us, particularly having lost our mam. Heaven knows whether she's still alive, let alone any other members of our family. Being unable to find our parents, I do feel in a state of bewilderment, wondering where we could possibly live, were we to return to Manchester.'

Annie put her arms around Joanne, giving her a pat and a hug. 'Our local billeting officer knows where you are, therefore I'm sure you'll hear from her soon, lovey.'

How could that happen when their mother had no idea in which town her daughters were now living? Nor had they any idea where she was living either. If they ever did hear from her,

26

Joanne wondered if Megan would be at all interested in going back home? And would she personally find the courage to tell her mam she'd fallen in love with a GI and how she ached to go to America to join him, rather than go home to Manchester? In addition to finding their mam and dad, would she ever find Danny, their brother, whom Joanne believed no longer lived with the farmer who first took him in. Receiving no response from him either when she'd written to say where they'd been moved to, following their departure from that area in Keswick, Joanne wondered whether he'd been sent some place else. What a muddle their lives were in. Where and when would their family ever meet up?

★ ★ ★

Danny was involved in taking a hike with a small group of friends around Derwentwater, a crystal glass lake. Not a breath of wind stirred in the heat of the day. How he loved this beautiful area of Keswick and the magical panoply of fold upon fold of mountains in a landscape that seemed to stretch into infinity. The ribbon of this dusty track linking the skeins of drystone walls could lure him to venture onward and upward into the unknown, were he free to roam. Far away in the distance were the hills of Scotland and the Solway Firth. Here, as they walked on through a copse of tall trees, he admired the awesome sight of Blencathra, a proud, benevolent mountain.

Many travellers, as well as themselves as young-sters, were urged into climbing these beautiful

27

peaks to celebrate their fitness, including Grisedale Pike, Helvellyn, the highest giant, and the mysterious Castlerigg Stone Circle. The presence of these brooding mountains always enthralled him even when they were loaded with snow, or wet grey clouds. The mountains often appeared sullen but today were filled with a benign merriness of sunny beauty. How happy it made him feel despite often having heard the sound of bombing over by the coast.

The war had started well for him, living and working on that friendly farm close to Blencathra until Willie Mullins had messed things up for him. He now worked part-time for a farmer close to the camp and still enjoyed walking if not climbing, having suffered an attack by Mullins. Thankfully, that selfish lad was too lazy to be interested in joining them today so he was free of yet more pestering. A part of Danny felt he'd like to stay out here in the countryside for ever, while another part of him ached to return to his parents in Manchester.

It was when they returned to camp that he was called to the camp leader's office, shocked to hear himself accused yet again of stealing fruit and veg from a local farmer. Horrified, he loudly protested. 'It weren't me, sir. I never steal nowt. I'm innocent, having happily worked for this farmer for some time. Why would I pinch owt off him and risk losing my part-time job? It were more likely Willie Mullins what stole it. He allus puts the blame on me, as he so likes to do for owt he pinches.'

The camp leader glared at him, sour-faced

and disbelieving. 'What proof do I have of that? I found a box of food close to your bed and Willie confirmed that you'd committed that theft, always complaining you were short of food. That young lad was also marked with bruises, admitting that when he'd challenged you about this crime you'd started a fight.'

'That's a lie!' Danny snapped. 'He must have hidden it there. I certainly didn't. We had a fight when he tried to drop me off the cliff we were climbing. He's the one who eats too much and steals things, not me. I'm not a bloody thief.'

The leader gave a snort of disbelief. 'I do not approve of bad language or arguments, lad. I appreciate you two do not get on terribly well. No doubt you fight him in order to keep him silent, as you've no desire to be charged with this theft. Fortunately, I have no wish to call the police, which would damage our reputation even worse than yours. You must simply apologize to that farmer and politely return this fruit and veg.'

'I'll not apologize for summat I didn't do.'

'Then you will suffer a suitable punishment,' he sternly remarked.

To his utter dismay, Danny then found himself locked in the coal cellar below the leader's office, a stark and dreadful place. Close by the room in which he was confined, he could hear the barking of a bad-tempered bull terrier who lived chained to the wall. In the past Willie would constantly insist that he must be the one to come down here to collect the coal needed for the huts, which Danny had always found pretty

29

scary. That dog would growl and attempt to pounce or bite him, unless he possessed a scrap of food to divert its attention. Now he had nothing to offer and could but pray he'd be kept clear of that dog and be freed soon.

He lay on a cold bed with one blanket for the rest of that day and night, his mind dreaming of his mother, father and sisters. Joanne and Megan had lived quite close to him for a while but then had been moved on, where to or why he'd no idea, never having received a letter from them since he too had been moved. At times he felt very lonely and worried about ever finding them. He did receive the occasional letter from his mother and sometimes a parcel of comics as if he was still a young boy, which he nevertheless quite enjoyed, *The Beano* and *The Dandy* being his favourites. There'd not been any word from his father, or any mention of him at all from his mam. How he missed his family.

It was the following morning, when Danny was finally released and provided with a most welcome scrambled egg breakfast, that the camp leader came trotting over to hand him a letter, a smirk of a grin on his face. 'Good news, laddie. Be aware that once the war in Japan is over, permission will be granted by the Government for you to be taken home to Manchester by train. Willie here, your old classmate, will go too. So make sure you improve your friendship, laddies. Not that I'll miss either of you when that time comes,' he said with a chuckle. He patted each of them on the back and walked away to leave them sitting scowling at each other.

This news gave Danny hope he'd be back with his family soon, once this war had finally ended. Or did he wish to stay here in this beautiful countryside? Not right now. He'd completely gone off that idea.

4

In the weeks following, Jubilee House became less packed than it used to be. Many of the civil servants, military personnel and refugees had left, some finding jobs or transport to take them back home thanks to the local authorities. Still not having received any letter from Teddy, Joanne badly regretted not being invited to join him in America. He was so far away she sorely missed him, all hope of a future together rapidly fading. She was no longer convinced that he loved her. Perhaps he just enjoyed having sex with women, including that one hanging on to his elbow, so maybe he'd assumed he could have it with her too. Not at all certain what he'd done to her and whether he'd succeeded in seducing her, being fairly innocent on such matters, Joanne deeply worried that she might have a serious problem as a result. It really didn't bear thinking about.

Gazing through the breakfast-room window as she cleared the tables, puffs of bright clouds bounced over the sea that shivered with white waves, looking beautiful as always. How it reminded her of the time she'd spent walking on the beach with Teddy, constantly kissed and fondled by him. Oh, and her love for that GI was so strong she still ached for him to write and offer to marry her. That would resolve this possible problem she had and make her future so much happier.

'We've still not received any letter from our

mother,' Megan whispered, as she came to help with the washing-up. 'So can we stay here?'

'I've been struggling to decide that too. We need to think what we should do with our lives now this war is over. Once we've finished our morning jobs we'll take a cycle ride to Stanley Park then enjoy a walk around, since it's a Saturday and you're not at school today.'

'That would be lovely, sis. It ain't gonna be an easy decision to make.'

'Don't worry, we'll talk things through, love.'

Breakfast being over, Joanne spent the next hour clearing and collecting cups and dirty plates, bustling back and forth, the two landladies upstairs busily dealing with bedrooms and bathrooms. The small dining room now empty, she gave that a clean too and set the tables in preparation for dinner. Once that was done, she went upstairs to tell Megan she was ready to go and they put on their cardigans and strong shoes then went to fetch their bicycles from the shed in the backyard.

'We'll cycle along Chapel Street then Hornby Road to the gateway to the park. I'll just check the tyres.'

While pumping them up, she saw Bernie, the landladies' nephew, hovering by the kitchen door. Having only just turned eighteen, he'd thankfully been too young to be called up during the war, but had worked with the local Home Guard. They'd become reasonably good friends over the years but he was a bit boring in Joanne's opinion, very much a gawky boy with a spotty complexion. Admittedly, his square face was now much smoother, with thick brown hair flopping over his brow, if still a little scrawny in build. There was a neat smartness about the clothes he wore now. They could be quite appealing and at times his grey eyes would hold a hint of shrewdness in their depth. But he was not exactly fun, exciting or good at jokes. Just quiet and conventional with strong ties to his aunts and the work he did for them, often helping with the cooking and various other tasks. Joanne had felt obliged to dance with him after Teddy had disappeared that day. Not something she had any wish to do again, never having viewed him as a possible love of her life. With a start, she realized he had caught her staring at him. Filled with embarrassment, she quickly turned away but not before she had noted how his expression looked most doting, which struck her as extremely odd.

'If you're off on a cycle ride, can I come with you?' he asked politely.

After giving Bernie an indifferent smile, Joanne pointed out they were going off to have a private conversation.

'You aren't planning to leave us like these refugees and other guests, are you?' he said, looking dismayed at such a prospect.

'It's difficult to decide what we should do so we need to talk it through. Speak to you later, Bernie.'

He watched them ride away with a gloomy expression on his face.

★ ★ ★

34

Stanley Park was filled with a fine mist, swirling about like a bolt of gossamer silk. Not that this blocked the sound of aircraft landing in the aerodrome just beyond what had once been the bowling pitch. After locking up their bikes close to the café, the two girls set off to walk round the lake in order to escape the noise. The cool wind gathered momentum and turned into a dampening shower, the sting of rain on Joanne's face making her feel this dreadful weather was adding to her sense of agony. Would she ever recover?

The time she'd spent with Teddy had once seemed so sweet and filled with hope. Now all that had vanished since he still hadn't written to her. Being young and having behaved most foolishly in trusting him, Joanne thought she might never trust any man ever again, let alone find the happiness she longed for. She felt miserable and sluggish, constantly rushing to the bathroom fearing she could be sick. Fortunately, that hadn't happened so far, but she had very little appetite and was rapidly losing weight. Each night in bed she would quietly weep from the sadness of her lost love and her parents, which made her feel completely torn apart. Sensing that her heart could break, tears again spurted in her eyes and ran between her fingers as she attempted to wipe them away. Looking shocked, Megan quickly led her to sit on a bench.

'What's wrong, why are you crying again, sis? What is it that's worrying you?'

When her tears were spent Joanne sat for a moment in silence, feeling rather like a small mouse caught up in the rumble of sound from the aerodrome as they sat beneath this ash tree. It was then that she saw a squirrel emerge from a branch above her, its small sleek body glinting as it nibbled insects when the rain stopped and there came a bright glimmer of sun, no nuts anywhere around. It scampered down and dashed off to nearby fields, scavenging for fruit and vegetables, rather like a greedy thief stealing what didn't rightly belong to him. They both burst into laughter. Thankfully she wasn't a mouse or a squirrel, although possibly a foolish young girl. Taking a deep breath, Joanne finally confided in her sister the misery she felt in losing her American boyfriend, carefully making no mention of what he did to her.

'Ah, I thought that might be why you weren't looking good or eating well and keep weeping each night in bed,' Megan responded fondly. 'Do try to cheer up, lovey. Mebbe that GI will write to you one day.'

'Oh, I do hope he does, once he's settled in back home and found himself some employment. It could take a while for him to go through the necessary process he mentioned.' A long delay was proving to be a strong element of concern, in fact something of a panic, not having had a period this month. If Teddy truly did love her and was doing his best to arrange for her to join him, he would surely write or maybe come looking for her one day, which would probably be here in Blackpool. Another good reason for them to stay on here. Her life then would be so much happier. Right now it could go completely

36

wrong and Joanne had no wish to speak of this problem to her sister. 'I must learn to be patient and cheer up,' she said with a smile.

Giving her another warm hug, Megan went on to speak of her personal delight at being offered a place at a local high school, come September, and her wish to attend. 'To be honest, I've no desire to leave our lovely aunts or lose the offer from that school. Would you be willing to give up this job and return home? I do hope not,' she stoutly declared. 'I desperately want to stay here, being the only place I've enjoyed throughout the war.'

A flicker of sadness and sympathy washed over Joanne. At the start of the war, Megan had been petite and shy, rather awkward and unsure of herself, feeling far too young to cope with the trauma of evacuation. Now she was a comely girl with a round, pretty face and a dimpled smile. Really quite bright so did deserve to attend that high school. And it was perfectly understandable that she was happy living with these landladies, feeling very much cared for. Things had been so different for them in the past.

When they'd first been evacuated out to a bleak part of Keswick back in 1939, they were made to stand and wait at the railway station whilst the local people decided whom they were prepared to offer accommodation to. Being working class and a bit scruffy looking after that long journey, they were the last to be chosen. Her brother Danny, aged only eight at the time, had been selected by a farmer while she and Megan were chosen by another farming couple.

Joanne had protested, claiming that being siblings they should stay together, but the billeting officer had ordered her to keep quiet. Having no idea where her brother was sent, she'd written to her mother, hoping Evie could discover that, which she did.

Joanne and Megan had hated the farm they were originally taken to, being treated like slaves and required to work hard on the land. If they didn't do as they were told they'd be deprived of the poor food they were granted only twice a day. They'd felt constantly hungry, often being given only bread and dripping for their evening meal. Nor were they ever allowed into the house. They had to sleep in a barn, sharing a small makeshift bed on the dirt floor with no heat or light save for a single candle. There was no toilet or bathroom available, just a potty, which they had to empty every morning. Each day they would rise early and have to walk miles to school, no lift by horse or cart ever offered them. When it was bitterly cold weather they'd frequently fall ill with colds, their hands chilblained. Joanne came to believe they'd been accepted as evacuees simply to provide those greedy people with money paid by the Government, as well as the work they required them to do.

'Do you remember the problems and anguish we suffered at that first place we were billeted?' Joanne asked.

'Only vaguely,' Megan admitted.

'Well, each month Mam would send us comics and parcels of food, and a warm scarf or jumper she'd knitted for us. I was always excited to see a parcel arrive then felt utterly furious when that couple handed it over to their own children, never to us. I frequently wrote home to explain this horror to Mam, then realized my letters were withheld by that farmer's wife, which was why I never received a reply. I did finally manage to send her a letter, thanks to our local teacher who gave me an envelope and stamp and posted it for me in town. I told Mam that if we weren't moved somewhere better, we'd run away.'

Megan gave a frown. 'I do remember your excitement when you saw Mother standing outside in the yard one day. I found that amazing.'

'I was filled with joy,' Joanne said with a loving smile. 'I dashed straight over; realizing Mam had come to rescue us. I threw our clothes into a suitcase within minutes. She was, of course, engaged in a furious row with our so-called foster parents and then marched us off.'

'She walked us for miles to find a bus and a train. We then went home but didn't stay long as we were soon evacuated again,' Megan said, pulling her face in a glower of disapproval at how their mother had sent them back to Keswick and what happened as a result. Something her beloved sister had no wish to speak of or remember. 'I agree we've been through an absolute nightmare and never seen her since. Thankfully these two kind landladies, Aunt Annie and Aunt Sadie, took us in when we were brought here to Blackpool, and are most kind and welcoming.'

'They are indeed.' On certain occasions, whenever she'd felt herself or Megan were badly treated, Joanne had gone to see the local billeting officer and insisted they should be moved. Eventually they'd been billeted here in Blackpool, which had proved to be a good thing. 'I suspect they gladly took us in because they aren't married and have no children of their own, just Bernie, their adopted nephew. However, you need to be aware that these landladies may no longer wish us to continue living with them, occasionally mentioning a wish to retire.'

'Oh, surely that won't happen.'

'We should bear in mind that it might.'

They went on to talk at some length, worrying over where they could go and live if that occurred, having no conviction they would ever find their mother. Joanne still missed her badly and felt in need of her support. Making a decision about whether or not they should leave was not proving to be at all easy. And brooding about her own problem would do no good either.

Joanne gave a sad little sigh. 'The question is, will the billeting officer send us back to Manchester now the war is over? Will he find where Mam is living, assuming she's still alive, or put us in a state children's home? Not a prospect I wish to consider. I'll make some enquiries and see if I can find out where she is. If not, I could pay a visit to Manchester and search for her by calling on various friends who may have an idea where she's now living or working.'

'If you succeed, we still have to decide if we really do want to go back home, wherever that may be. As I say, I'm not certain I do,' Megan stated firmly. 'Your love for our mam is fairly

40

obvious, but sadly I have very little memory of her. And convinced she may have deliberately neglected us, I very much prefer the affection I feel for these two landladies we think of as our aunts.'

'Mam was always most caring so why would we not be pleased to see her again?' Joanne stated gently. 'Don't worry, lovey, she could probably find you a good high school in Manchester. I'll most definitely look into finding her but right now we'd best head back to Jubilee House and happily stick with living here.' Stepping out with fresh vigour, they collected their bikes and cycled back. A warm breeze ruffling her hair, Joanne felt a comforting glimmer of determination and fresh hope.

5

It was a Friday afternoon when Evie and several of her women colleagues were instructed to visit the boss in his office. She happily went arm in arm with two of her friends, Enid Wilson and Lizzie Parkin. 'We may be granted a rise in pay now the war is over,' she said.

Enid gave a grin. 'Let's hope so. We definitely deserve that after all the work we've done.'

'And Mr Eccles is generally a pleasant man, though a bit depressed having lost his brother and son,' Lizzie whispered.

Seated at his desk, Mr Eccles failed to meet their happy smiles by keeping his gaze fixed upon his clasped hands. 'I do thank all you ladies for the excellent work you've done throughout the war. I must now release you from these labours in order to give preference to our return-ing soldiers. Your task is over so you are free to retire, being no longer required to do your bit.'

Panic reverberated through Evie. Blast and damn this mill owner, such a goddam-son-of-a-bitch. He probably cared more about men than women now the war was truly over. Her friends stood frozen in silence, no doubt aware they had no right to object to these soldiers being sorely in need of a job. But they too badly required an income, as did she. Tears spilled down her cheeks. Why would they sack her, considering the problems she was facing? Evie suspected that

42

when Donald arrived home he would not be fit enough to work and she would still have three children to protect and care for, or so she hoped. How on earth would she manage that without an income coming in? 'You surely can't be serious,' she sternly remarked.

Finally meeting her furious gaze with a sympathetic smile, he said, 'This war is over, so you dear ladies must now concentrate upon your domestic duties. The textile industry is not doing particularly well at the moment but soldiers, sailors and airmen on their way home will obviously require their old jobs back. You can work to the end of this month then must collect your final wages and card when you depart. I can but apologize for reality.' He then ordered them to return to their looms.

As they all walked unsteadily out of the office, Evie heard some of the women start to grumble to each other, some weeping, others looking shocked and dismayed. They did very little in the way of weaving for the rest of that day, as they kept sharing the worry of where else they might find employment. According to the general conversation buzzing around throughout the day, it was clear that other factories had also laid off women workers, so new jobs would not be easy to find considering the high number of unemployed and the return of so many men from the war.

When their shift ended and Evie walked home with her two friends, Enid said, 'How on earth can I continue to pay the rent without a wage coming in?'

Evie informed them that her niece too had lost

43

her job at the tyre factory. 'She's sought jobs at various shops, warehouses and factories, explaining her skills and experience as a result of the war, but so far has received no offer anywhere. I can but hope that if we look hard enough we will succeed, bearing in mind we too have considerable experience after all these years of hard work we've done.'

'I do hope so,' Lizzie agreed. 'I've lost my husband but not my childer, so need to keep earning a living.'

'Me too,' Evie said. 'Although my husband will be home soon, he won't be at all well.'

'We should have seen this coming as many of those brave soldiers do deserve their jobs back,' Enid muttered. 'I'd never got around to thinking how that might affect us. Nor did I expect it to happen so quickly.'

Listening to her two friends, Evie felt a sickness soak within her, not convinced she would succeed in finding employment. She felt entirely numb and stormed back to her one-bedroomed flat in a fine old temper. She slammed the door closed, flung her coat on the floor in a veritable rage. Clenching her fists, she drummed them against the kitchen wall, feeling absolute despair. One minute she'd been celebrating the end of this war, now she felt apprehension ricocheting through her at the prospect of a woeful future.

Over the next few days, whenever Evie's shift was over she went in search of employment, initially striving to find work in another factory, warehouse or mill, which she would prefer. No one was interested in taking her on, being a mere

44

woman, even though Evie had worked hard all her life in various cotton mills. She'd always started at seven each morning, involved with Egyptian cotton and testing it with her thumb. Some of it was often a bit rough and infested with fleas. After being spun and woven they'd be washed out in the bleaching process. Now the textile industry was in a slump. Knitting, sewing and lacemaking were also hobbies she enjoyed doing, having been taught by her mother when she was a young girl. It crossed Evie's mind that working for herself might prove to be less of a hassle. But would it earn her sufficient money? Probably not. With a sigh, she went on to search for alternative jobs in shops and department stores, including Kendal Milne, Lipton's and Maypole grocers, as had Cathie and Brenda. She failed to receive an offer from any of them. Even young men returning from the war were struggling to find employment, the state of the country not being in a good condition. Post-war life seemed to be falling apart.

As well as searching for a job, she was also desperately in need of a home suitable for her family. Not that finding a property here in war-torn Manchester would be easy either. An absolute nightmare. As a consequence of the 1940 Christmas Blitz and enemy bombers coming night after night, Hardman Street, Lower Byrom Street, a part of Duke Street, Piccadilly and many others had been attacked and were now pretty derelict, houses burned out by incendiary bombs. There was little sign of much in the way of repairs being done yet, let alone any new builds.

It came to Evie one day that the solution could be to ask the tackler in charge of the looms in her part of the mill if he could help to get her old job back. Harold Mullins was not an easy man but would surely understand the difficulties she was facing. Tragically his wife Jane, once a friend of hers, had been killed early in the war, no doubt as a result of the bombing. His son Willie had been evacuated with Danny, since they'd both attended the same school when they were young. Surely Harold Mullins was a great believer in the cotton industry, as was she, despite the hard times they were facing? Calling to see him back at the mill, Evie asked if they could have a word. 'I'm sorely in a quandary over how to resolve my problem of finding a new job, so wondered if you could help me get this one back or offer me some advice.'

Giving her a blink of interest, he agreed. 'Aye, we could 'appen meet up at the Dog and Duck at seven this evening. I'm not against that.'

This was not at all what she'd expected, assuming they could just talk here at the mill, but it didn't seem appropriate to refuse to meet him there.

★ ★ ★

Evie arrived early and, sitting in this public house near Potato Wharf, ordered herself a glass of shandy, all too aware of the disapproving glances from the men standing at the bar. Women were not supposed to attend pubs on their own so would Mullins, the gaffer, actually arrive and be willing to help

46

her? He hadn't sounded too convincing but then he never did, always a man more obsessed with himself. Gazing out of the window, she saw a bustle of people hurrying along the street, rain splashing over their unwary legs, car horns hooting at them if they attempted to rush across the road. The weather seemed to suit the bad news she'd received in losing her job and the brickwork looked battered and black with smoke, as a result of the dreadful bombing that Manchester had suffered over these last six years.

She recalled how much lovelier the Dog and Duck had been when she was a young girl and used to come here with Donald. Being her boyfriend, they'd sit, cuddled together, to enjoy a drink or a little snack. In those days she'd had clear skin, honey-gold hair, brown eyes as rich and dark as velvet with long, curling lashes. Now she felt wrinkled and worn out, with a core of anxiety she was doing her utmost to hide. What state would Donald be in when he finally came home? Would he still be the gentle, quiet man she'd fallen in love with and happily married, or listless and with health difficulties as a consequence of the anguish of war and his years held as a prisoner? He certainly wouldn't be well enough to work — a fact she must make clear to Mullins.

She was aware that in addition to the war issue of employing ex-soldiers, the mill owner was concerned that the textile industry could be going downhill because of foreign competition. Generally, yarn or cotton was sold through merchants who visited Manchester for that specific purpose. They'd as soon go to Liverpool or India for their product, with not a jot of commitment or loyalty in their bones, their task being to get the best deal they could for their clients. Having failed to find any other job, Evie had done quite a bit of thinking, attempting to pay attention to how well other mills operated, compared to this one. Did it need to update its looms, or increase and strengthen its markets by selling more products abroad than in England? And maybe change what they produced, now that the war was over.

Whether any of this would be the right thing for her to say to Harold Mullins was very difficult to decide. His temperament was indeed self-obsessed. He used to storm through the mill finding fault with everything women did and then return later all syrup and smiles, probably because he'd gone off to get himself a glass of whisky. He would then call them 'dear gels', his tone attempting to be complimentary. But not an easy man. Were it not for the difficulty she was in, she wouldn't attempt to seek his assistance.

'So you've getten problems. It don't surprise me in the least.' She heard him snort as he sat down beside her nursing a glass of beer, which made her jerk with shock, not having seen him enter the pub. 'Ye can't trust a woman as far as you can throw her.'

Evie stared at the fleshiness that sagged his jawline, the dark receding hair, his eyes slightly bloodshot, indicating a liking of far too much alcohol. She noticed a harshness and an arrogance in the twisted smile he gave her. Gathering her courage, she quickly explained her situation

48

and failure to find the employment she was in desperate need of. She'd brought a list of all the factories, shops and offices, etc. that she'd called upon and explained how she'd failed to receive a single offer from any of them.

Giving a snort of laughter, he told her how he'd once changed jobs, not having seen eye to eye with his previous employer and had ended up with this lucrative post as a foreman. 'I can quite see you'll have problems with your husband and childer when they finally return home. My son Willie should be arriving soon. No doubt he'll miss his mum, but can't say I'm broken-hearted over losing my wife.' He moved on to speak of how she'd been prone to hysterics and unnatural jealousy, calling her a slut of a wife who had found herself a fancy man. 'The bloody pair of 'em med a fool of me.'

Poor Jane, once such a good friend of hers, had claimed her husband had never been faithful to her so she had indeed found herself a new man. How could he blame her for that? Evie began to feel slightly uncomfortable, this not at all being a subject she wished to discuss. 'I'm so sorry she died in the war, despite whatever problems you had. My issue, however, is that I must be the breadwinner, at least until my husband fully recovers from having been a PoW. So I desperately feel I should be allowed to continue working at the mill. You must appreciate my concern to care for my son and daughters and make their lives good. I doubt it will be easy, considering how long it is since I last saw them. And, as you know, Danny and your son Willie have been friends since their early school days.'

He pricked up his ears, frowning in concentration. 'I'd forgotten that. It's good to hear about the friendship of our sons and weren't you and I friends once too?'

A wrench of memory cringed within her as Evie recalled having a date with this difficult man when she'd been barely sixteen. He'd tried to attract her in such an obsessive way, it had completely killed their so-called friendship, so far as she was concerned. Thankfully, he'd had no objection when she'd refused his next offer of a date and started courting her friend Jane instead. Since being the tackler in charge of their part of the mill, and she needed his help to retain her job, this was a reality she had to face. 'We were friends once,' she blithely admitted, giving him a polite smile.

'So what could you offer exactly, in order to keep this job?'

Taking a breath, Evie said, 'I'm aware that the owner fears the mill is going downhill now that we're post war and in danger of closing. It's been embroiled in weaving parachutes but it could move on to make good quality shirts to supply to large stores like Kendal Milne, or perhaps lace for pretty dresses and curtains.'

Harold showed little interest in these suggestions. 'I very much doubt Mr Eccles would be interested in employing women to make lace or owt, for that matter. It's the chaps we should employ now.'

'I appreciate some women will happily step down to make way for returning soldiers, but those of us still in need of an income should surely be allowed to keep working. Many are well qualified, as am I.' In Evie's opinion women must remain strong, not become weak as babes. She felt a strong desire to resolve her own problems as well as gain the respect of Mr Eccles for all the other women needing to keep their job. Had she said the right thing to persuade Harold Mullins to help this come about?

'I have some sympathy over your personal problems, which can't be easy to deal with. Unfortunately, there's no possibility of you getting yer job back.'

Her heart sank. 'Really? Are you sure? That sounds disastrous.'

'The fact is that Mr Eccles, the mill owner, has suffered the loss of his brother who was largely the one who ran the mill, and his son. He now has little desire to continue working there himself, being quite old. Nor has he much hope of selling it as the textile industry is starting to decline. If a mill goes bump it's generally because it's bankrupt, and he does plan to retire, possibly before that happens.' Leaning closer, he gave her a grin, revealing a couple of broken teeth. 'However, as a matter of fact I could offer you employment in a little business I run.'

Startled by this offer, Evie gave a puzzled frown. 'I didn't realize you owned a business. What sort is it?'

Tapping his plump nose, he gave a chuckle. 'Whatever I tell you, don't reveal details to anyone. Putting it bluntly, I accept bets from clients who are keen on gambling. I'm aware it's not legal but it's still popular and considered an important part of life for many. I like to keep a close eye on my clients, meking sure I get paid whatever they choose to invest. At this stage there's allus summat going on to liven me up. Considering I'm still busily engaged at the mill you could assist me to build it up into a more lucrative business. That would be useful, bearing in mind folk are more likely to appreciate a pretty woman dealing with this issue, rather than a chap. Eventually I too will lose my job, once that mill closes down.'

'I . . . I'm open to suggestions,' she stuttered, feeling slightly alarmed by the way his puckered face was mere inches from her own, the smell of alcohol on his breath most foul.

'Quite. What have you got to lose? It would only be a part-time job but you could earn a reasonably decent wage, so long as you make the necessary collections of debts from my clients.'

Evie felt a flicker of doubt that she'd any wish to be involved in this weird job offer he was making, not at all the kind of work she'd hoped for. 'I'm not certain I'd be any good at that.'

''Course you will, being a strong, determined lady. And as an employee I could permit you to rent one of the houses I own. How about that?'

She was stunned by this possibility and gazed at him in amazement. She was undoubtedly desperate for a home for her family as well as an income. Maybe she shouldn't fuss about this job even if it was only part-time and had to be kept secret. 'Are you making me an actual offer?'

'Aye, if yer willing to do what I ask.'

52

'I very much appreciate your generosity, Mr Mullins. I badly need to find a house to rent and shall do my best to oblige you,' she told him politely.

'That's good to hear. You can call me Harold, as we were once friends.'

'That was a long time ago and now I'll simply be your employee. I am, of course, expecting my husband to arrive home any time soon. I expect you were friendly with him too, so he'll be happy to know that you're willing to help us,' she tactfully pointed out.

'Aye, well, you'll need to keep this agreement under yer hat and say nowt about whatever I ask of you, in view of the authorities' attitude towards betting. They'll come round to changing these daft rules eventually. And since I'll be carrying on working at the mill till it closes down, I'll keep tabs on yer and see how you get on wi' this job. Any folk who are neglectful will have to be contacted time and again to make 'em pay up. Just remember that them what don't work, don't eat. Now, do you fancy a refill?' he said, giving her a glittering wink.

Evie noticed how his gaze slid over her, his fingers flickering as if feeling the urge to touch her. Feeling desperate to escape this possibility she politely declined his offer. 'No thanks, I haven't yet finished this glass of shandy, not at all a good drinker.' Taking a quick sip, she went on to say, 'I would like to know where that house is, please, what the rent will be and when I could move in? Then I can get it ready for the arrival of my family.'

He gave her details of the address and the cost of the rent he demanded, not cheap but reasonably acceptable. 'It might require a bit of cleaning and painting, but you're welcome to do that and can move in right away,' he said, handing over the key.

Thanking him profusely, Evie's heart pounded with relief and excitement. Eager to visit this house and discover what attention it needed, she gave him a nod and a smile, jumped to her feet and scurried away. It was then that it came to her she hadn't properly understood all he'd said about the work she was expected to do for his business. Nor had he offered any proof if and when the mill would close down. Had she done the wrong thing by asking for his assistance? Should she have gone to speak again to Mr Eccles, the mill owner? Probably that would have been a complete waste of time, having been dismissed along with other women and that poor man had lost two members of his family. He'd be unlikely to take any of them back, particularly now he intended to ultimately close the mill down. She could but hope she'd done the right thing by accepting Mullins's offer. Finding a job, whatever it was, and a new home for her family, was surely all that mattered.

6

June 1945

'I'll come with you to help search for your mother,' Bernie swiftly offered when Joanne made the announcement she'd visited the billeting officer who'd admitted he'd no idea how to contact this Evelyn Talbert, no longer being in possession of her current address. They were all sitting eating a delicious steak and onion pie in the kitchen one suppertime, which he'd cooked. Now with his sleeves rolled up Joanne found herself staring at his tanned arms, muscles round and strong, wondering why she was suddenly impressed by this image of him. Probably because she was savouring this good food, Bernie Flynn not at all a young man she wished to involve herself with. Taking a breath, she was about to deny that his assistance was required when she was interrupted by Aunt Annie.

'Do thank him for that offer, dear girl. It would be an excellent idea to have our nephew's support and protection in what is currently a bleak city, particularly as you've no idea where your dear mother is living so it could be a long and weary search.'

'Oh, I do so agree,' Aunt Sadie said. 'Do you wish to accompany her too, Megan?'

'No, 'course not,' she loudly protested. 'I have

55

a lot of homework to do so don't have time.'

Noticing the disapproval in her sister's lovely face, Joanne hastily assured Megan it was not necessary for her to come. 'Of course you don't need to accompany me, lovey. I take Aunt Annie's point that it won't be an easy task and no doubt there will be a good deal of walking involved, which would be too much for you, Megan.'

Bernie smiled at her. 'I, however, would be quite happy to walk my socks off.'

As the aunts clapped their hands to applaud his offer, Joanne felt obliged to politely accept it. He could be quite supportive, so why would she object?

They took the train to Victoria Station, which reminded her of the anguish she'd felt there as a young girl. She remembered how Megan had lost her precious doll when it fell from the rack where their bags had been stacked and its china head cracked and broke. Her sister had been heartbroken, crying for hours throughout the long train journey for the loss of her doll as well as her mother. 'It was so hard saying goodbye to our mam who steadfastly attempted to look brave when we were evacuated. We were taken far north from our beloved home and family, which made me feel so lonely.'

'A reaction I know well,' he softly said. 'I've never confessed this to you but I too lost my mother.'

'Oh, no! Do you mean she was killed?'

He gave a slight shake of his head. 'Nope. I reckon she's still alive some place but I've no idea where, as I'm obviously of no great importance to her. After my father was killed in the Royal Navy destroyer, HMS *Basilisk* near Dunkirk in 1940, she fell into a dreadful state of grief and then a year later ran off with one of his friends.'

'My goodness, what a dreadful thing to do, to abandon her son. You must have been utterly heartbroken. Me too, having lost contact with my mother, father and even my young brother Danny.'

'That's the reason I offered to help you find her, Joanne. Why would I not do what I can to help, when I fully understand the sense of loss you feel?'

'Much appreciated,' she said, and for the first time they shared a warm smile, offering each other comfort. 'I'm so looking forward to searching the place we used to live, quite hopeful that I'll at last find my mam.'

Once they arrived in Manchester they left the crowded platform and walked down Deansgate enjoying glancing at all the shops. Turning along Bridge Street, they passed the Pack Horse, then went all the way down Lower Byrom Street, trailing up and down several other streets too. Joanne found it quite devastating to see how many houses and factories had been destroyed and was appalled when she saw children playing games in the rubble and old air raid shelters. Narrowing her eyes, she carefully studied them all in case her brother was among them but sadly saw no sign of Danny. There were still sandbags lying around and no signposts, so searching

Castlefield for her mother was proving to be something of a nightmare.

When Joanne saw a woman walking some distance ahead wearing the kind of coat and headscarf she recalled her mother once wore, she desperately called out to her. 'Mam, is that you?' Turning to give her a quick glance, the woman walked away at great speed and disappeared round a corner, not troubling to respond.

'Was that your mother?' Bernie earnestly asked her. 'If so, I could run after her to tell her you're here.'

'Obviously not. If it was, she'd have come rushing to me with her arms outstretched to give me a hug. The problem is that I'm no longer certain of what she'll look like after all these years,' Joanne stated despondently.

'Will she recognize you?' he asked, giving her a wry smile. 'You're a lovely girl now, no longer a child.'

Joanne felt herself blushing even as she frowned, wondering if that had been the problem or had she been mistaken in guessing that woman was her mother? Maybe she'd lost all memory of her? Surely not.

When they finally arrived at the street close to Potato Wharf where they'd lived when she was a child, Joanne looked in horror at the derelict mess of the many houses bombed out back in 1940 during the Christmas Blitz, including their own. She couldn't even find the house where her cousin Cathie had lived quite close by, or homes of any of their other friends. Shocked by the sight of the dreadful state the city was in and the

58

fact she could find no sign of anyone she knew, Joanne felt grateful when Bernie gave her a clean handkerchief to mop up the tears rolling down her cheeks.

'Come on, cheer up. Let's find somewhere for a bit of a snack. We could then start exploring the mills or any other places you remember she worked.'

Looking up at him with gratitude, Joanne gave a nod. 'Good idea. Let's go to the Crown.'

They ate an excellent lunch of cod and chips at the pub, which Bernie insisted on paying for. He talked about how he'd enjoyed doing a lot of cooking. 'I had to learn how to cook when my mum left home. Fortunately, I was sort of adopted by my aunts and they readily accommodated me, which was just as well considering I had no way of paying the rent on the house I was living in. Being fourteen years old, I offered to work for them, which they happily accepted and have taught me a great deal about cooking since.

'I remember when I once managed to find some real eggs from a local farmer that I made custard tarts for all our guests. The Poles ate the custard but left the pastry untouched. Aunt Annie was infuriated when she saw that and gave them a telling-off over not eating the delicious pastry, speaking to them as if they were naughty children.' He burst out laughing. 'It was simply ignorance on their part, of course, never having had a custard tart before, and they quickly did as they were told and gobbled it up.'

Joanne burst out laughing also. 'Well done. I'm sure they very much enjoyed it.'

'Oh aye, they did, claiming it was delicious. Now the war is over I've moved on to gain training for more useful jobs. I'm having a go at decorating, plumbing and some simple building work. No idea if any of that will be appropriate for me. My aunts are most encouraging and supportive, happy to fund such training, and, as I greatly appreciate their care, I do whatever they ask of me.'

'They are indeed considerate and generous ladies. I shall be sorry to leave them and am not convinced Megan will agree to do that, even if I promise to take her back for regular visits. My young sister is a very independent little madam with no memory now of our mother. I'm a sort of surrogate mum to her, the only person she's had to protect and care for her, particularly whenever she's been upset or in difficulty.'

'I reckon you've done a good job. You're a lovely caring girl no matter what problems you and your sister have suffered during this dratted war. How are you feeling now, health-wise?'

This not being at all a subject Joanne wished to discuss she did not respond and quickly moved on to speak of where her mother used to work. When she took him to the mill she discovered to her dismay that it had been bombed and burned in a fire. Moving on to search every other possible mill or factory, Joanne called in them all to ask if her mother worked there, explaining she was called Evelyn Talbert, known as Evie. The response from the various secretaries or managers was always a sad shake of the head, as if they were asked countless

60

times where certain persons were, save for one mill where she was told her mother had once worked for them. Feeling a burst of joy, this excitement soon subsided when she was told Evie had now left, being sacked along with most other women. And nobody knew where she was working or living now.

Having spent hours searching and getting nowhere, Joanne felt close to despair, all hopes fading within her. 'And where is Danny, my dad, or even my cousin Cathie? We've got absolutely nowhere.'

They went on to explore the odd hostel and canal boat, in case she'd moved to live in one of those. Trekking up and down more roads, streets and yards where old friends had once lived, Joanne found those too were either destroyed or empty of anyone she knew. By late afternoon she agreed it was time for them to return home to Blackpool. Nothing was at all as it used to be here in Manchester. After walking dejectedly back to Victoria Station, Joanne remained silent throughout the entire journey, feeling utterly exhausted but surprisingly comforted when she nodded off to sleep with her head on Bernie's shoulder. Not for a moment did he object to that.

★   ★   ★

Davie, a good friend of Evie and Donald, had safely returned from the war when demobilized from the East Lancashire Regiment, and readily helped her to carry all her belongings in his old

Ford van. Not that she had any furniture, having lost it all when their first home had been bombed. He drove her along Liverpool Road and up Byrom Street to a crowd of back-to-back houses close to Wood Street and Deansgate, an area that had thankfully not been destroyed by explosive bombs. It was at least within reasonable distance of Victoria Station; now back in action after suffering a landmine fall on a platform early in the war. Would that be where her son would arrive, or the station on Liverpool Road or Piccadilly? She must make enquiries to find that out.

'Here's number six, chuck,' Davie said, parking his Ford van then starting to lift her boxes and bags out as she unlocked the door. Carrying a load of things in, he glanced around with disdain. 'I reckon you'll have to tart this place up. At least it's a bit bigger than the one room you've been occupying lately, chuck.'

Looking around to examine it, not for the first time, Evie gave a sigh. 'You're right, Davie, it does require quite a bit of attention. I'm determined to ensure that my family will return to a life of comfort, once I find them. As I'm no longer living in the place they once knew and loved, I'll work hard to make this more spick and span.'

'Good for you and I'll be glad to help, not having much work on myself just yet.'

'I couldn't afford to employ you.'

'That's all right, wasn't asking you to do that. If you can afford to buy some white paint, or whatever colour you prefer, I could decorate

62

these walls for you.'

'Oh, that would be wonderful.' She fetched her purse and handed him a couple of pounds. 'See what you can get with that. I really appreciate your help, Davie.'

'Rightio,' he said, then, giving a grin and a wink, he finished the unloading then went off happily whistling, promising to be back the next day to start the painting.

Evie knew that this house was not as large or comfortable as the first home they'd rented and lost during the Christmas Blitz in 1940. It had a messy living-kitchen, two bedrooms and a lavatory in the backyard they would have to share with several other families. Having investigated it when Harold Mullins first offered it to her, she'd worked out that the main bedroom would be for herself and Donald. Joanne and Megan could share the small spare room and she'd bought a sofa bed for Daniel, which she'd had delivered and placed in a corner of the living-kitchen.

None of this was ideal but hopefully they might eventually find a better house one day. That would not be easy right now, there being a desperate shortage of property in all cities that had suffered from bombing. This one was at least equipped, with a bit of furniture, including necessary beds in the rooms upstairs. Not that there were any carpets and nothing but blackout curtains over the mucky windows. Nevertheless, she was deeply grateful to Mullins for supplying her with this cottage, as well as the new job she'd be starting first thing on Monday morning, so she must make no complaints about the mess the house was in. She was also deeply grateful for Davie's offer of assistance.

He turned up as promised the next day and quickly set to painting the kitchen walls white, then moved on to other parts of the house. Evie spent every spare moment over the following days cleaning and scrubbing. Not convinced she'd given Davie sufficient money to paint every room, she frequently asked if he needed more but he would shake his head and gave a chuckle.

'Neither of us is rich, chuck, but we're coping well. I did make sure I bought a cheap version so you concentrate on your jobs and I'll see to this decorating. It needs to look good for Donald and your kids when they arrive home.'

Once he was done, every room looked much cleaner and brighter. Evie gave him a large currant sponge cake she'd baked for him as a token of her appreciation. 'You've done an excellent job, thank you so much.'

'Eeh, thanks, chuck. We're a great team. And do let me know when Donald comes home.'

'I certainly will,' she said, and gave him a smile as he trotted off.

She stocked the larder with some of her children's favourite food: dried eggs, Rowntrees KitKat, cheese and wheatmeal bread if little in the way of fruit, sweets, sugar or treacle, rationing still being in place. Once they were due to arrive she'd buy some chicken and vegetables and other tasty food. She had made an attempt to buy them new clothes, then realized she'd no idea what size they took now they were so much older, so had to abandon that idea. Evie made a mental note she could take them shopping to the Flat Iron Market, which had low-priced clothes, or else she could sew her girls a dress each. How exciting that would be, loving sewing and knitting as well as lacemaking.

No longer employed by the mill, her request to keep working with other women to make lace had been ignored by Harold Mullins. Certain machines at the mill had been idle throughout the war, there being no demand for lace in those days. Still in good condition it was a shame she'd not been allowed to operate them. Evie thought she might one day return to making lace herself by hand and try selling it on Campfield Market to earn herself more money. But it could take a while to build herself the stock.

Right now she had to acquire the necessary skills to do this completely different and difficult job, which would hopefully make her a reasonable income as well as having thankfully supplied her with this home for her family. But being only a part-time occupation, she might find some opportunity to work for herself. An interesting proposition.

7

Taking her favourite walk along the beach, Joanne loved the wonderful view of the sea as well as collecting a few beautiful shells and pieces of driftwood from under the pier, which she thought of as treasures. She would wash the shells and paint the driftwood in bright colours, or create an image of seagulls and boats, sensing that would give them a more interesting appearance. It surprised her when Bernie suddenly came to join her.

'Hello, Joanne. I saw what you were doing while I was watching the boats and am happy to join in,' he said, starting to pick up a few more shells to pop into her carrier bag.

Lifting her hair from her neck to let the breeze run through it, she glanced up at him with some reluctance, wondering why he had followed her. This being a lovely summer's day she felt quite unable to think of any justified reason for dismissing him even though she had a desire to be on her own to think things through.

'Thanks, Bernie, I have managed to find a few.' They walked along in silence, collecting more pretty shells. When she'd filled her bag he took it from her, claiming it was far too heavy for her to carry. Seeing his pale grey eyes glitter with admiration Joanne was filled with a sudden gush of panic. He did seem to be growing far too interested in her. She was even more surprised

66

when he next asked her for a date.

'I know that you like dancing and wondered if you'd care to accompany me to the Tower Ballroom. That would be fun,' he said, giving her a grin.

Oh, my goodness, did she wish to dance with this lad? She certainly had no intention of falling for him, still living in hope of becoming engaged to Teddy. Wouldn't it be dangerous to allow Bernie to become too fond of her? But what could she say? Hadn't they been sort of good friends these last few years? And he'd been most supportive by helping her search for her mother in Manchester, as well as sympathetic when they'd failed to find her? But she felt the urge to refuse this request as politely as possible, telling herself she should do her utmost to prevent him from attempting to court her, still fixing her hope on Teddy. Bearing in mind who he was, she must remain cautiously polite towards him. 'Maybe we'll give that a try on some occasion. I'll let you know when I feel ready to have a dance,' she said, tossing up her chin with a flicker of a smile.

To her surprise, a day or two later, she also received the offer of a date from Wing Commander Ramsbotham. Being such an attractive and lively young man, how could she refuse him? He was far more exciting and good-looking than Bernie. That night when they settled in bed, Joanne told Megan how she'd accepted his offer and declined Bernie's.

'Why are you being so stupid?' her sister demanded, sounding most scathing.

'Why would I not accept? Wing Commander Ramsbotham is a very attractive man,' Joanne stoutly declared.

'Rubbish, he's a pain in the ass. Bernie is so much kinder and more polite.'

Joanne rolled her eyes. 'He does appear to be quite smitten with me. He keeps offering to clean my shoes, check the tyres on my bike and if I stretch up a little to the high kitchen cupboard he'll ask what it is I want and can he reach it for me. He's very funny! And, of course, he followed me down to the beach the other day to supposedly help me find shells when really he wanted to ask me out. Not at all what I wished him to do.'

'Oh, for goodness sake, why not encourage Bernie to be your next flame instead of that randy RAF chap? Being our aunt's nephew you mustn't be rude to him. And you were far too flighty when those GIs showed interest in you, obsessed with *love*,' she mockingly stated.

'Don't talk nonsense.' Joanne felt slightly irritated by her sister's teasing attitude. She was such a highly intelligent girl and often dismissive of her despite her being her much older sister. She could, however, be making a relevant point not to be rude to Bernie, and a little against the decision she made. She was a bright lass.

'I'll give it some thought,' she said. She turned over in bed and shut her eyes tight so they wouldn't spill out tears yet again.

Had she been flighty? Being naive, headstrong and foolish to let herself fall madly in love with Teddy, eagerly waiting for the day he'd write and ask her to marry him. Many young girls had felt equally obsessed with those GIs during this dreadful war. It was true that like all his mates Teddy had clearly enjoyed having a fan club of girls gathered around him. All those guys felt in need of adoration, having been caught up in the fighting, bombing and enduring great danger. Like many other girls she too had stupidly allowed him to seduce her, all because she believed that he loved her. Maybe he didn't care for her at all. Had he thought of her as flighty, not just shy and prudish, greatly appealed by the adoring emotion he'd seen in her eyes and duly taken advantage of her? Was it just as well that he'd left, or was she in serious trouble and very much in need of a man to protect her?

★　★　★

The Tower Ballroom was beautifully lit with red and yellow lighting. When the Wurlitzer organ came sliding up, the man seated before it happily playing, the carefully sprung dance floor was soon packed with people in order to encourage everyone to keep dancing. Some were seated above in the balconies so they could simply watch. 'Shall we dance now or take a glass of bubbly first?' Wing Commander Ramsbotham asked as he led her to a table.

'Oh, no wine for me, thank you, just a cup of tea and a cake.' Joanne had tactfully agreed to accompany him to an afternoon tea dance not an evening one, taking her sister's advice that this would be far more appropriate and safe.

'Call me Clive, dear girl. That's my name,' he chuckled. Ignoring what she said, he ordered a bottle of wine. Then, taking her hand, he led her out onto the dance floor.

There was something about the way he held her close, pressing his thighs against her legs and his cheek against hers that set off a small alarm within her. Had Megan been right to warn her against accepting this date? He kept a firm hold of her for several more dances till eventually she politely suggested they return to their table and requested a cup of tea.

Taking a long drink from the glass of bubbly wine he'd poured for himself, he then poured a glass for Joanne. 'Cheers! Chin, chin.'

She lifted her glass to click his, as was demanded of her, but nervously set it down again without taking a single sip and gratefully thanked the young waitress who delivered her a teapot and a selection of cakes in a stand.

He laughed, the sound of his humour not at all pleasant, filled with a blast of cynicism. 'Come on, take a drink. Don't deny yourself such a delicious treat.'

'I prefer this afternoon tea, thank you, very much the kind of treat that suits me perfectly.'

Glancing about him with a faint air of derision, he said, 'Why don't we slip away to somewhere more private and enjoy a little fun together? Wouldn't that be more entertaining than this ballroom?'

Wasn't privacy what she'd often dreamed of in the past with Teddy? Now, this man demanding the opportunity to be alone with her was not something she considered at all appropriate. 'I'm not certain about that.'

'Why not, dear girl?'

From the expression in his blue eyes it was clear to Joanne what he was implying. He obviously fancied her and assumed she was fascinated by him too. The thought flickered in her head that if she agreed to let him do to her whatever he wished, could she then lay the blame for this child she carried upon him and gain herself a marriage that could save her reputation and spare her a desolate future? Would that be a good thing? He was an attractive man if quite a bit older than her and probably quite well off. He was, however, rather weird, remembering how he'd pinched her sister's bottom. Wasn't that why Megan strongly disapproved of him? Taking a deep breath, she mildly remarked, 'I assumed we were just coming to the Tower Ballroom to enjoy a dance and afternoon tea, not whatever you're suggesting.'

'Why would you not be happy to join me in a different hotel to the Jubilee House? I'm fully aware you were highly captivated with those GIs. I assume that's because you love having a man around to enchant you. And you are most captivating, a very pretty girl in that short, tightly fitting blue dress. Very sexy.'

Something in his tone jolted her as Joanne felt herself flush with a mix of embarrassment and annoyance. The implication seemed to be that he considered she was open to titillating attention from all men, in particular those in the Army or Air Force. No doubt he too loved having a fan

71

club of girls, being filled with a strong sense of his own importance and was possibly something of a pervert.

'Would you believe those Americans greatly interfered in our lives, robbing me of my latest conquest whom I'd been dating for quite a while. I remember one date I had with her when a GI turned up and gave her a kiss, blast him. That pretty girl dumped me in favour of that blasted chap, as so many have done.'

He went rabbiting on about the GIs and Joanne firmly shut her ears to his complaints. She stared at him, noticing a cold hardness in his eyes and a certain arrogance in his twisted smile. Some instinct made her turn her head away and to her surprise she saw Bernie standing in the doorway watching her and looking a little concerned. He did seem to be making a habit of keeping a close eye on her as if anxious to ensure she was safe, even this afternoon in spite of her refusal to accept his offer of a date.

'Actually,' she said, interrupting Clive Ramsbotham, this cocky wing commander, 'you wouldn't believe how happy I am that this war is now over and I'm no longer pestered by cheeky men. I've no wish to be harassed by you either, sir. Fortunately, an old friend is waiting for me so I must return to work now. Thanks for the tea and goodbye.' Highly amused when his jaw fell open in shock, she jumped to her feet and smartly walked away. When Joanne reached Bernie at the door in the far corner, she linked her arm with his, burst into a giggle and said, 'Do help me escape from that dreadful man.'

'My pleasure,' he said, giving a chuckle too, and they happily trotted down the stairs then along the promenade back to Jubilee House.

Fortunately, cocky Clive quickly departed and over the following days Joanne readily agreed to take a few walks with Bernie, feeling much safer with him. She always made sure Megan accompanied them, believing that to be far more appropriate. Bernie did at times seem to be increasingly attentive, often bringing her small bunches of wild flowers to express his growing interest in her. Joanne was stunned one afternoon following a show he'd taken them to on the North Pier when he attempted to kiss her cheek. She quickly turned away so that he caught her ear instead.

'Sorry,' he said. 'Just wanted to let you know how I appreciate your company.'

She heard Megan give a little giggle as Joanne politely accepted his apology. He was apparently attempting to be reliable and kind. Did that mean her sister was right to encourage her to go on a date with him? But how could she trust any man, let alone fall in love with this one?

* * *

All necessary jobs now done, thanks to Davie's painting and Evie having made the house much more clean and neat, she rose early on Saturday morning, took a little cereal and toast, then quickly washed up. She felt eager to meet her niece Cathie at Campfield Market and tell her what she'd achieved. It was as Evie put on her coat and headscarf that there came a knock on the door. As it banged open, she heard the call of an all-too-familiar voice and the sound of loud footsteps approaching. To her dismay, she saw Harold Mullins marching towards her. All too aware he could be most domineering, Evie felt a spark of resentment that he believed he had the right to walk in without an invitation. This would be because he was the owner of this small house, even though she'd already paid him the first week's rent and hadn't yet begun working for him.

'I hope you don't want me to start on this job today, as I've spent the last week busily smartening up this house and am now on my way out shopping,' she informed him politely, feeling a shudder of discontent within her.

'Hold yer horses, lady. You may be in a hurry but don't rush off. As you know I'm putting a bit of business your way. I've quite a few clients who've so far refused to cough up what they owe me. Here's the list of those who essentially must pay their betting bills,' he said, handing her a sheet bearing a long list of names and addresses. 'You can start calling on them right now, then the rest on Monday morning and insist they pay up.'

Evie met his unyielding gaze in consternation, realizing she was not in a position to refuse. There was probably much more to this job than she'd imagined. She hadn't at all taken into account that some folk would avoid paying his betting company. 'How do I do that?' she asked in alarm.

'With firm determination and politeness, at which you're most efficient. And tek no notice if they claim to be poor or hide away pretending they're not home. Keep hammering on their flaming door till they let you in. Then deliver the payments you receive to me this evening and every evening thereafter.'

'Heck, not sure I'll be any good at this,' she said, dreading the prospect of being demanding of people in poverty or difficult strangers addicted to gambling to hand over to her what they owed to Mullins, let alone walking the streets each evening to his house in the dark. Why had she ever agreed to take on such a task? The reason was obvious. Because of this house he'd offered her to rent, she reminded herself, glancing around with pride at the improvements already achieved. Something she'd been desperately in need of.

Giving her a smarmy grin, he said, 'Aye, you'll have to be good at this job, lass, otherwise you'll be bloody sacked and chucked out of this house.' Having made this cutting remark, he marched away.

8

When Bernie again asked her to attend a dance with him at the Tower Ballroom, Joanne felt sorely tempted to accept. Maybe she should be making a fresh start in life, as well as finding an answer to her problem. 'OK, why not? You're right, I do love dancing. We'll give it a go,' she said with a smile.

It was a delight to see Reginald Dixon come sliding up seated before the Wurlitzer organ this time, which he'd used to play at the Tower before joining the RAF. 'He often came to give concerts,' Bernie told her. 'Now he's planning to return for good, no doubt once he's been demobbed. Good to see him here.'

Holding her quite professionally, Joanne was surprised to find what a good dancer he was and easily kept in step with him. Presumably living near the Tower Ballroom had provided Bernie with plenty of opportunity to learn how to dance, often coming along to the afternoon sessions, as he did that time he rescued her from that dreadful wing commander. She happily danced with him, thankful that he was nowhere near as demanding or flirtatious.

Over the summer she'd taken several more walks with Bernie on the beach. On occasions he would escort her and Megan to the Winter Gardens to listen to music playing or watch various shows on the North and Central Piers or at the

Grand Theatre. Her sister rarely accompanied them these days, it being almost September and she was generally engaged in preparing herself for this new school. Aunt Annie had made her the required uniform and was teaching her how to knit and sew. Aunt Sadie was engrossed in finding her good books to read from the local library and encouraging her to draw and paint. They were so supportive of her sister, Joanne wondered if she should seek their help too.

Aware of how Bernie was holding her close as they danced, she could feel the warmth of him, which was raising an odd sort of expectation within her. Bernie did seem to be most friendly and there were moments when she almost felt the urge to become quite fond of him. Not that she believed that would ever happen, although could he provide the answer to her problem? She dismissed this nonsense with a sigh. He was a little more considerate and attentive than Teddy had been and happily content to work with his aunts. Yet there was a boring sameness about him, showing no plans to make changes to his life. He did sometimes gaze at her closely for no good reason, his eyes clouding a little beneath his furrowed brow. She gave a shiver. Why on earth would she wish to imply that she liked him much at all?

As if seeing a sign of anguish in her face, he said, 'I know you've not been eating too well lately, are you feeling any better?'

'I'm fine,' she stoutly remarked.

Noticing how she kept looking around, avoiding his gaze, he gave her a grin. 'You look very

77

pretty in that floral frock and with those clips in your curly hair. Did you agree to accompany me because you wanted to show yourself off, as you obviously like to do with us chaps? Well, why not when you look so gorgeous?'

About to protest at his indication that she liked to flatter herself she instead burst out laughing, feeling madly light-hearted and a little touched by this comment. 'How well you understand me. I do like to look elegant, which isn't at all easy having little money to spend on clothes. And as I no longer trust men I simply do my best to improve whatever cheap frocks I can find. You look quite good too in that smart navy suit with a white shirt and blue tie.'

'So I'm no longer the tangy mess I once was?'

''Course you're not, silly lad,' she said, feeling relieved that he did look much better. She'd never wished to be seen going out with him when he was a gangly youth with messy skin. 'You have greatly improved if not as handsome as some of those GIs.'

'Ah, am I the wrong man for you then, not being that fellow you desperately wanted?'

Joanne felt a waft of embarrassment. Had she said entirely the wrong thing by mentioning those Yanks? 'Are you asking me to confess that I'm in love with one of them? Oh, dear, would that make you jealous?' she remarked teasingly.

'Why would I not be?' Then, pulling her closer, he gave her cheek a gentle kiss. Instantly Joanne pushed him away, her heart hammering with fury at how he dared do such a thing, and marched back to their table at the side of the ballroom. Steadfastly avoiding meeting his shrewd gaze as he settled beside her, she felt alarmed when he continued to question her.

'Does that GI still fancy you and do you believe he'll send word for you to join him in America? Please tell me, as I do feel the need to know.' He asked the question quietly, a kindness very evident in his grey eyes.

'I very much doubt it,' she responded sternly. A part of her felt as if she wished to weep. How could she confess her need for Teddy because of the problem she was suffering, having missed three monthly periods? She couldn't risk losing hope of him sending for her, not after all the time they'd spent together, let alone how she desperately wanted him to accept her as his adoring wife after what he'd done to her. Feeling far too locked up in anguish to think of a suitable response and wishing to escape this issue, she quickly changed the subject. 'Tell me what you were involved in during the war, not having been called up.'

He gave a grin. 'I was enrolled as a fourteen-year-old by the Home Guard, trained and provided with a dispatch rider's Army trade badge. I constantly cycled around delivering important messages as instructed. We were at first a bit short of weapons but were trained to march and drill with a form of dummy rifles. Eventually we did have proper firearms supplied, and a special khaki uniform complete with an LDV armband. I was happy to be a local defence volunteer, happy to do my bit to help the various troops and protect our area. Keeping a watch for the possible invasion of the enemy over the sea was also an important part of our day.'

'How brave of you. So what do you plan to do with your life now this war is over? Will you take up sailing and fishing? And have you found anyone who fancies you?'

'What a question!' Remaining silent for some moments, he sat sipping his half-pint of beer. Joanne suspected that she'd asked the wrong question, never having seen or heard him going off on a date with any other girl. Did that make him feel unwanted and lonely, which may account for why he kept asking her out as well as these personal questions? Perhaps he felt the need to find himself someone to care for him, having lost his parents. Then his next comment completely stunned her.

'I don't have a girlfriend but am quite fond of you, and concerned over what you suffered. The truth is, Joanne, I saw what that GI did to you down on the beach that day. I suspect he may have left you in a sorry state, in which case if you're in need of saving your reputation by finding yourself a respectable man to marry and protect you, may I apply for that position?'

★ ★ ★

Evie was up like a lark first thing every single morning. On the first Monday in this job she'd spent the entire day attempting to locate all the addresses on the list, having walked for hours around parts of Castlefield and Salford. Now, knowing where she had to call, she'd knock on

80

doors then politely ask for the payments due. Some folk would readily or sulkily provide the money; others slammed the door in her face or made all manner of excuses.

'Can't pay at the moment. Maybe next week if I win summat. I'll let you know,' was a frequently typical remark.

And so it went on, day after day, week after week. Evie felt wracked with nerves every time she approached sour-looking men who viewed her with diffidence and disdain. Others proved reluctant to commit themselves, despite being impressed with her good manners. After gritting her teeth and promising to call again, she would smile and move on to the next house. As darkness fell and very often it began to rain, soaking her through, she would deliver the money she'd received to Mullins each evening, as instructed. Generally, Evie would politely point out how she'd failed to collect as much as was owed, something she was apologizing for right now.

'I've done the best I can and succeeded in persuading some clients to pay up, but others don't even answer the door or else firmly state they don't possess the necessary funds.'

'I assume you tell 'em when you'll call again and that's why they hide?' he snapped.

Taking a breath, realizing she never said anything of the sort, Evie gave a weary smile. 'I reckon it takes days or weeks before some can find the amount they need.'

'You ain't doing too well then. You should call twice a week at different times so they never know exactly when you're coming. Try a bit harder to get the money off 'em that's due.'

'I doubt that will work, or that I'm very good at this job.' Evie felt she was working hard, yet Mullins didn't seem prepared to give her the slightest praise for her efforts, or be very helpful. But then, as he had clearly explained to her, she was required to do as he ordered. And he was most rude by constantly complaining that she fell short of his impossibly high standards. Giving him a polite smile, she went on to say, 'You clearly have a low opinion of my worth. Night after night you complain. I can see this must be a problem for you but I feel worn out by working hard in this so-called part-time job, and failing to achieve whatever you demand. Pestering people too often doesn't seem to work. You should probably have employed a young man, not me.'

Harold's face darkened. 'I'm not in favour of chaps. Much prefer a woman to work for me. I reckon you'll improve if you do as I say.'

'Whether or not you'll admit it, you're losing money hand over fist. Same as Mr Eccles is, the mill being outdated so 'appen if you'd listened to the suggestions I made, I might have kept that job and helped him to improve it. Please let me have it back, I'd much prefer that job to this one, as many other women would, since we love working in a textile factory. I'd be much better at that.'

His face was purple as he glowered at her, a blue line around his lips, and for a moment she was fearful he might actually be about to hit her.

But taking a huge indrawn breath and showing a great effort of will, he brought his temper under control. 'I'm damned if I'll allow you to tell me how to run things at t'mill, or in this business of mine. I've no financial problems, am doing fine, but need to earn more as I too could ultimately lose my job if the mill closes down. Tha'll have to mek sure tha does better, or you'll lose yer flamin' house as well as this job.'

He slammed his door shut in her face and Evie turned on her heel and stamped away. What a difficult man he was. It came to her that renting this house off Harold Mullins meant she was completely under his control. But no alternative properties were available, and she'd failed to find other work. Dreading to think how much worse this job could become she made a vow to keep searching for more suitable employment as well as a better house. Meanwhile, she had to accept reality and keep on working for this man to earn money to care for her family, once they all arrived. Oh, hopefully they would come home soon.

* * *

Joanne felt as if she was drenched in confusion, having unbelievably heard Bernie's offer. The idea he'd seen what happened that day on the beach when Teddy had made love to her before dashing away, left her frozen with anguish. Why on earth would he offer to marry her simply because of a difficult situation he suspected she was in. No doubt that was because being a local

83

defence volunteer in the Home Guard, bravely doing his bit during the war when he was young, he still felt the necessity to protect people.

It was Teddy, the man she loved, whom she wished to marry, certainly not their aunts' nephew. He couldn't provide her with any sort of future that would appeal or make her happy, save for a form of protection and security. Being a mixed-up lad with no well-paid job, why would she care about him? The only thing she could find in his favour was his improved appearance. He was better looking now he was older, for all he was still a bit lean and obsessed with doing his duty. But how could he truly prove to be *in love* with her?

Now, as she walked alone by the shore feeling a benign coolness with the promise of autumn in the air, her eyes scanned the silvered water and golden sand, as if expecting Teddy to appear at any moment. Whenever she thought of him, the ache in her heart became increasingly painful. Would that beloved man call and confess how he missed and needed her, not having realized until now how much he truly loved her? He might then decide to find a job here in Blackpool and work hard to build a future for them together.

'Give me the chance, that's all I ask. I do love you, darling,' he might say. Oh, how she longed to hear that.

Pressing her stomach, it felt fairly flat and slightly painful, so when would it swell and prove her condition? Surely quite soon, a problem she struggled to block out of her mind.

She gave a sigh, wishing her dream of Teddy's

return to beg her to marry him would become a reality. If the days were difficult, her nights were even worse. She was haunted by the memory of the smiles he gave her, the touch of his lips, the caress of his hands, as if he was here beside her. She dreamed of Teddy all night long, and each morning when she woke, Joanne would remember that he was nowhere around. Turning her face into her pillow, she would cry silent tears of despair, all too aware of her problem.

Being so wrapped up in these dreams she had no serious belief in Bernie's apparent fondness for her. 'How can you make such a ridiculous offer? I think you must be teasing me,' she'd gently scolded him, feeling a desire to give him a dismissive giggle but had cautiously avoided doing that.

'I believe you're in need of serious care and assistance,' he'd firmly informed her. 'I'm fully aware of your sense of independence and difficult situation but you are a sweet and lovely girl and I'm — well — as I said, most fond of you. Please consider my offer as I'm sure your affection for me will grow too. My intentions are entirely honourable.'

'No doubt as a sense of duty, which I've no intention of accepting,' she'd stated firmly.

When he'd fallen silent she'd made a firm decision to look after herself. For Bernie to imagine she would come round to growing fond of him, he must be living in cloud cuckoo land.

Now, Joanne stood staring out to sea in abject misery. A chill washed through her, rippling down her spine and making her shiver with cold, as she desperately searched for a shred of hope. Her life was proving to be heart-rending and desperately lonely, having lost the man she loved, and also members of her family. Somehow she must learn to summon up the ability to find a way of coping with her sense of loss, and deal with this worse problem she had. Being pregnant with no hope of finding a husband could be a total disaster to her life. Not at all a pleasant prospect. The only way to cope was to meet reality head on and make a sensible decision. Should she give up all expectation of finding happiness and respectability, snatch at the fondness Bernie allegedly felt for her and accept his offer to protect her? Could he be the answer to her prayers? Life could be a vale of tears, not a bed of roses.

9

'I can't believe this dratted war is finally over, after all these years,' Evie said, giving a huge sigh of relief as she sat enjoying a coffee in Campfield Market with her niece whom she hadn't seen for ages, being so busy. 'The atomic bomb in Japan sounded like an absolute tragedy but it's such a relief to hear they've surrendered and it's finally over, a situation we've all longed for.'

'It's wonderful and we'll soon be celebrating VJ Day, even more of a treat than VE Day back in May,' Cathie told her, giving a warm smile. 'The authorities are saying they will no longer feel nervous about allowing children to return home now feeling assured they'll be safe, and plan to start sending them over the next few weeks. When do you reckon yours will come?'

'I've been informed that Danny will be arriving soon. I can hardly wait for that day.'

'What about your lovely girls, will they return home too?'

With a wrinkle of concern, Evie gave a small shrug. 'No idea. I'm now off to speak to the billeting officer again and can but hope he's managed to find them. Of course I write regularly to Danny and am so looking forward to welcoming all my family home, particularly now

87

that I'm renting a proper house instead of a one-roomed flat.'

Cathie blinked in surprise. 'Really, how did that come about?'

Evie briskly informed her niece of her new address and how she was renting it from Harold Mullins who'd provided her with a much-needed job, even though it was not one she much enjoyed doing.

Cathie met this information with a slight frown. 'From what I remember, my mother having known him in the past when she worked at the mill, he's not an easy man to deal with. He can be very arrogant and, of course, Mam has something of an insatiable sexual appetite, which he found quite accommodating, if you catch my drift. She sensibly evaded the attention he offered and turned him down, so do take care, Aunty.'

'I'll definitely never allow him to attach himself to me,' Evie firmly remarked. 'I agree he is a bit bossy and this job he's granted me isn't easy, taking into account what he instructs me about demanding payments. Anyroad, I have to bear in mind the benefit of this house he's let to me. It's some distance from the wharfs where I first lived, let alone the mill where I used to work, but I'm settled in and have done a lot of work to clean and tidy it, gratefully assisted by Davie who did some decorating for me, bless him. You're welcome to come and see it any time, love. Right now, I can hardly wait for the moment Danny will arrive. Then hopefully my girls and Donald will come soon too.'

88

Evie called to see the billeting officer, eagerly hoping he'd found her daughters. 'My family is surely due home and I've managed to find a house to rent that can accommodate them and my invalid husband. Do you know when that might happen and where they all are? I'm fully aware of where my son lives but how do I find my daughters, who I've sadly lost contact with?'

'Sometimes accommodation is only temporary,' he delicately confessed. 'Billeting officers had to dash around begging people to offer foster care for evacuees, doing their best to find appropriate billets in cottages, farms or grand houses, but it didn't always work out as well as we expected. Some folk would happily agree; some felt they were being forced into accepting these children; others would do it just because they liked being paid good money. They would often complain if evacuees objected to what little they did for them and many children would find themselves frequently moved on. That could be because some youngsters wet beds, suffered from eczema or other problems.'

'I remember hearing that my girls had been badly treated through no fault of theirs,' Evie stoutly responded. 'I fetched 'em home, but when the bombs came they were naturally re-evacuated. Where the hecky thump were they sent?'

He gave a cough and an apologetic little sigh. 'I'd like to tell you that evacuation was organized most efficiently, but sadly it wasn't that simple. Keeping track of evacuees' movements has not been easy. They were generally ordered to send a postcard from wherever they'd been billeted and notices would be stuck up on the house or school stating where they were being held. But this plan did sometimes go wrong, posters and cards often getting lost.'

'Or restrained by selfish people.'

'True, and, as I said, children were frequently moved on. I'll make more enquiries, so far having received no details. We can but hope your family will turn up one day in Manchester and find you, Mrs Talbert. Thankfully the war in the East is now over so it could only be a little while before they're allowed home. I'll let you know if and when I find out anything about them, dear lady.'

Evie thanked him and walked away, doing nothing to wipe the tears that fell from her eyes. If only she had a clue how and where to search for them. At least aware of Danny's address, she quickly wrote her son a warm letter saying how much she longed to see him and that she would be waiting for him at Victoria Station whenever his local billeting officer sent him home. Oh, but how she ached to see her daughters. And of course her darling husband.

★ ★ ★

Aunt Annie surprised Joanne one day by asking if she and Bernie were becoming something of a match. 'Are you falling in love with our nephew, Joanne?'

Startled by this question, she shook her head.

90

Was he the kind of man she could look upon as possibly good husband material? Would these ladies approve if she did accept his offer, even though she didn't love him? 'I swear I have no strong feeling for Bernie, and I suspect that accepting his offer of marriage would be entirely wrong for me, Aunt.'

'Ah, so he has proposed to you?' Annie said, giving her a sparkling smile.

'Oh, I assumed he'd told you that,' Joanne said, furious with herself for having stupidly mentioned this possibility that so occupied her brain. She kept wondering whether the comfort she felt whenever he took her for a walk or kissed her cheek would ever result in her growing fond of him. Should she explain how she'd lost the man she truly loved and may be carrying his baby, therefore this offer of marriage could be ideal? Deciding against that, she politely said, 'Bernie is most caring and fun. He does claim that he adores me and wishes to build us a happy future together. I'm still quite young and with a situation I need to sort out, not least finding my family.'

'Dearest girl, I could see something was troubling you as your appetite has been so poor lately. Now I suspect it's because you are resisting the desire to fall in love with him. Once you have gained some happiness in life the world will be your oyster and Bernie would be a most caring husband and willing to assist you find your mother.'

'The fact is I politely declined his offer,' she said.

A rueful smile appeared on Annie's face. 'That

is your choice, of course, dear, but whenever I see you chatting or walking out together you both look quite content. Pay close attention to how you feel about Bernie when out and about enjoying his company. Now, dear, do come and eat a decent meal to firm up your withering body.' And giving her a smile and a light kiss on her cheek, she took hold of her arm and trotted her firmly off to the kitchen.

Joanne sat at the table doing her best to eat, remembering she had indeed enjoyed spending some time with Bernie, but how astonished she'd been when he'd declared his fondness for her and proposed. Not that she had any wish to mention to these ladies her current problem was the reason he'd made that offer.

'Your decision may change over time,' Aunt Annie said, coming to sit beside her. 'I once had a proposal when a young man I was falling in love with took me dancing. Unfortunately, my parents objected to him as he was a different religion to me and in their opinion a much lower class, as if that mattered. Sadly, I was compelled to care for our parents until they passed away. Dear Sadie stuck firmly by my side, not wishing to accept a date from any man, let alone a proposal. Finding you two girls early in the war has proved to be the joy of our life, having no children of our own.'

'Oh it has indeed,' Sadie said. 'And we may eventually retire, may we not, Annie?'

'We are considering moving to Lytham St Annes where there is, of course, an excellent high school that Megan could attend. When that will happen we're not sure. No doubt whenever it seems right to leave Bernie in charge of this boarding house, were he interested in that, perhaps with your assistance. So do take time to think it through carefully, dear, knowing how close you two are. He is a good man and adores you.'

Aunt Annie was perhaps making a valid point that in many ways they might well be perfectly suited, not that she truly believed he adored her. But could this be a turning point in her life, a commitment she must make to accommodate the child she was carrying? She shuddered at the prospect of finding herself incarcerated in a home for unmarried mothers where she'd be classified as a piece of garbage and treated atrociously. Like any young girl, Joanne secretly nursed a desire for a happy marriage and children, and the possibility that her illegitimate child could be taken away to be adopted was also a worry. What a mess she had made of her life. Setting her state of health above her desire for Teddy, her lost love, Bernie might well become the answer to her problem.

★   ★   ★

The next day, as she took her usual morning walk with Bernie along the beach in the glowing autumn sunshine, the words popped out of her mouth without any further consideration. 'I believe I've changed my mind and am now willing to accept your offer,' she told him softly.

Bernie came swiftly to a halt, his face lit with a

93

glittering smile, looking utterly thrilled. 'Oh, that's wonderful to hear. I was fearing I was about to lose you for ever. Now it seems I never will, thank the Lord.' Pulling her close in his arms, he stunned Joanne with the tender kiss he gave her. It set off a startling swirl of yearning within her, mixed with a sense of panic.

'The thing is, Bernie, we're very young. You're nineteen but I won't turn eighteen until the sixth of November and, as I can't find Mam, how will I manage to acquire the necessary permission?'

'We can definitely deal with that,' he said, again giving her a hug and another gentle kiss. He went on to speak of his plans to find them private accommodation and how they could either go on working together or she could find herself a different job, if she wished. 'I will continue to help you search for your mother,' he promised. 'We can visit Manchester whenever you think it appropriate.'

'That's most kind of you.'

The moment they returned to the boarding house he was grinning and Joanne was not at all surprised when he put his arm around her and announced to his aunts that she'd accepted his proposal of marriage. 'We don't wish to leave it too long so might need your permission, Joanne still being young. And she is sadly unable to find her mother.'

'Oh, my goodness, we'll be delighted to do that, won't we, Sadie?' Aunt Annie said, looking equally delighted as she gave Joanne a warm hug.

'We will indeed, what a lovely surprise,' her sister agreed.

Finding him reasonably attractive and desperate to protect herself, Joanne could but hope she'd made the right decision. He was also willing to again visit Manchester with her to help find her mam. Now she must tell Megan, who would no doubt be equally delighted.

Joanne did not reveal to her sister the reason why she'd accepted Bernie's proposal, feeling that would be entirely inappropriate. Her darling sister was utterly thrilled by the news, convinced it was an exciting decision she'd made, since she very much liked Bernie. 'I can see why you love him, he's a really dear young man and has adored you for years.'

Not for a moment could Joanne believe that. He was simply being kind and caring and a good friend. But considering her situation why would she not accept his help? Still fretting for the loss of the man she truly did love, Joanne remained resolutely silent, struggling to fix a smile on her face. She'd strived to be cautious or prudish, the way Teddy had classed her, but then had innocently believed in his love for her. How naive and foolish of her to allow him to seduce her. Now Joanne was coming to the conclusion that she needed to grow up, be far more sensible and protective of herself.

Quickly changing the subject, she said, 'I will keep looking for Mam. Bernie has volunteered to help again by visiting Manchester with me.'

A small frown wrinkled Megan's face as she gave a shrug. 'There's no rush over that. It's good to think that marrying Bernie means we can stay here in Blackpool. That's such a lovely thought.'

Joanne could well appreciate her sister's desire to stay here, having endured so much anguish in her young life. When they'd first arrived at Blackpool it had not been easy to find someone to take them in. They'd been driven around the town on buses, street after street while landladies trotted over to come on board and choose anyone they fancied. It was almost as if they were looking for suitable maids to work for them. There were, of course, tears or cries of protest when siblings were split up and, keeping a firm hold on her young sister, Joanne had been determined not to lose her. Consequently, they were once again the last to be selected. She'd felt quite moved when Aunt Annie and Aunt Sadie had given them both a gentle pat and a warm smile, clearly more concerned about the distress on their young faces rather than whether or not they would make good workers.

'I do agree that it was quite touching to see how kind they were. I remember how they gathered up our bags and took us to their boarding house where we were instantly fed, bathed and freshly clothed. As they have each made clear, it was a joy for them to take us in. You were only seven years old and not old enough to work for them. I too was fairly young but glad to do my bit. They've been very caring towards us ever since so I do understand what you're saying, love.'

'And they're now happily arranging your wedding, so can I be your bridesmaid?'

Joanne laughed. 'Who else could do that, darling?'

* * *

Evie stood on the platform at Victoria Station, filled with anxiety even as her heart pounded with excitement, a shiver running down her spine at the memory of all she'd suffered. A cool breeze became so brisk that it almost whipped off her neatly brimmed hat. Realizing she'd forgotten to attach a hatpin, Evie jammed it back onto her head and attempted to tidy her ruffled bobbed hair. Then she calmly smoothed down the jacket of the suit she'd bought specially for this occasion, albeit only second hand from Flat Iron Market. It was important that she looked her best, all too aware she'd aged considerably over the years, being only thirty-four when her children had been evacuated in 1939 and now turned forty.

They too would no doubt look entirely different. Goodness, would she even recognize them?

At that moment she heard the hoot of an approaching train and Evie's heart pumped hard, making her feel slightly breathless. Moments later, the platform was packed with youngsters, parents rushing around in a state of utter confusion as they searched for their children. Some were hugging and weeping with joy, while others regarded each other with a slight indifference. Where were her own little ones, or rather her youngsters? Joanne would be seventeen, almost eighteen; Danny fourteen and Megan eleven.

Before the war, Joanne had been a pretty, fair-haired girl, vivacious and fun loving. When the bombs fell she would hide under the kitchen table until she'd dressed herself in a warm sweater, coat and shoes, then would run down the street to the air raid shelter in a fit of panic. Evie could remember how upset Joanne had looked when being evacuated in 1939, clinging tight to her siblings. Megan had carried a Mickey Mouse mask as well as her favourite doll, Danny a gas mask over one shoulder and each of them had a small bag of clothes and food for the journey. A label had been pinned on their lapels to state their name. Danny's bright hazel eyes and small face had been a picture of excitement, as if he was expecting to relish an adventure, his light brown hair flicking over his head with a tendency to curl. What a handsome little boy he'd been. Glancing anxiously around, she could see no sign of him or the girls anywhere.

Dashing back and forth as she searched with an increasing sense of desperation, Evie bumped into a young lad. He looked quite tall and fit with broad shoulders and long lean legs, rough-looking hands, podgy fingers and broken nails. His brown hair was cut extremely short and he had a slightly crooked nose. Catching a glimpse of his hazel eyes, which bore an expression of cold stubbornness, she then saw a label fastened on the collar of his coat upon which was a clearly written name. It came to her in a burst of shock that this was her son.

'Danny?' she murmured.

'Mam?'

They gazed upon each other in stunned silence for some seconds, then Evie pulled him into her arms to give him a joyful hug. Moments

your head in a waved roll, topped with a lov[e]
tiara,' Aunt Sadie charmingly told her. 'You [?]
have beautifully abundant fair hair and gorgeou[s]
light turquoise eyes. I'm sure you'll look
beautiful when this wonderful day arrives.'

'Are you sure you have no wish to delay this
wedding until you've found your mother?' Aunt
Annie quietly asked, looking most sympathetic.

'That could take months or years, so what is
the point? And at least I have your support.'
Joanne thanked them both then hastily scurried
away, not wishing to be interrogated any further.
Oh, and how she still badly missed her mother
who wouldn't even know how and why she was
to be married at this young age.

★   ★   ★

[E]vie was happily making a great fuss of her
[d]arling son, so thrilled to have him home again.
[S]eating him at the kitchen table, she provided
[hi]m with a large dish of piping hot chicken soup.
[H]e looked so grown up, entirely different to the
[yo]ung lad she remembered but fit and well, if
[wi]th a shaft of anxiety in his face. No doubt he
[ha]d felt lonely and missed his family as much as
[sh]e did. Sitting on the chair beside him and
[wis]hing to give him another hug, Evie carefully
[con]trolled herself. She really shouldn't cuddle
[hi]m as if he were still a kid when he'd turned
[fou]rteen on 4 June. 'Are you glad to be home,
[?]?'

[G]iving her a grin, he nodded, rapidly scooping
[th]e soup into his mouth as if he were starving

later, when he withdrew himself from her grip
looking a little embarrassed, she wiped the tears
of happiness from her eyes. It was then that she
noticed the platform was empty with no sign of
her daughters anywhere.

10

The wedding was in the process of being planned, well organized by Aunt Annie and Aunt Sadie. A task they apparently greatly enjoyed doing. Joanne didn't find it easy to take part in such an activity. Aunt Annie had also been busily engaged over the last week or so making her a wedding dress of satin and lace. It had a heart-shaped neckline, a tight bodice and quite a short skirt that reached just past her knees. Sadie was happily sewing a pink silk dress for Megan, both ladies having generously provided the necessary clothing coupons in order to buy the required fabric.

Trying the gown on made Joanne feel as if she was a slip of a lass who was seriously cheating these lovely kind ladies and, not least, their nephew in whom she hadn't the slightest interest. Fortunately, her cleavage did not show and thankfully her stomach was still not too plump, yet she must now be almost four months pregnant. Would she deliver a tiny baby, only being a small girl herself? And how could she explain its early arrival to them?

Aunt Annie was holding pins in her mouth as she checked the hem. Once she was satisfied that she'd tacked it appropriately, she carefully lifted the gown off Joanne and, sitting back down to stitch it, began chattering about her plans. 'We intend to invite many of our neighbours and

friends to the wedding reception and supp[ly] them with home-made soup, Spam and chee[se] sandwiches.'

'Assuming we can cope with finding [the] necessary rations we could perhaps mak[e a] sponge cake,' Aunt Sadie suggested.

'Ah, good idea. Finding sufficient suga[r to] make an iced wedding cake would not prov[e to] be easy,' Aunt Annie agreed, even though [the] dear ladies had already generously used [their] ration books.

Hurrying to dress herself in her blous[e and] skirt, Joanne felt a shadow of pain slip th[rough] her belly, presumably because of the gui[lt and] anxiety she was experiencing. When an[d how] could she tell Bernie's aunts the truth abo[ut why] she'd agreed to marry him? Not that he['d] questioned her about why she'd allowed [him] to do what he did, let alone explain his [reasons] for being prepared to acknowledge this [child as] his own. A part of her felt humbled by [this] and filled with shame, considering Ber[nie] didn't love her.

'Now what about your bouquet, d[ear?] Would chrysanthemums be appropriate[?'

'I really don't mind. Whatever you th[ink.'] Why would she care less what bou[quet she] carried? Joanne simply longed for thi[s to] be over as quickly as possible, althoug[h how she] would feel about spending the weddi[ng] bed with Bernie was a prospect sh[e'd] blocked out of her mind. Far to[o awful to] contemplate.

'Oh, and we could curl your hair [...]

hungry, poor lad. After she gave him a large slice of home-made Eccles cake, which he also ate with great appreciation, he said, 'Aye, I am.' Then, wiping his mouth, he finally sat back to relax, having filled his belly with sufficient food.

'That's good to hear,' she said, as she poured him a mug of tea. 'What is most worrying for me is where my daughters are. Do you by any chance know?'

'Sorry, Mam, I don't. They were moved away from Keswick before I left that farm. Joanne said they must leave because Megan wasn't at all happy staying there and she'd write to let me know where they were moved to. Lord knows where that was. If she ever wrote to me, nobody bothered to send me her letter since I too was moved. Pretty dreadful, yeah?'

'I didn't hear from them either. Having lost our home and they too were moved, all contact has been lost between us. What a mess our lives have been. I expect the years of war haven't been easy for you either. You're a brave lad but why on earth were you moved to that bloomin' camp? Were you involved in a problem of some sort?'

Danny firmly shook his head. 'I did nowt wrong. Just got lumbered with blame for nicking fruit and veg when it were Willie Mullins who was guilty, that stupid lad who used to be my friend became a real pain in the ass.'

'I'm sorry to hear that.'

'He never was easy to know. A right bossy mess totally obsessed with himself. If I didn't agree with whatever he said or did, he'd turn furious and attack me, being so self-centred.

103

Willie was convinced that no one cared a jot about him, let alone his dad who rarely visited him. If he did come they didn't seem to get on well. Then if Willie didn't get what he felt he deserved or was punished for summat he'd done for a laugh, he'd put the blame on others, including me.'

'Oh dear! His problem could be because he was grieving for the loss of his mother, poor boy. Jane was my friend when we were young girls together. I found it tragic to hear of her death but then many lives have been lost in this dratted war.' Evie went on to explain how she was now working for Willie's father but tactfully made no mention of Harold having admitted his marriage was a complete failure and felt no grief for the loss of his wife. That surely wouldn't be at all appropriate when his son clearly did.

Danny blinked at her in dismay. 'Why the hell would you work for that man? Even his own bloomin' son doesn't care for him though is becoming equally difficult.'

Evie attempted to smile away the tight glower of disapproval on his face. 'I agree Harold Mullins isn't easy to work for, love, but he has rented us this house and I'm earning a reasonable income from him. It'll do for now till I find summat better, eh?' Seeing how he'd fallen silent she reached over to pat his cheek. 'Don't worry. Life should improve for you, and Willie, now this war is over and you're safely home. It will for me too when my family all return. Your dad will be home soon, thankfully alive if not too well. As for your sisters, I shall keep searching for

104

them and speak again to the billeting officer. Now, do you want anything more to eat?'

★ ★ ★

Two days before the wedding Joanne woke in the middle of the night to find herself bleeding. Horrified, she dashed to the toilet fearful she must be about to lose this baby. She felt a pain in her stomach and spent hours sitting on the lavatory in the bathroom awaiting disaster but could see no sign of any embryo, just a trickle of blood leaking out of her. In the end she provided herself with a cotton pad and staggered back to bed, falling instantly asleep being utterly exhausted.

First thing the next morning Joanne made the decision that she ought to visit the doctor, a fact that had been hovering in her mind for some time. Still bleeding she fearfully contemplated she must be undergoing a miscarriage. If that was the case would she still go ahead with this marriage? She slipped out of the boarding house before breakfast and hurried along Chapel Street to their local doctor, knowing she needed to arrive early to take her turn in the queue. Waiting proved to be quite an anguish but eventually her turn came.

'You are definitely not pregnant,' the doctor gently informed her; once Joanne had explained her predicament and he'd carefully examined her. 'This is a perfectly normal period. In fact, I'd say you're still a virgin, dear girl. Whatever you believe that fellow did to you, clearly didn't happen. He

105

probably just fondled you rather hard.'

Joanne stared up at the doctor with an enthralled sense of astonishment and relief. As he stepped away to pull off his gloves and give her a gentle smile, she quickly pulled down her skirt and removed the sheet he'd discreetly spread over her. 'Then why have I had no periods for the last three months or so?' she asked, utterly mortified at believing herself to be pregnant, which had resulted in a decision to marry Bernie in order to spare her the mess she was apparently in.

'You've clearly experienced a health issue. Have you not been eating properly for some reason?' he asked quietly. 'Periods can disappear for a time due to loss of weight, a fairly common occurrence during the war. Not simply because of rationing issues but often as a result of being distressed over the loss of a loved one, which affects the ability to eat.'

Joanne nodded, suddenly understanding this had been her problem. 'Let alone losing this GI I'd supposedly fallen in love with, I've lost all contact with my mother and brother after years as an evacuee. Not a pleasant experience.'

Giving her a sympathetic smile, he gently patted her shoulder. 'You're no doubt starting to recover from this sense of loss and have begun to eat much better. Put the past behind you and be thankful that your condition is perfectly admirable. All is well.'

Returning to the boarding house, her mind buzzing with confusion, Joanne saw Aunt Annie come marching over to meet her, dressed in a polka dot blue dress covered with a large apron.

'Where have you been, dear? We've been worried that you weren't around to deal with breakfast duties, as you usually are.'

'Sorry, Aunt Annie, I just felt in need of a walk to think things through. A part of me is filled with nerves over this coming wedding,' she admitted softly.

A sympathetic smile lit Aunt Annie's plump face. 'Nothing to fret about, it will be a simple event, not at all stressful. Bernie was also worried about your absence. You can reassure him too. Right now, you could pop upstairs to help make beds and clean bathrooms.'

'On my way,' Joanne swiftly assured her. She dashed off and spent the morning busily engrossed in various domestic jobs and the afternoon resting in her room, carefully avoiding speaking to Bernie, as she felt in complete turmoil.

She endured another sleepless night, this time not weeping but feeling a strange yearning for this alleged child of Teddy's she'd imagined she was carrying. She had felt a desire for him to prove his love by kissing and caressing her, although had foolishly given no appropriate consideration to what might happen by allowing him to go too far. Thank goodness he hadn't actually made love to her, even if he did press himself hard upon her and probably pushed his fingers inside, as he shouldn't have done. Joanne was aware she'd been so naive and innocent she'd no idea what he was doing or why. How obsessed with sex men could be.

By dawn the sky was a pale apricot streaked with clouds, the gentle gurgling of the waves failing to salve her sense of trepidation. Wasn't she expected to feel happy over this coming wedding? But having agreed to marry Bernie for what she deemed to be a good reason, she now had a dreadful mix of guilt and relief in the pit of her stomach.

Once breakfast had been served, washing, cleaning and all necessary tasks dealt with, they went for their usual late morning walk along the beach. Joanne remained silent as Bernie rattled on about how Blackpool's housing waiting list was growing quite long as soldiers returned and jobs were hard to find. ''Course, the country's broke, so we'll all have to work hard to restore it,' he said with a laugh. 'We'll build ourselves a good life even if it does take us a while to find a home of our own. You always look lovely, as you do now in that warm padded blue dress, woolly scarf and jacket.'

Joanne paused to stare out to sea, avoiding meeting his admiring gaze. 'I'm sorry, Bernie, there's something I need to tell you. The fact is that I've changed my mind and have decided I cannot marry you. I'm far too young and it's not at all what I planned for my life, now the war is finally over.'

Hearing him gasp she glanced up and saw how he looked utterly shocked and upset, which filled her with a strange sense of distress. 'I thought you were in need of a man to care and protect you. I'm most happy to do that.'

'I no longer require such help. All is well,' she said, then saw how his flint-like gaze flared, as if begging her not to make such an unwelcome remark. Even the shine of his brown hair in the morning sun, looking like sleek silk, made Joanne suddenly feel the need to smooth her fingers over it to comfort and apologize to him.

'Are you absolutely sure about that?'

'I am. The problem I thought I had is gone. I naively assumed the worst when Teddy embraced me but according to the doctor I'm still a virgin and perfectly well, although I did have a health problem now resolved. So what you saw was not as dreadful as you imagined. I'm so sorry.' She could feel a hot flush of embarrassment light her cheeks as he viewed her with shocked desolation.

Making no further response to what she'd bravely told him, he spun round on his heels and silently walked away.

Cancelling the wedding did not go down well with his two aunts either, who were dreadfully disappointed that their beloved nephew had lost her, declaring him to be heartbroken.

Megan too was distressed, accusing her sister of dismissing Bernie's love for her and as a result would also lose his friendship. Did that matter? Becoming trapped in a marriage with a man she didn't love would surely have been a complete disaster, in Joanne's humble opinion. Looking furious, Megan too stalked off, leaving Joanne feeling distraught and lonely, all too aware she may ruin her sister's life too by destroying her hope to stay in this lovely town.

Knowing she may no longer be welcome to stay in Blackpool, having hurt the landladies' nephew, returning to Manchester to find her mother was now most relevant in Joanne's mind.

She would stay a little while, for the sake of Megan. But if she failed to persuade her to come with her, she might lose her sister too, let alone any man to truly love her. Such was the sad reality of the foolish mistakes she'd made in her life.

11

Spring 1946

It was one day in early April that Evie was informed her husband would be returning home. Going to meet him a week later at Victoria Station she was filled with excitement. When the train arrived and in a flutter of smoke he stepped out of a carriage, she stared in stunned disbelief at this tall, thin man in uniform carrying his kitbag. He looked like a total stranger; gaunt, tired, and a tension very evident in him, a person she barely recognized. It came to her that he must still be suffering from health problems. Thrilled that her beloved husband had at last arrived home, Evie flung herself into his arms to hug and kiss him. He held her tightly too, a small smile lifting the pallid expression in his pale face.

Holding his hand, she walked him along Deansgate then down the alleys off Wood Street to their home. Pushing open the door, she called out to Danny. 'Your dad's home, love. Come and say hello.'

Seated at the kitchen table Danny made no move to step forward or give his father's hand a shake. Noting the blankness in her son's face, Evie realized that he probably resented never having heard from him. Donald reached into his kitbag and pulling out a toy dog, handed it to him as a gift. 'I remember you allus liked animals, so reckoned you'd like this.'

'I'm nearly fifteen now, sir, not interested in toys, ta very much.'

A small silence followed this comment and seeing a sourness punctuate Donald's dark eyes, Evie quickly took him over to sit in the armchair by the fire. 'Let me make you a cup of tea, darling. You must be pretty shattered but I'm so delighted to have you back home.'

Glancing around, he gave his head a shake. 'Don't really see this as our home. Not much impressed with it at all. Why did you stupidly lose the one we loved?'

Evie felt stunned by this callous remark. Was he making out that the reason their old house had been bombed was her fault? Hadn't she and other women suffered that problem as a result of the attacks upon this city, like many other towns had suffered? 'I too regret our first house having been bombed. At least this one is better than the various single rooms I've had to live in since,' she said, giving him a smile. She'd spent weeks improving it from when she'd first moved in months ago, desperate to make it look good when members of her family arrived. He didn't seem to appreciate her efforts. 'Finding paint to tart this up was not easy. Fortunately, your friend Davie Higginson helped with the decorating and is looking forward to seeing you again. Now, can I get you something to eat? Perhaps a lovely slice of cake to put you on till tea time?'

'Whatever you have available,' he murmured listlessly. 'My stomach's not capable of coping with too much food.'

Studying his appearance, Evie judged he was little more than seven stone, maybe less. She knew that when Donald had volunteered to join the RAF in 1939 it was because he had a fascination to fly. He was given a test and a medical, which he passed, and was accepted as a trainee pilot. Back then he'd possessed admirable qualities. Now he looked battered having been a prisoner of war. Evie was told by one of the chiefs at the Resettlement Service that he'd been captured after his plane was hit and rapidly fell out of the sky. He and his small crew had dived out wearing their parachutes. Two of his colleagues were killed but he had fortunately landed in a tree where he was captured, imprisoned and interrogated. He'd suffered starvation as a PoW that sadly damaged his stomach, poor man. What else he'd endured as a PoW Evie had no idea. On the two visits she'd paid him in hospital while under the care of the Civil Settlement Service, he'd remained silent on the subject, clearly having no wish to discuss such traumas.

Nor did he seem to be greatly interested in hearing anything about her own life. Not her work, this house or the evacuation of his son and daughters. Evie valiantly attempted not to harass him but kept herself busy doing quiet little jobs as he sat in gloomy silence for the rest of the day. All sign of his early smiles had vanished. He ate only half the slice of cake she gave him and when she supplied him with sausage and mash for his tea, he barely ate any of that either. Danny too looked stunned as they watched him push the food around his plate, hardly eating a scrap.

'Have I not cooked well enough for you?' she asked him anxiously. 'Or maybe you'd prefer something else? You do need to eat and put on a little weight.'

'Don't bloody boss me, woman,' he shouted. Then to Evie's amazement he picked up the remaining two sausages, wrapped them in his handkerchief and stuffed them in his pocket. 'I'm in need of a walk and a blast of fresh air. Can't bear being confined indoors.'

'I'll come with you. I like walking by the canal,' Danny said.

'Nay lad, stay put and do jobs for yer mam. I'm off to the pub for a drink and to get meself some cigarettes. 'Appen I'll also meet up wi' Davie.' And he put on his coat and marched off.

Evie sat in stunned silence for a moment, then seeing Danny looking equally upset at having been refused the offer to accompany his father on a simple walk, she took her son's hand and gave it a squeeze. 'Oh dear, he might be a bit snappy and impatient, but your dad's no doubt experienced a traumatic war and we'll just have to be patient with him and hope he eventually recovers.'

'I'd say he's got a mental issue,' Danny said. 'What he needs to realize is that we've all suffered from this bloody war too. The trouble is, he's bound to assume his situation was worse than ours, so we'll have to carefully avoid talking about it.'

What an intelligent and caring boy he was, Evie thought as she gave him a hug.

★ ★ ★

114

When night came Evie felt enchanted to find herself at last in bed with her beloved husband. Sadly, he made no attempt to touch or kiss her, merely said goodnight, turned over and fell asleep almost instantly. She placidly reminded herself how he was still unwell, noticing how he had a slight limp when he walked. Evie could but hope he would eventually recover and return to being the loving man he'd once been. Cuddling up close beside him, she happily drifted off to sleep. It was sometime around midnight that she was startled awake by the sound of him yelling. Switching on her bedside lamp, she saw that Donald was still locked in sleep but obviously suffering a nightmare.

Danny came rushing in to gaze at his father in stunned disbelief. 'Is he in trouble?' he whispered. 'What should we do?'

Not knowing how to answer this question, Evie gave a blank shake of her head. Then when Donald again yelled out, shouting and screaming and flinging his arms up as if attempting to protect himself, she gave him a gentle shake. Thankfully, this woke him up and, seeing tears in his startled eyes, she quickly found a handkerchief to wipe them away. 'Are you all right, darling?' she asked, smoothing her hand over his chest.

Staring at her as if he'd no idea who she was, without saying a word he turned over and went back to sleep.

'Heaven help him,' Danny said, as he slipped away back to bed.

In the days following it became clear that having returned from the war where he'd suffered injuries and been held for a time as a PoW, Donald had mental problems locked within him, as Danny had suspected. He was listless, self-obsessed, anxious and largely exhausted. Each night, instead of wishing to make love or cuddle Evie, he suffered from sleepwalking and a constant string of nightmares. No longer the gentle, quiet man she'd fallen in love with and happily married. What was even more astounding was that he frequently fell into fits of rage whenever Evie or Danny did not do as he ordered, sounding most authoritative.

'I told you not to keep pestering me with too much food,' he yelled, as she guided him to the table for dinner.

'You really do need to eat more, darling.'

'Not this damned fatty pork or mushy peas. Do as I bleeding told you and leave me in peace,' he shouted.

Evie jerked in dismay as he picked up his plate and threw his dinner at the wall, blemishing its white painted surface with gravy, slices of delicious fried pork, peas and mashed potatoes. What a ruinous thing to do, let alone wasting perfectly good food and doing himself no good at all.

As she understood from what her friends and niece had said when their husbands or loved ones had returned home, men did not expect their womenfolk to hang on to their freedom and independence. They behaved as if they were still very much in charge of a troop, as Donald was doing, treating Evie and his son as if they were a part of it. Nor did he take into account the daily work and responsibilities they had to deal with,

116

let alone his own need to eat well, despite the difficulty in finding rationed food. Evie realized it was going to take some time for him to settle down. He'd once possessed admirable qualities, now he was clearly battered. Peace may finally have come to the land but she could find none in her heart.

★ ★ ★

At first, Danny felt that he missed the freedom to roam around the countryside, climb trees if not the mountains and enjoy the sparkling fresh air of the Lake District. Sometimes in his head he could see acres of heather interspersed with steep slopes and fierce crags. He also missed the horses, cows and sheep he'd helped to look after. Now he was beginning to happily settle in and felt quite close to his mother, even though he was much older than when he last saw her four years ago. That was the time she came to visit him. What a treat that had been and such a pity she never managed to come again, not having much money. He remembered how she went on writing to him for years after that, as well as consistently sending him comics and food. She had always been most caring, kind and loving, sympathetic of problems he'd suffered as an evacuee, so he felt delighted to be back home.

When meeting her at Victoria Station last autumn he'd realized that his mother looked much older than he remembered and a bit tired with violet bruises beneath her eyes, very much as if she was overworked and short of sleep.

Having convinced her that he had no wish to return to his old school, she'd readily helped him to find a job. He'd been happily working for a company shifting and loading goods onto canal tugs and barges for some months. It suited him well to be out and about and not stuck indoors. Working in a factory would have made him feel very claustrophobic, a sensation he sometimes felt in this grim little house.

Right now he was occupying the bedroom that was meant for his sisters. Once they were found and returned home from wherever they were, he'd be confined in that sofa bed in the living-kitchen in this miserable house. Not a pleasant prospect. But he would put up with that, feeling keen to see them again. He appreciated all his mother had done to tart this place up. Irritatingly, it still stank at times and the electricity or water would stop working. Now that he'd got to know his mother better he found she was proving to be a strong, determined lady, and still valiantly striving to find his sisters as well as care for him and his mentally deranged father.

It was a bitter disappointment that his father was not at all as friendly towards him as he used to be. Danny worried that he may have said entirely the wrong thing by refusing to accept that silly toy he'd brought. His memory and desire to see him again had been quite strong, recalling the games they'd played together before the war when he'd been a young boy. Donald had taught him how to play football and cricket, ride a bicycle and even swim. Always a fun and attentive father. Yet now he was proving to be a nightmare in more ways than one. Danny found him far too bossy, constantly issuing orders even worse than those he used to receive from Willie. Donald would pack him off to bed far too early, treating him like a young kid, not as grown-up or educated as he actually was. In reality, Danny recognized that he was as tall as his dad now, and much stronger and fitter. Was that a good thought or a sad one?

This morning was cold and misty, as he made his way along the towpath beside the canal to the tugs he worked on. He'd so far successfully avoided seeing Willie Mullins, the one-time friend he'd come to hate over the years. There were occasions when he'd felt some sympathy for him but what a bastard he'd been in so many ways. Today, Danny was shocked when Willie suddenly jumped out from behind a tree to stand before him, fists on his hips and a sarcastic grin on his face.

'Are you going off to work?'

'I am, so please step out of my way,' Danny told him calmly.

'I'm aware that my father is employing your mam when it should have been me. I'm having to spend a load o' time looking for a job instead of helping Dad as a bookie in his business. That's not right. Was this barney your idea?' he snarled.

Danny felt shocked by this accusation and didn't feel certain how to handle the situation since they hadn't been on good speaking terms for years. Far too aware of the attacks he'd suffered, he firmly held fast to his courage. 'It's nowt to do wi' me,' he loudly protested.

'What about your mam then? How did she manage to get this job, her knowing nowt about betting?'

'She's no doubt learned whatever is necessary. I suspect she knows nowt about what a bleedin' mess you are either, so I'm not surprised if your dad had no wish to employ you. I'll 'appen tell her that.'

'You flamin' well won't or you'll seriously regret it. I'd say your mother is a slut and viewing my dad as her fancy man. He certainly finds her most appealing.'

Danny growled. 'That's a lie. She's devoted to her husband, my father, who has now arrived back home and is not too well.'

Willie snorted with laughter. 'I reckon you should keep tabs on her and watch what she gets up to then. She's a right madam that woman and no doubt eager to do whatever me dad demands of her. She's even happily living in his house, which I believe she might well have shared with him before her family came home.'

Stepping closer, Danny gave a glower of fury. 'You're talking absolute tosh. I arrived last autumn shortly after she'd moved in and she was definitely living in it alone until I came to join her. It's not a good house but she's done her best to improve it. I don't believe a word you're saying and if your father lays a finger on my mam, I'll skin him alive, so I will.'

Willie stepped forward, giving a snarl. 'If you ever did that, I'd do the same to you. In fact, I'll teach you a lesson right now for supporting your scandalous mother who's stolen my bloody job.' And giving Danny a punch, he sent him flying backwards into the stinking murky water of the canal. Filled as it was with oil, filth, dead animals, weeds and other rubbish, rage and fear escalated through him. Water filled his throat as he sank lower, tasting like a rusty rat. Danny firmly clammed his mouth shut, reminding himself that he'd been taught to swim by his dad, and had improved his skills when living in that camp by Derwentwater. He pummelled his legs hard, struggling to avoid being caught up in the weeds and rubbish as a cold dark wetness sank within him. Would he manage to safely reach the surface?

12

'May we have a little word, dear girl?'

Busily engrossed in dealing with the laundry, Joanne turned to meet Aunt Annie's query with a smile. 'Of course, Aunt.' After pegging up the last sheet and pillowcase, she went to join her seated at the kitchen table and welcomed the cup of coffee she was presented with. Seeing how upset she looked, Joanne feared that this dear lady was about to comment on the misery evident in Bernie over these winter months. Would she attempt to persuade her to agree to marry him. Knowing she could never allow that to happen, Joanne took a deep breath and spoke of more practical problems. 'You look deeply concerned about something, Aunty. I worry it might be because you must have lost many of your rations and clothing coupons with the work you did for that proposed wedding. I assure you that I'm happy to replace them with some of mine, or repay you once I can afford to do that. Or maybe you could sell that wedding gown you made to someone else. It really is beautiful.'

Bearing a most stubborn expression on her plump face, Aunt Annie shook her head. 'Our concern is not the rations, coupons or the money involved in preparing for that wedding, rather the effect of your cancellation on our dear nephew. He is sadly in a morose state of mind. Poor Bernie is finding it most upsetting seeing you around every single day when you evidently no longer care for him.'

Aunt Sadie, coming to sit beside her sister, gave a vigorous nod. 'We do perfectly understand that as a young gal you perhaps made a mistake to agree to wed him. Yet having you stay on here is greatly disturbing for our nephew. He's constantly striving to avoid spending any time with you, not even the walks you used to enjoy together, obviously finding your presence quite heart-rending.'

Joanne met each of their concerned expressions with a flicker of appreciation. Having carried on working at the boarding house she was all too aware that her relationship with Bernie was no longer an easy one. He'd barely engaged in any conversation with her since she'd informed him that she wished to cancel their wedding, merely making the odd comment about the weather or work he was involved in. And he frequently disappeared and remained absent for hours at a time, off somewhere he never mentioned. Not having believed his proposal had been connected with any emotion he felt for her, she'd assumed he was simply busily living his own life not at all bothered by the decision she'd made. It felt quite upsetting to hear what these dear landladies were saying, with no smiles that were usually evident in their friendly, open faces. 'I . . . I hadn't realized it had such a bad effect upon him,' she remarked woefully.

Aunt Sadie gently patted her cheek. 'Darling Joanne, we've loved having you stay with us, being a sweet girl and evacuee. But we sadly cannot contemplate the prospect of you continuing to work with Bernie. Not at all appropriate so far as he is concerned, if you catch our drift.'

'I do indeed.'

Aunt Annie again chimed in. 'I'm afraid we must request, dear girl, that you seek a new life elsewhere. We do promise to continue to look after Megan and, of course, you can keep in touch with your sister and visit her whenever you wish. Just give us suitable warning when you are about to come. Right now we think you should seek employment in Manchester, perhaps in a hotel. We would, of course, be happy to give you a reference.'

'We'll sorely miss you, but must give priority to our homeless, orphaned nephew,' Aunt Sadie said with a smile.

'I can understand that, dear ladies, having given this possibility some thought. I'd put it off because I was concerned for my sister. I greatly appreciate your offer to continue to care for her, so I'll look into this matter at once. Please don't mention it to Megan until I've found something suitable. And thank you for your offer of a reference. Much appreciated. Once I've found appropriate employment I'll explain to her where and why I'm moving. I've no wish to upset her but promise to do exactly as you suggest. Returning home to Manchester could well help me to find our mother.'

'That would be wonderful,' Aunt Annie agreed.

'Do be aware that if I succeed with that, Mam will want Megan to return home too and could find her a good high school to attend in Manchester.'

Aunt Sadie gently nodded. 'We fully understand that is something we may have to accept and do but hope we could visit you both from time to time, should that come about.'

'You'd always be most welcome. I live in hope that I will find my mother one day. Until then I'm deeply grateful for your care of Megan.'

'Then we are agreed,' Aunt Annie said, then when Bernie walked in at that moment she quickly changed the subject by offering to top up Joanne's coffee cup and give her a lovely slice of fruit cake.

Politely declining, Joanne gave her a quick smile, saying she must get back to doing the laundry and discreetly slipped away.

Later that day, she set about writing to hotels in Manchester, firmly hoping to find a job, and in the days following carefully avoided any contact with Bernie. Joanne was delighted when a week later she received a letter offering her the opportunity to attend an interview. She tactfully informed Megan that she was popping over to their hometown to again search for their mother, making no mention of how she may ultimately achieve employment and then return to Manchester for good.

The interview went well and Joanne was successfully granted employment, having worked in a boarding house and gained the necessary experience. She would also be provided with decent accommodation up in the loft of this hotel. As she walked back to the station she kept staring around, her eyes searching for a glimpse of someone she recognized. Apart from Victoria Station, which had suffered during the war, she noticed an office block near Exchange Station had been bombed. There was also evidence of burned-out buildings all around and flattened-out areas that had once been occupied. Even Piccadilly looked something of a mess compared to how it used to be before the war. So many families must have lost their homes, as had they.

On her journey home, Joanne focused her mind on what she needed to say to her beloved sister, fearing that leaving Blackpool could create problems for them both. They would be sure to miss each other badly. But if Megan still wished to stay it would surely be to her advantage, as she would continue to be well cared for by those dear ladies. As for her own future, Joanne knew she must build herself a new life and could but hope she'd sooner or later find their mother and ultimately manage to tempt Megan to return to her true home.

* * *

Knocking on Harold Mullins's door to deliver the money she'd collected, as she was expected to do most evenings, Evie felt a tremor of anxiety, aware she'd not achieved as much as she should. It had been another difficult day in spite of having trailed around from house to house from early morning till late this evening.

The door opened and he surprisingly urged

126

her to enter his house. 'So what have you getten?' he asked.

'Sadly very little,' she answered politely, handing him the box that held the money.

'Eeh, heck, are you failin' in this job.'

'I'm doing my best but, as I've explained, it isn't easy.'

'Sometimes it pays to hold yer fire and hang around until folk turn up. I'd not rush away until whoever's avoiding you finally arrives home. I reckon it'd be right up your street. And what have you got to lose? If they don't pay you should threaten to call the rozzers, or police officers as we more rightly call them, reminding these idiots that they could be nicked for the debts they owe.'

The thought of doing that was not a pleasant prospect but, giving a nod and a smile, Evie promised to continue doing her best. 'I have waited on occasions, but if they spot me hanging around near their door, they quickly disappear again. Calling the police wouldn't be appropriate either, some people deep in poverty are possibly hoping to make a bit of money by taking a bet.'

'That's their bloody problem. A hefty gambling debt should be paid off. At least a sizeable chunk of it. Folk have to accept they must find some way to pay their betting bills even if they are on the dole. I too require funds to pay for what I need in life. I'm not yet convinced you're any good at this job, but you're a lovely lady so fellas probably would welcome you in their house, as do I.'

Giving him a startled blink, Evie noticed how

127

his eyes were glimmering, blatantly staring at her breasts. Alarm ricocheted through her as he flickered a mischievous smile. Not at all what she'd expected, as he would frequently be dismissive of her and put her down with a casually cutting remark. Now he appeared to be attempting to charm her. What a shuddering prospect that was. Taking a deep breath, she quickly backed away to the door. 'I must be off to see to my husband and hope to achieve more over the next few days, bearing in mind your advice. I'll do whatever you say is necessary, being very much in need of this job.'

When she did arrive back home she was shocked to see Danny engaged in a furious row with Donald. Her son did look rather odd, being dressed in clothes that were definitely not his and holding a parcel of his own that was dripping water all over the kitchen floor.

'It's not my fault I fell in the canal, it were just an accident.'

'You stupid boy. Look at the mess you're in,' Donald roared. 'You're a liability, not having the sense you were born with. Keep away from the flamin' canal in future.'

'No, it's where I work.'

'Don't talk daft. You're far too young to be working.'

'I'm not! I told you I'm nearly fifteen and old enough to get a job having left school. What's wrong with that?'

Hurrying over, Evie gathered up the parcel of wet clothes and gave Danny a hug before tenderly speaking to her husband. 'These things happen, folk do sometimes slip off a tug into the canal. It's generally not a disaster, just irritating and most fortunate that you once taught our son to swim, so don't tell him off.'

'I'll do what I bloody please,' Donald roared, jumping up from his chair to hover over her. Holding fast to the panic stirring within her, Evie managed to smile then gently gave him a kiss. 'Now, darling, would you like fish and chips for your tea, since I'm a bit late home?' And when Danny eagerly offered to run out and get them from the local shop, Evie busily set the table, watching with relief as Donald calmly settled back in his chair and lit himself a cigarette. What a muddle his attitude was.

★ ★ ★

Joanne quietly informed Megan that she'd been offered a new job at a hotel back in Manchester, and saw panic fill her young sister's eyes as she gave a gasp of dismay. Tenderly putting her arms around her, Joanne gave her a comforting hug. 'Hush, darling, don't fret. Listen carefully to what I have to say. I'm quite thrilled about this and will accept, as it could help me to find our mother.'

Joanne went on to explain how she found it difficult to stay here working with Bernie now that she'd cancelled their wedding, and how he was wanting her to leave. 'Our dear aunts gave me a good reference to help me find new employment and happily agreed to continue caring for you. I will, of course, come and see you as often as I can. If I'm fortunate enough to ever find our darling mother then I'll bring her to see you too and hopefully she'll agree that you can decide where you wish to live. Is that all right, lovey?'

Megan gave a little nod, looking very much as if she had no real wish for this to happen. So often in the past whenever life changed for them or something unpleasant had upset her she would react by badly weeping. Now she seemed a much more resolute and determined young girl, far more relaxed and content than she'd been as a young evacuee.

'I shall miss you so much, sis.'

'I'll miss you too, but, as I say, I'll come to see you quite regularly and write to you every single week. And if you ever want to come and visit me, just let me know and you could most definitely do that.'

'I will visit you whenever I get a bit of time off school, but I am fond of our aunts and this high school I'm attending, so I'm happy to stay here even though I'll feel lost without you,' she bravely stated, a small sparkle of tears suddenly flooding her eyes.

'I shall feel lost without you too, lovey, but we will always remain close,' Joanne assured her. She gave her a kiss on her soft cheek and gently wiped her tears away. How sweet and delightful her sister looked these days, generally dressed in her school uniform of green pleated skirt, blazer, tie and a smart white shirt. All provided by dear Aunt Annie.

Joanne felt quite sad about leaving these

130

landladies, even more so at losing the company of her darling sister. But it was very much the right thing to do, considering the foolish mistakes she'd made. It was time to put more common sense into her head and build strength and independence.

Megan helped to pack what Joanne deemed to be suitable clothes: hats, shoes and underwear, the rest of her sister's few belongings remaining in her care. 'You'll perhaps earn the money to buy yourself some new clothes, once you get settled into working at that hotel,' she said, looking slightly envious at such a prospect.

'When you come and visit me we'll enjoy a lovely day of shopping together,' Joanne promised, and with a giggle they shared a loving hug. 'At least you'll be safe here, well cared for and much loved by these aunts.'

On the day of departure Joanne recommended that Megan didn't accompany her to the station as that would be too upsetting for them both, to which she soulfully agreed. It was as she made her way to the door that Bernie at last came to. speak to her. His grey eyes looked oddly soulful as he steadily gazed at her. 'I'm sorry you've decided to leave, Joanne. I'd much prefer you to stay but do accept it is painful to see you every day, so that wouldn't be the right thing to do. Having made the decision to build yourself a new life I hope it goes well for you.'

'Thank you, Bernie, I hope you have a good life too.' She stood awkwardly before him, wondering if she should give him a comforting hug or shake his hand. Recognizing no possibility of being allowed to do either she gave him a little smile and picked up her small suitcase.

'I'll carry this for you if you need my help,' he said, 'and don't you wish to take your bike with you?'

'No thanks, I'd rather leave it here to enjoy when I come on a visit, and I can carry my own bag. It's not much of a walk to the nearby railway station.' Giving a little nod and smile, she walked away. When reaching the corner of the street, Joanne turned to look back at Jubilee House and seeing Megan standing with the two landladies outside the door, gave them all a loving wave.

As she walked to Central Station she thought of the many tourists visiting Blackpool who had been killed when a Botha plane had crashed into the station on 27 August 1941. The plane had collided with another over the sea and was duly wrecked. Debris and fuselage had fallen onto the station and over parts of Albert Road, South King Street and Central Drive here in the town centre. Many heroes and soldiers had saved people's lives but many were killed, including two military personnel and a passenger in the planes, plus station staff. Others were badly injured, failing to escape the aviation fuel that set a fire burning everywhere. Manchester too had suffered similar problems. Central Station was still in operation and with the war thankfully over Joanne felt in no danger. Once on-board the train, she sat in silence throughout the journey to her hometown, speaking to no one, tears rolling down her cheeks at the thought of leaving her sister behind. As well as the issues of bombing and aircraft accidents, there'd been other issues for them over the years, being evacuees. Not at all easy to deal with, particularly regarding what Megan had been through. She prayed that she would remain safe.

13

Over the coming weeks Joanne found herself working hard at the hotel as a waitress. She spent most of her time rushing back and forth between the kitchen and the dining room, taking orders from guests, the pressure of that much greater than she was used to, finding it somewhat confusing. Carrying hot bowls of soup would sometimes fill her with nervous anxiety. At first she would sometimes forget what they'd ordered or misunderstand and order the wrong thing. Eventually she was kindly instructed by the pleasant woman in charge to attach a pad to the waistband of her pinafore and write the details on that, talking to her as if she were an idiot, which maybe she was. Joanne was also instructed to know how each dish was prepared so that she could make recommendations to customers. It was necessary to be knowledgeable, polite and charming, even to rude customers, screaming children and people who declined to give her a tip.

Clearing and resetting each table after guests departed was a task she had no problem with, having done a great deal of that at the boarding house. In this posh hotel everything had to be laid out very smartly. There was a great deal of sparkling silver cutlery, china cups and plates, pretty napkins and also a small vase of flowers on each table. Not simply basic pottery, a load of sauce and tomato ketchup bottles, as there'd been in Jubilee House.

There were times when she longed to be back there, a much jollier place with sun often sparkling over the beach. Today, a grey chill seemed to hang about everywhere. She occupied a small room at the top of the building and even after a few months still felt very mixed up and dreadfully lonely. Had she made the right decision to come here?

Fortunately, she was granted a few hours off each afternoon and one full day a week, which varied from time to time, certain days and weekends being either quiet or very busy. Joanne spent her spare time roaming around looking for her mother and anyone she knew. This hotel being situated fairly close to Victoria Station, she would stroll down Deansgate through central Manchester to Castlefield. Watching the barges come up the canal basin filled with sand, coal, grain, oil, gravel, timber and other items was always interesting, the distant sounds of the city washing over her and the wind whistling under the canal bridge. When the sand was tipped out it made some of the land around look like a part of the beach in Blackpool. Oh, how Joanne missed that.

She would explore areas close to the River Irwell, the grimy old Medlock littered with old prams, boots and rubber tyres. The river had dye works, cotton mills and printworks close by and she visited those too, seeing no one she recognized. Other days she'd take a bus to Salford, Ancoats or Collyhurst. Not places she felt certain Evie would be living, but having failed to find her anywhere in Castlefield, she felt the need to spread her search.

At the end of each day her feet would hurt and her back ache and she'd thankfully retire to her room to read a magazine such as *People's Friend*, or a book she'd borrowed from the Central Library. As she relaxed in bed, she made a note of all the places she'd visited, marking them on the map of the city she'd bought, then write out a list of other possible areas. Having spent weeks on this task, Joanne was slowly losing all hope of success. It could be that her mother had died when their home or the mill where she'd worked were bombed. But just in case she was still alive, she'd keep on looking for her.

Joanne hadn't yet taken the trouble to become too friendly with any of the other members of staff apart from a young girl, Shirley Nuttall, the waitress she worked with. She didn't know a soul. She was sitting in the hotel kitchen enjoying a soft-boiled egg and toast for her breakfast when the chef came over to sit with her. 'Hi, there, I'm Andy, hope you're feeling settled in and are enjoying the food.'

'Thank you, yes, it's delicious,' she politely told him.

'You look pretty delicious too. I wonder if we could meet up for a date sometime, mebbe going to the pictures or a dance, whatever you fancy?'

Joanne stared at him in astonishment, recalling how little she trusted men having been dropped by Teddy, the GI she thought loved her, and that

136

Wing Commander Ramsbotham turning out to be a real pervert. 'Sorry, I'm rather busy doing other things, so don't have time for a date with anyone right now.'

'Oh, come on, you aren't in heaven wi' the door locked so can surely find time for a bit of fun? How about going to the Palais on Rochdale Road, or if you're a bit posh the Opera House on Quay Street? Just name where you'd like to go. I'd love to take you anywhere.'

Having finished eating her breakfast, Joanne got to her feet and gave him a dismissive smile. 'Dream on, I've no wish to go anywhere with you or any other man just now. I prefer to remain free of such demands,' she said and, lifting her head high, walked away.

Thankfully he didn't bother her again, which was a huge relief. Her chief concern was to find her mother, not a new boyfriend. The change in her life felt quite interesting but not easy. At least this was a job that supplied her with reasonably good pay, and being very caring of guests and having efficient serving skills she did receive a surprising number of tips. Joanne carefully saved every penny she possibly could, intending to take a day off to visit Megan a couple of times a month. Fortunately, Bernie was generally absent whenever she informed those dear ladies that she was coming.

★ ★ ★

It was one of those strangely cool summer days that brought a scent of anticlimax echoing within

137

Evie, as if the loss of a bright blue sun-filled sky had clouded over her, installing a feeling of dread about her future. She was sitting with her niece in their favourite café at Campfield Market, striving not to admit that Donald was largely uninterested in her, his wife of some twenty-odd years. He was no doubt grieving for the loss of his mates, some of whom were dead, and he sorely missed them, which she could well understand. She'd lost a few friends too. Donald had endured a tough war about which he refused to say a word, so she'd strived to be tolerant of his anxiety and sense of insecurity. At least Davie had told her that he enjoyed spending some time with him, though didn't always find him easy to talk to either. Such was reality.

'I fear Donald might never fully recover or return to his former self, regardless of the treatment he's been given,' she told Cathie, happily giving baby Heather a cuddle on her lap. 'I believe his aspiration to reveal the issues he had to deal with during the war and any emotion he feels for his children, let alone consideration for others, has completely disappeared. Nor is he willing to help me find our daughters.' Tears spilled out of her velvet brown eyes as Evie felt they no longer seemed to be of any interest to him.

'Why do you think that is?'

'He's locked in his own personal anguish,' Evie said, recalling the conversation she'd had with him that morning over breakfast when she'd confessed how she still sorely missed her daughters, having struggled for months to find

138

them. Donald's reaction had been completely dismissive. 'Why bother to search for them girls? They must be quite content wherever they are so that's where they should stay, otherwise they'd have come back home by now. Trouble is, I'm not at all happy about where I'm living.'

This comment had made Evie feel utterly devastated, the indifference in him towards his daughters making it appear that he was not as caring or loving as he used to be. She felt as if her family was falling into ruins. Donald tenaciously objected to the fact she kept worrying about her children, rationing, loss of her job and the difficulties she'd experienced in finding them a home. He would constantly moan about everything she failed to do for him, not convinced she kept things as tidy as she should. He spent some of his time fussing over tidying his own belongings, which were very precious to him. Each day he walked for miles, showing no interest in finding a job, but hated staying indoors for too long. Evie did once persuade him to do some shopping for her while she was busy working, but he strongly objected to the queue he was stuck in and refused to do that ever again.

It was true that like hundreds and thousands of other women she'd suffered many sleepless nights in a damp air raid shelter, endless restrictions, queuing and bombing, etc. Danny had been absolutely correct to say that having fought hard in a war for years, his father saw himself as the only one in need of care.

'My son too is finding it hard to accept this apparent stranger as his father, constantly complaining about his lack of interest in him, once his precious son. We worry it may never be possible to improve Donald's temper or achieve a happy family life, something I've dreamed of for years. Perhaps I shouldn't be telling you this, Cathie, but with my girls living in some remote place, who else is there for me to turn to for sympathy and support except you, love? I hope you don't mind.'

Cathie gently squeezed her hand. 'Of course I don't, Aunty. You certainly have my complete attention and love. Have you, by any chance, spoken to those teachers who escorted my cousins when they were evacuated?'

Evie shook her head. 'I never could find any, as they're no longer working at that old school. Not even sure they were around when Joanne and Megan were evacuated that second time, once the bombing started.'

Giving a small frown of consideration, Cathie said, 'I think I know where one of them lives, so I'll go and have a chat with her, if you like, and see if she remembers where they were taken.'

'Oh, thanks, love, that would be wonderful. I've spoken countless times to the billeting officer but he seems to have disappeared too now, the war being long over. What a mess I seem to be in.'

* ★ *

The next time Joanne visited Jubilee House, to her amazement she found it largely closed, only a few regular guests staying there, perhaps because

140

summer was over. Megan came running along the passage to welcome her with a burst of joy and a warm hug. 'So good to see you, sis.'

'And you, lovey. You look very fit and well.' Then noticing the dusty state of the staircase with bits of plaster and rubble lying around on the steps and a ladder going up to the loft, she asked what on earth was happening.

'Take a look,' Megan said, and pushed her up the stairs where she surprisingly saw Bernie's face suddenly appear in the loft entrance hatch, grinning down at her.

'Hello, I'm putting in a new bedroom,' he said.

'Oh, my goodness, that can't be easy but what a good idea.'

'He's a very clever man,' Megan proudly remarked. 'Pop up the ladder to take a look at it while I finish off my homework. Then we could go for a walk on the beach or along the pier if you like.'

When her sister scampered off, Joanne climbed up the ladder and peeped into the loft, hugely impressed by its size and appearance. What had once been a fairly scrubby storage area had now been cleaned out. 'Heavens, it looks much bigger and more classy than I remember.'

Bernie was clearly busily engaged in painting the walls. He put down his brush, rubbed his hands on his work trousers then helped her in. 'You're welcome to give me your opinion on the plan of this room.'

Looking at it in more detail, Joanne was amazed to see that a bathroom had been added, a fitted wardrobe built into the far wall and a

141

bright window installed with a view of the sea. 'Did you do all this work?'

'I did, with quite a bit of help and training from a friend,' he said. 'What do you think?'

'Oh, it's wonderful. Megan is right, you are indeed a clever and most practical man.'

Glancing at him, she thought how Bernie seemed to be even taller, fitter and better looking than when she'd last seen and worked with him some months ago, let alone last year when they'd supposedly been courting. His thick brown hair still flopped over his brow but his square face was clear of the spots and rashes that had bothered him when he was a young boy. He appeared quite friendly towards her now, obviously no longer concerned about her refusal to marry him. Maybe he'd found himself a new girlfriend, a thought that brought a strange flicker of gloom within her, not having the possibility or desire to find anyone for herself. Had she made the right decision to leave here when she couldn't find her mother, relative or any old friend in Castlefield? It felt a most lonely place to live. She then became aware that Bernie was explaining his next task.

'Once I've finished painting the walls and woodwork, the last job will be to make the entrance much wider and build up a small staircase. My mate Johnny, who lives down the road, has promised to help with that too. He's training me on how to do this building work, claiming an extra pair of hands to hold and hammer things and offer instructions is most useful,' he said with a grin.

'Good for you. I assume that set of steps will need to be quite small. Presumably it's then just a case of putting in new furniture. Whose room will this be?' she asked, returning his smile with one of respect.

'My aunts'. I'll then update and improve the room I occupy on the floor below, which makes sense. I have plans and ideas for other parts of the house too, not least putting in more bathrooms, which I'll work on bit by bit.'

'Excellent. I admire this ability in you. You're clearly good at this job.'

'The training takes quite a bit of time,' he said with a chuckle. The expression in his grey eyes then changed to one of concern. 'So how about you, Joanne? I hope your new job is working for you. And have you managed to find any news of your mother?'

'Not yet, but being a waitress at this hotel is fine,' she brightly remarked, having no wish to complain about the sense of despair and loneliness she felt.

Reaching over, he tapped his hand gently on her shoulder, as if recognizing some distress in her. 'It can't be easy,' he murmured and, to her stunned amazement, Joanne experienced a strange wish to fall into his arms. If she'd stayed on here and accepted Bernie's proposal, this could have been their bedroom as a married couple. Would that have been a good thing or not? She'd dismissed this young man and clearly put her life into something of a muddled mess. Would she ever calm down and find anyone to love and care for her whom she was willing to accept? Joanne thought she no longer had any wish to see that GI ever again. From now on she must stop fretting about the mistakes she'd made in the past. But if and when she'd find happiness was very much open to question. She certainly had no intention of ever attaching herself to Bernie Flynn. It was really time she found herself a friend and life of her own, as well as caring for her beloved sister.

★   ★   ★

Having spent the entire summer searching for her mother to no avail, Joanne came to the decision to ease off the time she spent looking for her, which had proved to be utterly useless. Much as she loved and missed Mam, she felt worn out and riddled with a sense of depression so resolved to freshen herself up. As a consequence, she started visiting the cinemas and theatres, sometimes with Shirley or other members of staff who generally welcomed her presence. On occasions, Joanne would find herself agreeing to accompany a young man, there being quite a few who worked here. These alleged dates were always a little disappointing, perhaps because these men were rather boring or wrapped up in themselves. Still carrying the memory of Teddy in her heart, she desperately attempted to banish it, but whenever they tried to give her a kiss or a cuddle, it never appealed to her and she'd tactfully resist.

Recalling the request she'd received from that young man working as a chef here at the hotel, which she'd firmly declined, she thought that maybe that had been a mistake and he could be a better possibility. When next she saw Andy the chef in the kitchen, she went over to say hello and give him a smile. 'That offer you made for you and I to have a date, I'm thinking I might now agree to give it a go.'

Looking at her in amazement, he gave a shrug. 'Too late, love, I've found somebody else, a gorgeous friendly girl called Shirley Nuttall, your waitress partner.'

'Oh, I see. Well, not to worry, it was just a thought. Shirley is a lovely girl, I do hope you get on well.'

''Course we will. She's most adoring. I gave you the chance to get to know me better but you weren't interested and obstinately refused. She didn't, so you've missed the chance.'

Hearing him start to laugh filled her with embarrassment as she quickly walked away. Dear Lord, what an idiot girl she was to be trying to resolve her sense of loneliness by finding herself a boyfriend. Her so-called friend hadn't even mentioned her own success. Joanne now came to the decision to remain single and ignore all men.

14

Autumn 1946

Autumn had arrived and, as Evie sat huddled on the wall down by the canal breathing in the smell of tar and coal dust, of cold damp water, mud and grass, she came to the decision it was time for her to visit Cumberland, her husband feeling a little better. Hopefully her niece had found out the information she needed from that teacher she'd offered to speak to.

When she went to meet up with Cathie at Campfield Market, Evie heard that she'd sadly failed to discover anything.

'Their teacher was aware those two girls were moved on a second time from Manchester to another foster home in Cumberland,' Cathie said. 'She did point out that some evacuees were also sent to Wales or the Fylde coast. Many were frequently moved around and were often lost track of. And as a few of her colleagues have remained in various places she promised to write to them in the hope of finding out where your daughters were possibly sent, but has found no solutions so far.'

'Eeh, love, that's a shame but thanks for trying. Let's hope your friend gets a response and some news about where they are eventually. That's summat to look forward to.'

'It could take a while,' Cathie commented wryly.

Evie frowned. 'Aye, I daresay it could and with all billeting officers now gone I've no wish to wait for months or years. I've long felt the need to visit Cumberland but as well as having to work hard I'm currently occupied with caring for my invalid husband, who has no wish for me to go anywhere so I've kept putting it off. I feel it's time for me to give it a go and visit various town halls, as well as the place Danny was located and ask if they have any information about Megan and Joanne.'

'That would be worth trying, although not easy and quite time-consuming,' Cathie warned.

'I'll need to ask Harold Mullins for a bit of time off work, which he'll hopefully allow me. Would you look after your Uncle Donald while I'm away?'

''Course I would, Aunty, just as you occasionally look after little Heather for me.'

★ ★ ★

Harold Mullins was not at all pleased by Evie's request for two days off. 'Nay, lass, there's too much work for yer to do. Why would I allow you any free time?'

'Because I'm still trying to find my daughters, which is very important to me. And just going on a Sunday would not work as most places will be closed, so if I could have next Thursday and Friday off that would be most useful. I always have Saturday free and will return on Sunday.'

Looking completely uncaring about her troubled thoughts, he gave a snort of disapproval. 'You

147

can't be serious to ask for this. Not after all I've done for you.'

'Good gracious, how can you say that? What right have you to object to this simple request? I'm still in difficulty over the loss of my family.'

'Your son and hubby have been home for some time and your daughters will no doubt turn up eventually. So as you're settled down in domestic bliss, why would I sanction you much in the way of time off, considering it would risk me losing money. I believe in addling brass. Do be wary of where these fancies lead you.'

'I assure you I'll catch up with calls upon your clients as soon as I return.'

'If I agree, I'd need evidence of approval for my generosity,' he said, chilling the atmosphere between them still further. Then, stepping close, his mouth twisted into a sardonic smile as he slid his hands over her hips to pull her close and give her a squeeze. 'You are an irresistible lady.'

Shoving him firmly away, Evie felt a strong desire to punch his private parts with her knee. His growing attention to her was proving to be something of a battle, the stink of beer or whisky in his breath making her want to throw up. 'Take note, Harold, that being happily married you should take your flaming hands off me,' she remarked coldly.

Giving a roar of laughter, he lifted them up to let her go. 'Just be aware that when you return from this trip you'll have to work longer hours to make up for lost time. Then come and hand over the money you've collected and show your

148

appreciation for granting you this time off,' he whispered softly.

After viewing the gleam of desire in his gaze muddled with an expression of disapproval, a sense of sickness fluttered through Evie as she hurried away. What a dreadful, intimidating man he was. Alcoholic, belligerent, aggressive and very much a bully. Oh, how she hated him and this damn job. Had she made entirely the wrong decision to work for this man? And how could she ever escape him? If only she had the time to try working for herself. The concern she was suffering from caring for her husband and son was not easy and this battle with Harold Mullins was making her feel worse. She must ensure that her life changed once her girls were found. Right now, no matter how demanding he was he'd get no so-called appreciation or thanks from her.

The moment Evie told Donald of her plan, he looked utterly staggered at such a dreadful prospect and made it clear he would not permit her to go. 'I'm still ill and in need of your care, so you ain't going nowhere. It would be heartless of you to leave me alone.'

'I think your health is gradually improving so I'm afraid I must, darling. Don't worry, I'll only be gone three days at the end of the week and Cathie has agreed to come to cook and care for you while I'm away, so you'll be fine.'

Thrilled as she was to have her husband back home, coping with him was not proving to be at all easy. Harold Mullins was not easy to deal with either. Evie was beginning to feel that her resilience was fading rapidly, partly out of exhaustion for all the work she was involved in, as well as anxiety over the state of her husband's mental health. She felt very much in a sticky mess.

★ ★ ★

Evie took the train to Cumberland, the golden beauty of the trees in autumn filling her with an almost guilty sense of peace. It was good to have a day or two free from that dreadful job and she felt an excited anticipation that she might soon find her lovely girls. When she reached the station at Keswick, she left the train, walked into town and managed to find herself a room in a small guesthouse that would not cost her a fortune. Keswick looked a pleasant, quiet place, save for the occasional sound of car horns and a number of people wandering around enjoying the shops and the beautiful panoply of mountains that surrounded this town. Its highlight was the possession of a surprisingly large lake, steamers packed with passengers who were very much enjoying a sail on Derwentwater, despite the coolness of the weather.

When she'd told Danny of her plan to come here, he'd mentioned the walks and climbing he'd been involved in on Blencathra, Castlerigg, Grisedale Pike and other places. Mainly he spoke of the farm where he'd first been billeted, situated within a mile of Keswick, a place she remembered well, being most impressed with it when she'd visited him all those years ago. He went on to inform her that his sisters had been settled in a house on the outskirts of the town the second time they'd been evacuated. 'They were happier there than they'd been at that farm they'd hated but were eventually moved elsewhere.' Asking him why that was, he gave a shrug. 'No idea. Mebbe they were flung out because it is quite a wealthy area so them folk 'appen didn't care for ordinary kids or what they got up to. Joanne posted me a note to say they were being re-billeted but had no idea where they were to be sent. Then, as I told you, I too was shooed out to that bloomin' camp for no good reason. What a nightmare that was, and I obviously lost touch with my sisters.'

'Didn't we all, love,' Evie had agreed.

Now she walked around Keswick, calling in various bed and breakfast houses, hotels, schools and shops, showing them a photo of her daughters when they were young, but received no good response. She then went to call at the farm where Danny had first been billeted, driven there by a young cab driver in his Austin car, most impressed when she saw it again, as she had been the first time. Evie loved the call of the curlew and the clean tang of heather. The fast running stream, known locally as a beck, meandered behind the farmhouse and the mystical green of the pinewoods. She saw a large garden packed with fruit and vegetables. Was that where Danny was charged with stealing? Surely he'd been well fed so should never have been charged by these people, or Willie. Most of all, she appreciated the sense of wild countryside and open freedom of these Lakeland fells.

When she knocked on the door it was the farmer's wife who answered, her husband no doubt out working out on the land. Politely thanking this lady for how they had fostered her son at the start of the war, Evie went on to explain who she was searching for and asked if she had any notion where her girls might be.

'Why would I have any idea where they were billeted?'

'Oh dear, I just hoped you might know. And I'm sorry you thought it necessary to send my son to a camp for problem evacuees since he's always been a lovely, sensible lad and said he'd enjoyed living here and helping on your farm.'

Giving a dismissive sniff, the woman said, 'Having been accused of committing a theft why would we allow him to stay?'

Evie stoutly responded by assuring the lady of her son's innocence. 'He was accused by an alleged friend who could well have been the guilty party.'

'I reckon there could have been more to it than that. Nothing I fully understood or wish to discuss,' she snapped and slammed the door shut.

Alarmed by the suggestion Danny might have been charged with something more than pinching fruit and veg from this farm, Evie felt her heart pounding as she got back into the cab and asked to be taken back to town.

The next day the young cab driver happily drove her to Threlkeld, Penrith, then down to Ambleside, but not the camp where her son was located, pointing out that it was now gone. Evie

152

accepted this reality and although she spoke to many people in various hotels, schools and shops, town halls and billeting officers in surrounding villages, she sadly found no information about her daughters. She spent a fairly sleepless and anxious night worrying over why Danny had made no mention of possibly being charged with some other offence. Did he have no wish to admit his guilt?

Early the next morning after at least enjoying an excellent breakfast, she caught a bus to explore Windermere, Staveley, Burneside, and finally Kendal. Knowing she must go to the station at Oxenholme the following morning to catch the train home, this last town was surely a good port of call in case this was where Joanne and Megan had been moved to. Trailing around feeling a little lost and confused, she suddenly found the town hall in Kendal and felt the urge to pop in to ask if there were any billeting officers still around.

'No, madam, I'm sorry, all volunteers are now gone,' a pleasant lady secretary informed her, Evie having briefly explained who she was searching for.

'Sadly, that seems to have been the case everywhere I've looked for them.' Feeling weary and heartbroken over having achieved nothing except more dreadful news, she turned to walk away and was then startled by the lady's next comment.

'Of course, many children who didn't settle here were moved on to Fleetwood, Southport and Blackpool. Have you investigated those?'

Staring at her in stunned amazement, Evie suddenly recalled that her niece had mentioned that many children had been sent to Wales and the Fylde coast. Goodness, why hadn't she taken note of that, although how could she possibly succeed in exploring all those possible towns, let alone in Wales? Still, this piece of information might prove useful. 'Thank you for that, dear lady. I certainly will.'

★ ★ ★

How Danny regretted his mother going off to the Lakes. Would she discover all he'd suffered back then, problems he'd managed to block out of his head having no wish to remember or discuss them. They were far too stupid and unreasonable. Left alone without his wife around to help keep him calm, his father was looking even more depressed. Feeling some sympathy for this sense of despair very prevalent in him, Danny attempted to be friendly and chat.

'Tell me about the anguish you suffered in the war, Dad. It must have badly affected you. Did you lose any of your mates?'

Meeting his son's curious gaze with blank despair on his face, he gave a small nod. ''Course I did. My best mate had his foot knocked off by shells and holes in his leg. I picked Larry up and carried him down the track. When the doctor came he amputated his leg off. The next day he died, having bled too much.' He then fell silent.

Aware of the pain in his father's face, Danny

could think of nothing appropriate to say except, 'How awful and so brave of you to try to help him.'

'That's not the only issue I suffered. There were plenty more I prefer not to remember or speak of, not least the torture and brutality as a prisoner of war. The guards loved to starve, beat and kick us. I'd lie in a crumpled mess on the floor and wish I could vanish into a different world.'

'Thank God you didn't,' Danny stated quietly.

'Don't talk rubbish, lad. Look at the mess I'm in and don't pretend for a moment that you give a toss about me. Nobody does. And you never do a damn thing I tell you to do. Like now. Go and buy me a paper. Make me a cup of tea. Clean this kitchen floor then wash up.'

Danny gave a sigh, wearily irritated that his father was again becoming most domineering and showing little patience or interest in him. He felt very much under his control, as if he was being treated as a servant or a low-rank soldier. Even though Cathie had called in frequently these couple of days to help do various domestic tasks and cook for them, it was never enough so far as his father was concerned.

The next morning, Evie still not around, Donald came pounding into Danny's bedroom about six o'clock and sharply demanded that he should instantly rise and make breakfast.

'It's a Saturday, Dad. I've worked hard all week so surely I'm entitled to have a bit of a lie-in today. Can't we wait till Cathie pops over, as I'm sure she will?'

'No, lad, that's a rubbish job you have on the canal, not a sensible one at all. Do as you're told now!'

Danny felt a strong urge to argue with him and deny this, quite enjoying spending long busy days loading and organizing deliveries on the tug, serving an apprenticeship that was hard work but felt very worthwhile. Yet how could he convince his father that having turned fifteen he was now almost an adult, certainly not a child any more and surely had the right to do what he wished in life. But could he refuse to do what his father asked? He dragged himself out of bed and staggered downstairs, managed to find some bread and provided him with toast and jam, which didn't go down at all well. Thankfully when Cathie arrived a little later, she set about cooking Donald some bacon and eggs.

Feeling desperate to escape, Danny said he wasn't hungry, felt in need of a walk and hastily dashed off. When he saw Willie playing a game of football with his mates on a rough piece of spare land not far from an air raid shelter and a bombed factory, he watched with interest. They looked like they were having fun enjoying this sport, something Danny was not involved in, having lost touch with the friends he'd once known here in the Castlefield area of Manchester. Making a sudden decision that he felt badly in need of some fun in his life, he marched over to them to make a request to Willie.

'I wondered if we could stop fighting, arguing and bullying each other and try to be mates again, as we were advised to be back at the camp.

156

The thing is, I'm a bit bored and would like to take part in this game and get to know some of these lads.'

'By heck, that's an interesting suggestion to make,' Willie said. 'Of course, in order to take part you'd have to join our gang. Have you any idea what else we involve ourselves in, apart from playing footie?'

'Would you care to tell me?'

'Aye, I 'appen will, once you've been accepted as a member. First, to prove you're brave and skilled you need to skim down into that damaged air raid shelter and come out the other end.'

'Rightio.' Danny quickly did as he was bid, which wasn't difficult even though he encountered a few rats, mice and stinking rubbish down there. Quickly bouncing out, he asked if he was now accepted.

'That's your first challenge. Now tha must climb over that wall up to the top floor of that old factory, then tie a rope round yersel' and slide down. Up to the top and back within ten minutes, OK?'

Giving a gulp, Danny sensed this challenge could be even worse than climbing that cliff in Cumberland. 'I don't have any rope,' he said. Laughing, Willie gave a jerk of his head to one of the members of his gang, ordering him to hand one over. Some of these lads looked a bit frail and sickly while others were quite robust. Being working class and some of them having lost members of their family, they appeared to be attempting to overcome feelings of hostility over what they'd suffered in today's world. Danny too had that attitude to life right now. How he missed his sisters, and his father was sadly a pain. Thank heaven he was fortunate enough to have a good mother.

It took every ounce of courage and strength he could find to scramble over a wall then step up the broken staircase to the top floor of the factory, which was pitted with holes. The prospect of dropping down one was a far worse concept than falling into the canal. Eventually reaching the far end, he fixed the rope onto the frame of a window, hoping it wouldn't break. After wrapping it around himself and saying a silent prayer, he spun down at speed. It was halfway down that he realized this rope was several feet short of the ground. When he reached the end of the rope, taking a breath of strength, he skilfully managed to jump down and drop onto his feet without breaking a leg. What a relief that was.

To Danny's surprise and delight, he was cheered and thumped with pleasure when he marched over to the lads in the gang. 'You're welcome to join us,' they yelled, and even though Willie gave him a smirk of sour laughter, he too agreed.

'Thanks for letting me join. I hope it'll turn out to be interesting,' he said, giving them all a grin. Wouldn't being a member of this gang bring some excitement and fun back into his life? Danny felt very much in need of that.

15

Being a waitress, not a cleaner, Joanne was generally granted a few hours free each afternoon, once breakfasts were over, everything cleared and tidied away and tables laid in preparation for the evening meal, which she was also busily involved in. Saturdays were now classed as her day off, Joanne insisting upon this so that she could visit her sister twice a month on a school-free day.

Today she chose to pay a visit to Campfield Market. There were many markets in Manchester including Smithfield, Shudehill, Grey Mare Lane and others, places she'd regularly investigated, but this was her favourite. One she'd regularly attended when a child with her mother, as she had done several times over the summer, feeling very much alone. It was a chilly September morning with rain drizzling down as she hurried into the market hall where it was more dry and warm. She could hear stallholders calling out their wares, children laughing and people chatting. Joanne began to search for a small gift for Megan, intending to visit her again the following week in time for her birthday. Staring at the lovely dolls her sister had once adored, their mother having bought her one here, she sighed with regret that it had been sadly broken on the train. Megan was now far too grown-up to be interested in such toys any more. Instead she bought her a lovely beaded purse with a silk lining and a chain handle, something Joanne was quite sure she'd love.

Thrilled with this and seeing that the rain had stopped, she went out to look around at all the market stalls lining the pavement from Tonman Street to Deansgate. Joanne treated herself to a few sweets, these still being on ration, and a new lipstick she felt in need of. Having enjoyed exploring the market she then went over to the café to treat herself to a coffee and a cake. As she settled herself at a table she suddenly heard the sound of a familiar voice. Turning around she stared in stunned amazement at her cousin.

'Cathie? Goodness, I can't believe it's you,' she cried.

Whipping around to return her gaze in equally astonished delight, Cathie jumped up to fling her arms around her. 'Oh, Joanne, I can't believe you're here. How wonderful to see you, my long lost cousin.'

Hugging each other tight, they both wept, then finally sat together and Joanne quickly asked the question that had haunted her for years, explaining how she'd been searching for her mother since the end of the war. 'Do you know if Mam is still alive and if so, where she lives?'

Cathie beamed. 'I do indeed. Would you believe that dear lady is currently exploring the Lake District in search of you. We're expecting her back sometime late tomorrow. I'll go and see her on Monday and will so enjoy giving her the news that you're home. I'll take you to see her whenever you're granted any time off work.'

'Oh, that would be wonderful. What a special

day this has proved to be.'

They went on to share issues of the war and how her mother had been obliged to constantly move around having lost her home and her job. Joanne was also sorry to hear of the loss of her cousin's sister as she cuddled Cathie's adopted baby Heather. She made little mention of what she and her sister had suffered, preferring to speak of the happy time they'd spent in Blackpool and how she'd now found employment at a local hotel here in Manchester. Making no comment on the reason for that either, she handed Cathie the address. 'It's not far from Castlefield and I've been searching months for Mam, with no luck. How wonderful to see you.'

It felt so good to have at last found a member of her family, and hopefully soon her mother, father and young brother.

★ ★ ★

When Evie arrived home late on Sunday afternoon, she felt very much in need of a private conversation with her son and was quite relieved when Danny told her that Cathie had provided them each with a good chicken lunch and soup and sandwiches for tea. His dad had now gone off to the pub for a drink, as he so loved to do. 'Good to see you, Mam. I assume you found no sign of my sisters, which doesn't surprise me. Don't worry, they'll 'appen turn up one day,' he said, giving her a peck of a kiss on her cheek. 'I'm off now to meet up with my mates.'

'Hold on a minute, lad, I need to tell you

161

something.' Sitting him down at the kitchen table, Evie patted his hand and explained how she'd called at the farm where'd he'd been billeted. 'I only met the farmer's wife and she told me you were sent to that camp having been accused of committing another offence. So what was it that you never mentioned? Were you caught up in some misdemeanour, love?'

A flush of fury pitted his face, turning it ash pale. 'No, I did nowt! Don't believe a bloody word that woman said.'

Leaping to his feet, he looked as if he was about to run off, but Evie pulled him back down onto his seat. 'If you were innocent, why were you not able to convince them of that?'

'How could I? It were far too bleedin' complicated and I were wrongly charged.' Obstinately refusing to discuss the details, he stormed off, paying no attention to his mother's call for him to stay. Giving a sigh, Evie almost regretted asking him this question. The last thing she wanted was to upset her son, absolutely convinced he was not guilty of whatever that so-called other offence was. At least she sincerely hoped that was the case.

When he returned an hour or so later, Evie gave him a cuddle and assured Danny of her belief in his innocence. 'If you ever wish to discuss this problem with me, love, just let me know. Otherwise, we'll shut it out of our heads, right?'

'Thanks, Mam. I blocked it out of mine years ago, knowing very little detail about it and it was just a load of codswallop.' Then with a frown he

162

said, 'I feel a bit like Dad at times, not wishing to remember the traumatic effects on my life during the war. He's told me a little of what he suffered, but not most of it. He says there are scary and horrific things he shuts out. I do see the point of that.'

Evie stroked his head and gave him a kiss. After wishing her goodnight, he went up to bed, not saying another word on the subject.

★ ★ ★

It was early on Monday morning that Cathie came bouncing in while Evie was clearing up after breakfast. Danny had gone off to work on the tug and Donald still lay asleep in their bedroom. 'Eeh, hello, love. Good to see you. Would you like a cuppa? Thanks for looking after my family.' She was about to confess her failure to find out anything about her girls but it was then that her beloved niece gave her an excited hug.

'Guess what, I have some wonderful news for you. Would you believe that quite by chance I've found your darling daughter?'

Dropping the cup of tea on the floor, Evie gave a scream of delight. 'What? Oh, how amazing! How did you meet her? Where is she? And is she well?'

Laughing, Cathie happily picked up the broken cup and mopped up the tea, then settled Evie calmly down in her chair to briefly explain where they'd met and how Joanne was now working here in a hotel. 'She looks such a lovely girl, so pretty and lively. Oh, and she's desperate to see

163

you. I could arrange for you to meet this afternoon when Joanne has her daily break from work.
Can you manage to take a little time off too?'

'I can indeed, with or without Harold
Mullins's permission,' Evie stated boldly. 'Oh, I
can hardly wait.'

★ ★ ★

The moment she saw her, Joanne ran to throw
herself into her mother's arms. 'Thank God
you're alive and well, Mam. I've tried so hard to
find you for years. How I've missed you.'

'I've missed you too, love, hoping and praying
my children were all safe.' Evie's throat felt as if
it was choking with emotion even as joy escalated
in her heart. She was thrilled and stunned to see
her daughter looking so much more grown-up
than the vision she had of her as a child.

Tears ran down each of their cheeks as they sat
cuddled together on a bench by the old lock on
the River Irwell. Cathie had suggested they meet
here, viewing it as a suitably quiet and private
place before Joanne went to meet the rest of her
family. They'd both approved of this idea and
now spent over an hour talking, sharing some of
their memories of the war. Evie spoke a little of
the anguish she'd had to endure, describing how
she'd tragically lost their house, money, clothes
and pretty well everything she possessed, living
in a bedsit and spending night after night in the
air raid shelter. 'That had a dirt floor, a few
benches and no heat or light. I'd sit there listening to sirens screaming and wailing. I reached the

164

conviction that I might lose you for ever.' When she asked what problems her daughter had faced, a look of confusion came into Joanne's face, as if these were issues she really had no wish to discuss. An attitude very like that of her husband.

'Megan and I didn't always find being billeted in some places at all good. Pretty scary at times, even after our second evacuation. Thankfully, things improved when we were taken by train to Blackpool and fortunately fostered by two lovely landladies.' Joanne went on to say how they'd enjoyed living with Aunt Annie and Aunt Sadie at Jubilee House, and that she'd started working for them once she was old enough. 'We had lots of fun in Blackpool, dancing in the Tower Ballroom, skating in the Winter Gardens, visiting theatres, piers and riding donkeys on the beach,' she said with a laugh.

'That's good to hear. Finding time for a bit of fun during that dratted war could surely prove to be a great relief. Your brother too has enjoyed walking, climbing and helping on a farm, but also had some problems he's no wish to speak of. I've not told him yet about your return. Danny will be so thrilled to see you, love, and hopefully your dad will be too. Unfortunately, Donald is in something of a sorry state, still an invalid after all he's suffered,' she said quietly. She went on to explain how Joanne's father's poor health situation had come about. 'He does have some mental issues too but I'm doing my best to help him recover and get over those. It just might take a little time.'

'I do hope he gets better soon.'

'I'm sure he will. Now, do tell me about Megan.'

Joanne went on to explain how she was happily attending a high school, now being a most intelligent twelve-year-old girl. 'The sad truth is that having little memory of you, Mam, her wish is to stay in Blackpool with these aunts whom she's quite fond of and she does like her new school.'

Dismay pummelled in Evie's heart. She'd sent her children away as evacuees being anxious to save their lives. Now it sounded as if she'd damaged her own. How could she face not having both of her daughters come home? 'I'm so relieved to hear that she's happy and doing well, but so longing to see her again. She was only six years old when I last saw her.' Tears again filtered down her cheeks and Joanne gave her a tender hug.

'I shall be taking the train to visit Megan next week, Mam, in time for her birthday. I'll let you know the exact day if you wish to accompany me, otherwise I'll hopefully persuade her to come back with me.'

'I'll definitely come with you, lovey. Can't wait to see her. Now I'd like you to come home and meet your dad and brother,' Evie said softly. 'I appreciate you may not wish to stay, being accommodated in that lovely hotel and we're living in a small, messy house, but it will be so good for you to see the rest of your family.'

'It will indeed, Mam.'

* * *

Meeting Danny proved to be an absolute delight for Joanne. Her brother looked utterly enthralled to see her then melted into her arms, pressing his cheek against hers being quite tall now, not at all the small boy he'd once been. 'It's wonderful to see you again,' she said, smoothing her hand over his brown hair, so much darker and shorter than it used to be when he was a young child.

'How is Megan?' he asked, a glimmer of concern in his hazel eyes.

'She's fine.'

'Thank God for that. I have worried about her, being so young.'

'Me too.'

When Joanne approached her father it felt as though she was meeting a stranger. She was astonished to see how thin he was, his dark brown hair having turned grey and his shrunken face creased with wrinkles, a cigarette dangling from his mouth. Seeing a glimmer of affection in his dark eyes, happiness flickered through her. 'You do remember me, I hope, Dad?'

'I do, love,' he said, giving her a warm smile as he tossed the cigarette into the fire. 'You've lived in my head and heart for years. Have I lived in yours?'

'Of course, every evening I'd look at that photo of you and Mam on your wedding day and would wish you both goodnight. That kept me happy.'

'I don't suppose you missed us too much, having fun living in Blackpool?' he sternly remarked, a severity entering his face.

'I greatly missed you and was determined to find you both.'

Giving a chuckle, Evie told him how their lovely daughter had enjoyed dancing at the Tower Ballroom. 'Dare I ask if you did that with a boyfriend?'

'I don't have one,' Joanne stated firmly.

'I do hope you didn't lose one you'd fallen in love with at some point these last few years?' Evie remarked gently. 'That would be a shame for a pretty girl of your age.'

Joanne found herself blushing, a part of her feeling a sudden desire to reveal the anguish of what she'd gone through while she knew it was important not to do that. She had no inclination to ever admit the fanciful notion that she'd believed Teddy to be in love with her when he'd just wanted fun. Sex was definitely a taboo subject. And she certainly had no intention of risking her good name by revealing what she'd foolishly allowed him to do to her. Firmly shaking her head, she steadfastly insisted that she definitely had no boyfriend. Even as she said this, she could see doubt resonate in her mother's sharp eyes. Were these elements of anguish she'd no wish to discuss shimmering on her face?

It fleetingly crossed Joanne's mind that she and her mother could each feel they'd lost the man they loved, if in different ways. Teddy had simply left, but though her father had thankfully survived he was mentally damaged, a disaster that could be even more painful for her dear mother. Giving him a hug, Joanne savoured the fact that at least she'd found her beloved family, and their love for her was most evident, even her father's. How lucky she was.

Now she looked forward to telling Megan that she'd found them and that this could be the time for her to consider coming home.

★ ★ ★

'I have some wonderful news for you,' Joanne whispered, holding her sister's hands, when they sat together on the edge of her bed the following Saturday. Whenever she visited Megan they would enjoy some fun time together. They might visit the Tower Ballroom, the Derby baths or the Odeon cinema. Her sister would sometimes be involved in the odd sport activity with the other girls from her school, which Joanne would happily watch and cheer her on as she played. Today she'd wished her a happy birthday and been pleased to see how she loved the beaded purse she'd bought her. Before offering to take her out to celebrate this some place, she happily announced how she'd at last found their mother.

Megan blinked, staring at her in stunned silence for some seconds, then finally asked, 'Where and how did you manage to do that?'

Joanne quickly explained how it was quite by chance that she came across her cousin Cathie at Campfield Market, that she'd been delighted to see her and had happily arranged for her to meet her mother first, so they could have a quiet chat together. 'That was wonderful! You know how I've sorely missed her all these years. Mam then took me to meet Danny and Dad. That was a delight too. I'm pleased to tell you that she's here now at Jubilee House, and is desperately waiting to see you, lovey, hoping you'll agree to return home with us. She has, of course, promised to find you a good high school. Won't that be lovely for you to be back home with your family after all this time?'

'Why would I do that when I'm perfectly happy here?'

'Because she's your mam and loves you dearly.'

Megan gave a frown. 'I've no memory of her, nor of my dad.'

'But you do remember Danny, your beloved brother, and he too can't wait to see you either.'

'Oh, has he come here too?' Megan asked, a flicker of excitement at last lighting her eyes.

'No, darling, he works on a tugboat and wasn't granted any time off today for this journey. Mam only works part-time so didn't feel the need to get permission or say a word about this trip to her new boss, being desperate to see you.'

It was then that the bedroom door opened and Evie stepped in. Gazing in delight at her young daughter, she said warmly, 'Hello, Megan. How wonderful it is to see you at last after all these years of searching for you since the end of the war. I'm here thanks to your sister.'

Megan gazed at her, not saying a word or moving an inch.

Coming over to kneel beside her, Evie gave her a warm hug, tears of joy sparkling in her eyes. 'You are my darling youngest child. I love you dearly and have badly missed you, as well as Joanne and Danny. I'm aware you have the wish to stay here, being fond of these ladies, but how could I wish to live without you any more? And, as your sister has pointed out, your dad and brother are equally eager to see you again. I hope you'll be pleased to meet them too.'

'Of course you will, won't you, lovey?' Joanne said.

Receiving no response, Evie smiled and went on to say, 'I've spoken to the landladies downstairs and they accept that I desperately want you to return home with me. They say you are most welcome to visit them whenever you wish. Miss Fairhurst, your Aunt Sadie, has offered to make us a lovely lunch to celebrate your birthday, which is most kind and generous of her. I'm not able to stay overnight, I'm afraid, as I have to care for Donald, your father. Later this afternoon we must catch the train back home to Manchester at the Central Station. Can I help you to pack, love?'

'No, I'm not going anywhere.'

16

When they arrived back in Manchester, having spent the entire train journey with Megan in a disgruntled silence, Joanne smiled when she burst into tears the moment she saw Danny and flung herself into his arms. They'd always been close siblings. Picking her up to swing her round, he gave a spurt of laughter. 'By heck, it's good to see you again. I do hope you're well, Megan love.'

''Course I am, considering all the hockey and netball I play. But I've now had to leave my school and sport teams.'

Seeing her fall into a much more distressing burst of tears, he gave her another hug. 'You might manage to be accepted at your new school although being mixed it's mainly lads who play sport. I play with my mates,' Danny explained. 'So you might have to find yourself some other solution or a new hobby.'

'Don't worry about that right now,' Joanne hurriedly said, attempting to comfort her. They had enjoyed a lovely lunch to celebrate her birthday, thanks to Aunt Annie and Aunt Sadie, but her sister had been deeply traumatized at being taken away from what she considered to be her home and friends. And she was still looking no better.

'I'm sure you'll find it's a good school when I take you there tomorrow,' Evie said. 'The

172

teachers say they'll be happy to welcome you. Now do say hello to your dad while I go and fetch you a bit of supper.'

Casting a sideways glance at her father, Megan remained silent, watching in awe as he gave her a warm smile and pulled her into his arms. 'Hey up, what a treasure you are, love. Have you nowt to say to me, little one?' he asked.

'I think she's a bit tired and shy,' Joanne said, seeing how she pulled herself free of him, giving a little tremble. In reality, Megan had no memory of her father. Nor did she find it easy to be friendly with any men or boys, save for Bernie. She'd hated it when Wing Commander Ramsbotham had pinched her bum, in addition to what had happened to her back in the past. 'As you see, Dad, she's no longer a little one being quite tall now. She's turned twelve and a very bright girl.'

'Aye, I reckon you're right there. You were nobbut a toddler when I last saw you, chuck, and remember giving you lots of cuddles. Seeing you makes me feel so much better now we're at last all back together. I'm wishing you were all three still young and in need of the caring dad I once was. I hope I will be again, once I've resolved my problems.'

Joanne gave him a hug. 'I'm sure you will, Dad.'

Megan remained stubbornly silent as she sat at the kitchen table to drink the glass of sarsaparilla and eat the slice of Eccles cake her mother gave her. Joanne too enjoyed this supper, then when they were done said, 'I'll take her up

173

to bed now, shall I, Mam?'

'No, I'll take her, lovey. I know you have to get off back to the hotel. Megan is going to share my bed. Dad has agreed to move into the spare room with Danny since that has two single beds.'

Not showing any interest in responding to this or willing to speak to either of her parents, Megan tightly grasped hold of Joanne's hand. 'You take me up please, sis,' she whispered. A decision Evie was obliged to accept.

Once having helped her to unpack her suitcase and settle her into the double bed she would be sharing with her mother, Joanne said, 'It's not the perfect place for you to sleep but can't be helped and I'm sure you'll be all right.'

'I do wish you could sleep here with me instead of our mother,' Megan whimpered, grabbing hold of her sister and begging her not to leave.

Joanne gave her a tender kiss on the cheek. 'I can understand your reservation, lovey, but you will find Mam most kind and caring once you get to know her a little better. Sadly, I can't stay, not even tonight. I must go back to my hotel. I don't have permission to stay overnight any-where, needing to be up shortly after dawn to start preparing and feeding the guests their breakfasts. I will pop over to see you tomorrow afternoon, being allowed a little time off. And as you know I do get all of Saturdays free, so we can meet up regularly to have fun or just enjoy a coffee and a chat.'

'When can we go back to Blackpool to see our aunts and my friends? I do want to do that soon.'

Stroking Megan's hair and gently covering her

up with the sheet and blanket, Joanne firmly promised they would visit them whenever they could afford the time and money for a train journey. She too felt the desire to do that for no good reason. But returning for ever would not be an easy decision to make. Once satisfied that being exhausted after a day of trauma and travelling, her sister was falling asleep, Joanne slipped back downstairs. Their father having gone off to the pub and Danny to meet up with his mates, she welcomed the possibility of another private chat with her mother.

'I'm sorry Megan is in a difficult state of mind but she feels desperately sad to leave those two ladies whom she's grown fond of over the years.'

'Eeh, I do understand that and no doubt she dislikes the fact I sent her away to be evacuated, making her feel neglected,' Evie remarked mournfully. 'I'm not having an easy time with my husband either. Donald too can be a bit silent and distant, although it was good to see him welcoming you all. 'Appen I should try to save the world following this messy war, eh?'

Joanne gave a chuckle as she settled beside her on the horsehair sofa, not at all a soft or comfortable place to sit let alone sleep. No wonder Danny had resisted doing that. 'Just concentrate on saving your marriage first, Mam,' she said, thinking how relations between her parents did seem to have gone a little cool, and would maybe go worse now they were about to occupy separate beds. 'I know you'll be most caring of Megan but she's a very independent-minded girl, having blocked out all memory of the past. So do appreciate that you'll have to patiently wait for her to become a little more friendly and caring of you.'

'I accept that could take a while. Nor has she shown much interest in her father.'

'She's still young and feels more comfortable with her girl friends, never having good experience with men throughout the war, so many of them quite bossy. I have to admit I too have a lack of trust for them, having made a few mistakes in my life.'

This comment seemed to perk her mother up. 'So what did you do that caused you to move from your job in Blackpool to that hotel in Manchester?'

Giving a wry smile, Joanne quietly admitted how she'd declined to accept a proposal from Bernie, the landladies' nephew. 'As our so-called relationship had collapsed and we were no longer working well together I agreed that leaving was the right thing to do,' she said, not wishing to explain that he'd offered to marry her because of the anguish and mess she'd been through with that GI.

'Oh heck, what a shame. I only had a few words with him but he seemed a nice enough lad. What was it about him that didn't appeal to you? Do you reckon he still hopes you might one day trip down the aisle with him, once you get a bit older? Have you put such a possibility into his head?'

'I most definitely haven't, at least I do hope not.' Joanne gave a quick intake of breath and fell into a silence, not having considered this to be at

176

all likely. Had she been rather dismissive towards him? She'd carefully avoided Bernie when they'd visited today, as she always did. He was generally absent, no doubt working with that friend of his someplace. But she'd almost felt that she missed seeing him, having enjoyed their chat in the loft bedroom he'd created the last time she'd met him. This was a sensitivity she should put right out of her mind and not feel any pity for him when he was doing fine with his life, as was she. 'Right now, I'm quite happy to remain single,' she declared firmly.

'You might change your mind, love. A happy marriage with a nice chap can give you a good life. It worked well for me. I sadly missed Donald when he was lost in the war. A vital part of his life as a pilot was working with a crew who would stick together, living in a hut throughout the length of a tour, very much dependent upon their support and friendship. Tragically, casualties in the crew were high and he's grieving badly for them, as well as suffering whatever it was they went through when captured by the enemy. Hard to know any of that. Such is the effect of war. I'm most anxious about his state of health but do my best to care for him since I still dearly love him.' She gave a bewitching smile.

'I do too,' Joanne said.

'That's good to hear. I regularly buy him the odd bottle of beer and a packet of Gold Flake cigarettes, which are what he most feels in need of, not having much of an appetite these days. I'm trying to persuade Donald to get better at eating, and at Christmas I hope he'll attend the annual party to be held at the local church hall. Bearing in mind that you love dancing and fun, you could surely come too, and 'appen stay with us over Christmas. Megan too would hopefully like to accompany us to that party.'

Getting to her feet, Joanne gave her mother a hug. 'That would be lovely. I'll do my best to join you. Now I must be on my way.'

'Aye, 'course you must, love. Would you like me to fetch Donald from the pub and ask him to walk you over to the hotel?'

Fortunately, she had brought their bicycles back with them from Blackpool this time, convinced Megan would need hers to ride to school, and having her own would be useful too. But she'd foolishly left it at the hotel. However, she'd no wish to make a fuss about that. 'No, I'll be fine and must be off now before it gets too late. Goodnight, Mam. See you tomorrow.'

Joanne did not find it at all pleasant walking alone down the cold dark streets, wishing she had come on her bike as she saw small groups of lads standing on corners smoking or drinking. Hurrying along, she glanced at some of them, wondering if Danny might be amongst them but unfortunately didn't spot him. Dashing quickly up the street she heard an odd scraping noise and kept glancing behind her, worried that one of those lads might now be following her. This suddenly didn't feel at all a safe place to be. And considering the sorry state of her sister, she couldn't help but wonder if it had been the right decision to bring Megan back home. Thankfully, she reached the hotel quite safely, giving a sigh of relief. Moving in with her family over Christmas and taking part in that dance would be a good idea and much more fun.

★ ★ ★

Evie lived in deep belief that Donald would eventually recover, but he was showing no sign of that so far. Megan too was something of a problem. Having no memory of a life with them as her loving parents it was almost as if she didn't entirely believe they cared a jot about her. She would happily chat in private with her beloved brother and sister, whenever Joanne called in, but only make the odd polite comment to herself or Donald. She would complain about the wet weather or politely ask if her mother would please pass the salt whenever they ate a meal together. But she never engaged in a proper conversation, behaving as if she was being forced to live with strangers.

Striving to make it plain that she absolutely adored her and was eager to cheer her up, Evie spent the days and weeks following engaging herself in taking her daughters out and about. They visited the Gaumont Cinema and other flicks, the Hippodrome on Oxford Street and went for a regular swim at the Corporation Baths on New Quay Street. Evie greatly enjoyed them but did begin to worry when she found herself rapidly running out of the money she'd been saving in case she lost her job or felt in need of working for herself. She might risk putting herself into financial difficulties, but caring for her children and being anxious to give them a good life was surely more important.

Megan was generally silent and not even greatly impressed with the school Evie had found for her, despite it being a good one, simply because it was mixed, packed with boys not just girls. Hopefully she would grow used to this eventually. Sadly, she was no longer able to take part in her much-loved sporting activities because, as Danny had warned her, these were mainly meant for lads at this mixed school, not girls. Evie was greatly concerned, seeing how Megan missed having any friends to play games or chat with. The poor girl appeared to be sinking into depression and not becoming friendly with anyone.

As Joanne happily joined many of these trips she attempted to cheer up her young sister and did occasionally speak of her own anxiety for Megan, explaining how she was still a little homesick for her aunts, school and friends back in Blackpool. 'I'm not convinced she'll easily settle here, despite your wonderful efforts to show your love and care for her, Mam,' she said tactfully.

'It could take a while but I'm sure she will eventually.'

Giving a sigh of despondency at the problems she was having to cope with, Evie focused her attention on the fact that her darling family were at least back in her life. Now that Christmas was almost upon them, she took her daughters to the Flat Iron Market to buy them each a pretty frock for the Christmas party. Finding one striped in pink and violet she held it up around Megan.

'You'd look very pretty in this, pet,' Evie told her. 'Why not try it on.'

'It's a bit too fancy with no sleeves or collar,' Megan complained.

'I could make you a lace collar to put on it, if you like, lovey?'

'No thanks, that would make it look even more posh.'

'Would you like to try this one then?' Joanne asked, holding up a simpler blue frock with long sleeves and warm pleated skirt. Megan gave a nod. She slipped behind the curtain into the small fitting closet, tried it on and happily agreed she liked this one best.

'Well, that's a grand decision,' Evie agreed. 'You look beautiful in that frock, darling, I'm so proud of you.' She happily purchased it, trying not to assess how her savings were becoming dangerously low, and resolutely decided to make Megan a lovely white lace collar for this pretty blue frock. 'So what do you fancy, Joanne?'

Joanne chose a red dress with a satin skirt, a patterned bodice with a scoop neckline and three-quarter sleeves. 'This is gorgeous,' she said, swirling round to show it off when she tried it on. 'Are you sure you can afford this too, Mam, or should I make a contribution?'

'No need, love. I wish to buy you each a present for Christmas that you really like. Right, now that's dealt with let's go and treat ourselves to a bit of lunch.'

It was as they were sitting enjoying cheese on toast that Evie jerked in surprise when she saw Harold Mullins approach. 'Hey up, so tha's tekken another day off when tha should be working yet again?' he said with a snarl of contempt. 'I'm fully aware you miss the odd day off whenever it takes yer fancy.'

Finding herself cringing with fury, Evie attempted to give him a polite smile. 'It's a part-time job I have with you so I'm entitled to some time off to suit myself. I'm working much better and saying nothing about what I do, as instructed by you. And, as you can see, my daughters have finally arrived home so I've been spending much-needed time with them. You surely can't blame me for that?'

Taking a glance at each of the girls he gave a blink of surprise. 'Ah yes, I'd heard they'd arrived. By heck, what pretty young lasses they are. I bet plenty o' fellas would tek a shine to them, not least my son. I'll tell Willie he might meet them at that Christmas party.'

Seeing the glimmer of interest in his dark eyes, Evie felt herself stiffen with alarm. She had no wish for this dreadful man to encourage his son to involve himself with her girls. Not at all a comforting thought. Fortunately, neither of them made a response nor troubled to even glance at Harold. They were too busy chatting and happily giggling to each other to listen to a word he was saying, which was surely a good thing. Warning herself to carefully protect her daughters, she diligently changed the subject back to her work. 'I assure you I'll collect all the necessary debts, starting first thing on Monday as I generally do. Good day to you, Harold.'

'Make sure you do,' he snarled, and sliding his

gaze once more over each of her daughters and Evie herself, he gave a smirk and walked away.

How she hated this bloomin' man. When Evie had worked at the mill she'd been aware that Harold enjoyed having a fan club of girls assembled around him at all times because he cared for no man other than himself. Since he was all gloss and no substance, he apparently felt the need for their adoration. Even the mill boss had apparently discovered he wasn't at all as trustworthy as he pretended to be, running a business that was illegal. As did his poor wife Jane. Perhaps she too had grown tired of nurturing his ego, and sadly been replaced by a newer model. Nor did Evie have much faith in his son Willie, who'd apparently been a pain to her own boy. She doubted she'd ever trust either of them as long as she lived.

17

Christmas 1946

The small hall, not at all as glamorous or exciting as the Tower Ballroom and very much cooler, was nevertheless packed with people happily laughing, dancing and singing to the upbeat music of 'I've Got My Love to Keep Me Warm'. After that came jazz to which people danced the Jitterbug, Boogie-Woogie, Charleston and then a guy singing 'Swinging on a Star' in the style of Bing Crosby. All great fun. The band went on to play 'All I Want for Christmas is My Two Front Teeth'. Joanne and her mother laughed and clapped as Megan enjoyed this lively dance with Danny, both happily kicking their legs up and down. After that Danny went on to dance with various other girls. Megan too received many requests while Joanne sat with her mother at a table, each enjoying a glass of wine to celebrate Christmas.

'I'm deeply disappointed my Donald refused to attend this Christmas party with us,' Evie said. 'He would surely have enjoyed watching you and his younger daughter dance, love. Sadly, he's becoming increasingly silent and distant, locked in his world of pain.'

Joanne attempted to say something comforting, wishing to reassure her mother that once he'd managed to put some weight on, Dad would surely begin to feel much better. 'I've heard that PoWs often can't bear to stay indoors or confined spaces so it's a shame he didn't think to come out tonight. It might well have done him good.'

'I agree, but he paid no attention to my effort to persuade him. He can be a bit snappy and impatient but very obsessed with visiting the pub for a pint of beer, mebbe in a bid to calm himself down. No doubt that's where he's gone tonight,' Evie said with a sigh.

'May I have the pleasure of this dance, please?'

Looking up, she smiled. 'Why not? Good to see you, Davie. I thought you might be out with Donald.'

'I often am, but not this evening. Sorry he isn't here and I hope he won't object to us having a bit of a dance.'

''Course he won't,' Evie said, and Joanne chuckled as they happily sailed off dancing in a most stylish fashion.

Joanne too felt pleased to accept a few invitations, even from perfect strangers, some of them young and pleasant, other men rather old. Not that it mattered as they were often the much better dancers. But it was when the band started playing Glenn Miller's 'In the Mood' that she was surprised to be asked to dance by Willie Mullins. Giving her a smile and holding out his hand, he said, 'I reckon we could have a dance, eh?'

He sounded not at all polite and, aware of the problems he'd caused for Danny, this invitation was not at all welcome. However, as those two lads were now allegedly reformed friends and Willie was the son of her mother's employer, it didn't seem appropriate for her to refuse.

He held her rather tightly in his arms, saying how pretty she was and most charming. Joanne was wearing the red satin frock Mam had bought her for Christmas. Very special. Megan was prettily attired in that pleated blue dress with the neat lace collar her mother had made for her. Making no response to this comment, she teasingly asked, 'Have you come with a girlfriend to this party or simply your father?'

'I came with my latest conquest, a young girl of seventeen I've recently been dating. I've chucked her now, having got bored with her.'

Joanne felt a strong desire to giggle at this comment. What a self-opinionated young lad he was. No doubt that poor girl had become equally bored with him. He was quite smartly attired in a brown checked suit, white shirt and bright blue tie, his dark hair slicked very tight and short above his broad forehead. But there was something slightly discomforting about his cocky attitude. Nor was he very good at dancing, bearing a tension in his face as he stepped back and forth, swinging up and down and often treading on her toes. Joanne bit her lip, attempting not to say 'ouch' whenever that happened. His hold on her was growing tighter, pressing his hand hard upon the back of her waist, so that she endeavoured to create a safer distance between them.

Looking around, she could see that her mother was now dancing with his father and met

186

her weary gaze with a blink of sympathy in her own, neither of them apparently enjoying the experience. No doubt Harold's request had sounded very like a summons, very much the last person on earth she'd wish to dance with. No wonder she badly missed her husband being present.

When the dance thankfully ended, Joanne gave Willie a nod and turned to walk away, but he caught hold of her arm to prevent her leaving.

'I'm not against us having another dance, or if yer fed up wi' dancing we could we go for a walk instead, eh?'

Giving him a glance of disbelief, Joanne firmly shook her head. 'Don't be ridiculous. It's a cold winter's evening and we're here to enjoy this dance and party, so why would I agree to do that?'

Swinging his eyebrows up and down and sliding his tongue around his lips, he playfully said, 'I could give you a little pleasure and keep you warm if you did.'

'No thank you,' she tartly remarked.

As the next music started, he pulled her close and gave her a kiss, pressing his sweaty mouth against hers. Utterly shocked, Joanne pushed him away and slapped his face. 'How dare you! You've no right to do that to me.'

He grinned cheekily at her. 'I'm a man and you're a woman, so why would I not have that right?'

Joanne gave a snort of disapproval, all too aware of her determination not to allow any man to fondle her after what she'd suffered in the

187

past. Strangely, she remembered the fun she'd enjoyed with Bernie at the Tower Ballroom and how he was much better at dancing than this stupid lad, and had never done anything rude or inappropriate to her. If only he was here instead of this idiot. Realizing what a conceited young lad this was, his tone of voice quite sharp and arrogant, she made the decision to be appropriately dismissive of him. 'You're a silly young lad, not a sensible grown man,' she said and, giving him a dismissive laugh, marched away.

When she reached her sister, Megan welcomed her with a wry grimace. 'Hope you're OK, sis. I saw what that lad did to you. I don't like the look of him either.'

Fortunately, Willie seemed to have found himself another girl to dance with and to her delight Joanne saw her mother dash over to the door, her father having arrived. That was so good to know. Evie slipped her arm in his, kissed his cheek and moved happily into his arms for the last waltz. What a delight it was to see them enjoying this dance and such a treat to find her entire family together at last. Even Megan looked happy watching them, as did Danny.

The evening ended with the tune 'Have Yourself a Merry Little Christmas', which had been sung by Judy Garland in the film *Meet Me in St Louis* back in 1944. The two sisters and Danny happily joined in the singing. What a fun evening it had been.

★ ★ ★

188

Evie found it wonderful to have her entire family home for Christmas, making this very much a precious time. And her husband had made love to her following that dance. What a delight that was, a desire in him that had not appeared for such a long time. Not sleeping in the same bed didn't help so she made a decision to look into changing that, and lived in hope that his emotional need for her would continue. Right now she must concentrate on preparing for Christmas.

She'd baked a cake and a Christmas pudding, bought a reasonable size of goose for their Christmas dinner. She'd also purchased a small Christmas tree, pinned paper chains upon it and decorated everything with tinsel, even stitched a new lace frock for the small fairy she always stuck on the top of it. Joanne had helped her to hang strips of paper chains around the walls. It was not easy making this small, miserable house look attractive and there was even a slightly sour smell, no doubt because it was a bit cold. Being the only one she'd found available it was at least convenient, situated close to Deansgate and the city centre, so she sternly reminded herself not to worry as she'd done her best to decorate and improve it.

On the day before Christmas — her birthday, and having been named after Christmas Eve — she rose early to prepare breakfast, planning to bake some mince pies. It was when Evie reached for a loaf and started hacking off chunks of bread for toast, the kitchen feeling damp and dark, that she attempted to turn on the light and found the electricity had stopped working. The taps had too, no water coming out of them. Perhaps that was because being December this house was freezing cold. It was then that she noticed rain running under the door soaking the kitchen rug and that a hole had burst open in the white painted kitchen wall, rain pouring down it. The black range, usually alive with bright fire, was also dead. It generally provided much-needed heating and cooking too was done on this coal-fired kitchen range. Now nothing seemed to be working at all. She felt baffled about why all these problems had come about and how to resolve them.

'It's flamin' cold. Light this bloody fire, woman. You should keep us warm,' Donald snapped, walking into the kitchen.

'I'll light the fire,' Danny said quickly. 'Oh, the coal scuttle is empty.'

Picking it up, Evie rushed off down the backyard to refill it and was shocked to find their coal-place was empty, not a scrap of coal left. The coal rationing allowed them only two and a half tons in total per year and what she earned didn't always provide her with sufficient to buy more than a small amount at a time. Evie would normally put just a few pieces of coal on the fire in the range on cold evenings, dampening it down at night and during the day when she was out. Now that her husband was in need of being kept warm in this freezing cold weather, running out of coal was not a good prospect for him, let alone losing the possibility of being able to cook the Christmas dinner.

But why had all the coal disappeared when she'd recently bought sufficient for the holiday, and why had the electricity gone off too? Oh dear, had she not paid the necessary bills? Evie generally had to give the money to Harold as he was the owner. She must check that and somehow find more coal, otherwise Christmas could be a complete disaster.

'We've no coal left,' she announced sadly, shivering as she dropped the empty scuttle back by the range. 'Where it has gone, I've no idea.'

Danny gave a furious scowl. 'Actually, I saw Harold Mullins in our yard yesterday, 'appen he's taken it.'

'Oh, my God, you could be right, Danny. He is a difficult, selfish man. I suspect he didn't pay our electricity bill either, despite my handing him the necessary money due.'

'Bloody 'ell, what a bastard he is,' Donald snarled. 'You should stop working for him, Evie.'

'I wish I could. Right now we'll just have to knuckle to, clean up the freezing rain spilling everywhere and do what we can to be festive, despite this mess,' she stoutly remarked. 'With no electricity we can light the odd candle, as we did during the war. Though how do we keep warm with no coal for the range and upon which I need to cook?'

'I'll go and find some coal or wood, Mam. I'll scour the canal and railway sidings to pick up what bits I can find. Leave that to me,' Danny said. He grabbed a sack from the shed and dashed off in search. Megan staunchly scurried out with him.

191

'What a treasure he is,' Evie said. 'But poor Megan. She's still missing all her friends and has been sent to a school that doesn't seem to appeal to her, let alone having suffered a sense of neglect during the war. Now she's facing another awful mess. This being our first Christmas together in years I'd hoped it would be the best. It could be Christmas from hell if I can't cook a good dinner or keep us warm. Why does everything go wrong despite my best efforts?' She found depression sliding over her and tears blocking her eyes.

'Shall I go find that bleedin' man and give him a belt to make the point we need him to pay what bills he should?' Donald snarled, giving her a cuddle.

'No, love, you can leave that to me, since I'm the one who works for him. Mind you, I shall look for another job in the New Year, and if I still don't find one will mebbe try working for myself. Why not?'

After grabbing her warmest coat and hat, Evie went out to call on Harold Mullins and check whether he was guilty of stealing their coal, as well as not paying the due electric bills. No answer came as she knocked on his door. Shivering with cold, she peeped through the window but could see no sign of him, so where the hell was he? Feeling the need to investigate his coal situation she hurried down the road then went round the back street up to his yard. Sadly, that door too was locked, which didn't help at all.

Filled with panic and resentment, Evie marched away in fury. It was as she reached home that she saw Danny carrying a sack well stacked with coal and Megan carrying a box of wood. They were both happily grinning and looking rightly pleased with their success. With relief, Evie did not dare ask how or where her son had managed to do this. No doubt he'd found bits of coal and wood lying around the canal or railway sidings, or else close to some mine.

'What a star you are,' she said, giving him a hug.

Once the fire in the range was burning well, she slid the kettle on the centre of the hob to make them all a much-needed cup of tea. Evie spent the rest of the day cleaning, baking the mince pies and doing more cooking, assisted by Joanne when she arrived. She was delighted that her elder daughter would be staying with them over Christmas, Danny prepared to sleep on the sofa bed in the living-kitchen so that the two girls could occupy the spare room. When night came, Evie made sure the fire was properly dampened down to keep a slight warmth in the house overnight. And before going to bed she boiled water to fill a solid hot water bottle for each of them, and gave them all a goodnight kiss. With delight, her beloved husband was now back sleeping with her and they again made love. What a treat that was.

Early on Christmas morning, Evie livened the fire up, stuffed the goose in a large pan and placed it in the small oven in the range to slowly cook. She spent the next few hours happily preparing and cooking roast potatoes, vegetables, sausage, stuffing and heating the fruit pudding. When they all sat down to savour the delicious Christmas dinner, she gave her family a warm, loving smile. 'So wonderful to have you all here. Thank goodness this hasn't proved to be a disaster, thanks to Danny. Then turning to Donald she said, 'A glass of sherry, dear? Oh, and here's a large box of Gold Flake ciggies for your Christmas pressie.'

He chuckled. 'Eeh, what a treat. Why not? Happy Christmas, love.'

Christmas Day proved to be uproarious, exciting and uplifting, if slightly exhausting. They listened to the choir singing on the radio, then played at jigsaws, Monopoly, quizzes and charades. Joanne proved to be excellent at this game, lifting her fingers to give an idea of the number of words and performed wonderful gestures, miming words or phrases they had to guess. It proved to be great fun. At the end of the day as they sat together on the horsehair sofa with Megan cuddled up beside her, Evie ceased to worry over the dying fire or how they would find more coal or logs, the ruined decorating, or the still damp rugs. What a lovely day it had proved to be and how wonderful it was to have spent it with her darling family.

18

In the days following, Evie was delighted that Megan slowly came round to being a little more friendly towards her, perhaps as a result of this lovely Christmas and the jolly excursions she'd taken her on before that. It had not been an easy time in other respects, electricity and sufficient coal still not available. Evie would make sure her daughters, son and husband wore several layers of clothing as well as providing them each with a hot water bottle to warm their feet when they went to bed. But even those would go cold by the early hours, the worst part of a winter's night. Now, as she called at clients' houses to collect more debts owed to Harold Mullins, she struggled to decide how best to challenge him on these dreadful issues he might well have created for them. She very much feared it was not an easy decision to make, all too aware what a difficult man he could be. Maybe she should take the responsibility for paying domestic bills, and find a lock for their coal-place.

As evening approached and the moment she had to deliver the debt payments, she hovered by his door still struggling to find the necessary courage. It was then that she saw her niece's friend, Brenda, walking towards her. She was a young girl she'd got to know through Cathie and for whom she'd done much to help, having heard a little of what she'd suffered in France during the war. Just as she'd helped her niece cope with her problems too.

Brenda gave her a cheerful smile and asked if she'd enjoyed a merry Christmas. 'You look a bit irritated. Do you have a problem?'

Giving a sigh, Evie swiftly explained how she believed Harold Mullins had messed things up for them by robbing them of electricity and water. 'Mebbe he'll put the blame on me since I work for him.' Blushing, she hesitated, not wishing to explain exactly what this illegal job entailed, carefully slipping the list of clients into her pocket.

'Don't blame yourself, it should definitely be his responsibility as the owner of that house. I agree he's not an easy man but you're a most protective and caring lady so don't lose faith in yourself.'

'Thank you, dear. Actually, my son said he saw Harold in our yard and suspects he also nicked our coal, all of which had vanished. Sadly, I don't have proof of that, so I'm striving to find the courage to tackle him on that subject too,' she said, nibbling her thumb.

'Ah, I live in a flat just a few doors away and saw him carrying a wheelbarrow loaded with coal the evening before Christmas Eve. I did wonder where he'd got that from.'

'Oh, my goodness, is that true?'

'It is indeed. Why would I not tell you what I saw?' Brenda said. 'You've been so helpful to me over the years, I'm happy to help you too, Evie. Stand up for what's right. If you need my support on this point, just let me know.'

'Thanks, dear girl, you've given me exactly the courage and proof I needed,' she said, giving a nod of appreciation as she watched her walk away.

When Evie knocked on the door this time it was swiftly opened and Harold stood frowning before her. 'You look a bit irritated. Have you not collected enough money from debts to hand over?'

Evie stoutly met his sour expression with one of her own. 'I believe I have. The thing is, Mr Mullins, I'm not sure I should hand this money over, considering the problems you caused for us over Christmas.' She then bravely stated that as the owner of the house they rented he was probably the one who'd failed to pay the bills, despite her having handed over what she'd believed to be the right sum of money. 'And I reckon you also nicked the coal I'd bought. Now I'm struggling to find the money to buy more.'

There was a moment's silence then he burst out laughing. 'How can you prove that?'

'My son saw you take it and a friend witnessed you bringing it home on the evening before Christmas Eve, which was when we lost all our coal. So unless you can convince me of your innocence, I shall retain the sum it cost me in payment for what you stole.' Handing over only a portion of the debts she'd collected, Evie saw fury glare in his dark eyes.

'Flamin' rubbish! You can't keep the rest of that money. It belongs entirely to me.'

'Oh, yes she can,' said Brenda, stepping up to slip her arm through Evie's. 'I was that witness, so don't for a moment think you can demand every penny back from this lady. Nor can you challenge me either. Having dealt with drastic situations in France throughout the war, nothing you say or do will scare me for a moment. I'm an expert on survival and courage.'

'Don't think you can scare me either,' Evie remarked bravely. 'Just accept reality by paying what you owe me, being guilty of this theft and mess-up.'

'You'll bloody well regret making such a charge,' he roared, and slammed the door shut in her face.

Evie spent the rest of the week searching for a new job. She called again at all factories, mills, warehouses, shops and department stores, only receiving a shake of the manager's head, or a grumble that the country was in a mess and near bankrupt. Austerity still being very evident, businesses too were in financial difficulty. There was a rise in prices despite rationing and still the problem of a housing shortage. She found that so many factories had been destroyed or closed there was very little work available for anyone, not even men.

'Where could I find a new job?' she asked Davie, her old friend, catching sight of him when she came out of the Co-op, having failed to get a job offer there too.

He sadly gave a shrug. 'No idea, chuck. The British Legion did attempt to achieve jobs for ex-servicemen, with little success. Some employers do obey the law, feeling the need to be generous, but many chaps have found themselves sacked after only a few months.'

'Goodness, many women too were sacked and sent back to the kitchen sink, once the troops returned. The brave new world they'd fought for not at all what they'd hoped for. Why on earth does that happen to these soldiers too?'

'They're often told they are no longer well qualified, being out of date, so not worth employing.'

'That's so inappropriate. Mebbe they need to work for themselves. Me too if I don't find a better job,' she stoutly responded.

He gave her a sympathetic smile. 'That could be a good idea. But be aware that those men who wish to start their own business find they're obliged to gain a licence, as well as obey loads of rules and regulations set up by politicians and bureaucrats who have very little idea how to run a business. And those chaps who have been working in the same trade since the start of the war believe they should have precedence and often prevent a shop or business from opening. That's happened to several of my mates.'

Giving a bleak sigh as she said goodbye and walked away, it came to her that she may have to stay on with Harold Mullins for the moment, until she had found a way forward. A most depressing prospect.

★   ★   ★

Joanne gazed in alarm at her mother as she came home looking badly in need of sympathy and support. She'd called in to see her, it being

Friday afternoon, to pick up Megan from school and take her out for tea. Her sister was now upstairs busily doing her homework. 'Goodness, you look worn out, Mam. Have you had a difficult week with that Harold Mullins creating more problems for you?'

'He is indeed. Good to see you, love,' she said, giving her daughter a hug.

'Shall I make you some coffee? Then you can tell me what's wrong and why you're still working for him.'

'Eeh, I could do with a cup and to have a natter with you. He frequently tells me off for not collecting enough debt payments for him. On Monday evening I didn't hand them all over because of what he owes us.' Evie went on to describe what she'd charged him with, thanks to the support of Brenda, the friend of her niece. 'I don't much care for this flippin' job I'm caught up in, not at all interesting. Nor do I get on well with Mullins,' she said, flopping down on a chair. 'But having spent the entire week again searching for a new job in between the work I have to do for him, I've failed to receive a single offer. What a mess I'm in. And as there's nowt I can do to find employment, let alone get back working at the mill in this difficult post-war world, I simply have to accept reality. I'll 'appen find summat better to do with my life, eventually.'

'Hopefully you will. I desperately feel the need to help you get away from working for that chap you clearly dislike, Mam.' Joanne poured hot water from the kettle into their coffee mugs,

200

anxiety pounding within her.

'I've constantly strived to find a way to escape. I might achieve that by working for myself.'

'Here's your coffee, Mam. Do tell me how you might manage that. I'd really like to know what you have in mind.' Joanne watched in awe as Evie placed a stuffed pillow on her knee that was lined with bobbins and needles and began to twist and plait a large number of threads, adding to the pattern of lace attached. 'Golly, I remember you doing this when I was quite young.'

'Oh, aye, I've always enjoyed lacemaking, knitting and sewing. It's a fun thing to do and I'm trying to get back to it, there being many problems working for that chap. Mebbe I'll soon manage to earn enough by working for myself and will then be able to resign. Otherwise I'll hang on, being desperately in need of a good source of income, and determined to care for my family. How is your job going and do you have any problems?' she asked, giving a smile before she began to sip her coffee.

Stifling a sigh, Joanne insisted she enjoyed working as a waitress at the hotel, making no mention of the sense of loss she felt in leaving Jubilee House and the fun of Blackpool. To her surprise a part of her even missed Bernie, which was utterly ridiculous and just proved what a boring life she was living. 'You shouldn't be too obsessed with us, Mam, your long-missing family. I am well accommodated in that hotel even though I've no intention of spending my entire life there.'

'I'm still trying to find us a better house, one that isn't owned by that flamin' chap, but I've had no luck so far. Mebbe one day the local authorities will find me one. Once I do, you'll be welcome to join us, darling.'

'Don't worry about me, Mam. I'm pretty grown-up now so must make my own decisions in life. Who knows where I'll live and work next. Megan, of course, is still badly missing Blackpool and her school and friends. But no longer demanding to leave Manchester, as she's growing quite fond of you,' Joanne tenderly informed her.

'Eeh, that's good to hear, although her attitude is a bit blow hot, blow cold. I do hope she'll settle down. That would be such a relief.'

As a contented silence settled over them, Joanne happily watched her mother stitch. 'Whatever you're making looks amazing and a beautiful shiny white. What will it turn out to be when it's done?'

'A lovely lace tray cloth. Then I might stitch a blouse in a lovely blue or green for darling Megan. Which colour do you think she'd like best?'

'Blue would be good.' Closely watching her slip the threads around, she said, 'You really are most talented. How did you learn this?'

Evie laughed, her round face lighting up with joy. 'I was taught by my mum. She was a most clever lady and sold many of the shawls and silk cloths she made, so why would I not try to do the same? Lacemaking can be a bit complicated but basically these bobbins are the thread carriers. They have a bulbous-shaped shank to give weight and keep the thread taut. The lace is created by weaving, plaiting and twisting these threads, pins holding them in place. That's putting it simply, and I happily make the pattern. I would also enjoy knitting lace scarves and garments, if I had the appropriate equipment to spin the thread.'

'You're so clever. I do hope this works for you,' Joanne said with a smile of admiration. 'You could perhaps teach me to do some of this work.'

'Why not? Let me know if and when you'd like to give that a go. But you must swear not to mention to a living soul the possibility I might start working for meself. I don't intend to let anyone know how badly I dislike that Harold Mullins. It's most appropriate for me to be polite to him and I've no choice but to go on working for him until I'm in a position to leave and have found us a better home.'

'That might take a while, Mam. The thing is, I'm earning quite well, so could contribute some money to help you get started on this business of yours.'

'Nay, love, don't waste your savings on me. I'll get there in time. As for you now being quite grown-up, lovey, you need the freedom of your own life. I fully recommend you look after yourself. And when I've found somewhere better to live and accommodate Megan, Danny and my lovely husband, I'd like to think you'd be happy to come and stay with us or visit whenever you wish,' she said, giving her a loving smile.

'I look forward to that, Mam. But if you need any financial help, do let me know.'

Danny was stunned when he found himself watching the gang caught up in a bit of crime, which they viewed as fun. Bombed and abandoned buildings had been a treasure trove for looters throughout the war, many personal items having been left there, the owners having lost their lives. Even if folk were simply protecting themselves in an air raid shelter they often discovered that items had been stolen when they returned home. Because of their boredom or the loss of their parents or other family members to care for them, this gang of young hooligans, as they were often called, amused themselves by pinching whatever they fancied. They often did this with the idea they could sell things on to someone else, rationing and poverty still very much an irritating issue for them. Because of their hunger they'd pinch broken biscuits or a bottle of Tizer from a market stall. Each morning they'd arrive early outside a baker's shop to hang around waiting for yesterday's stale bread to be tossed out into the bin.

Danny carefully avoided becoming involved but tended to feel a pity for them, some members of this gang not having a home to live in and would sleep huddled down under a bridge by the canal or the lock, at times in the dark narrow streets and alleyways around the canal basin. They'd shiver and shake, breathing in the smell of tar and coal dust, cold damp water, mud and grass. Feeling the need to build themselves a fire to keep warm they would often scrounge coal from storage yards, or knock timber out of fences. Danny had needed to do that when his own mother had found their coal stolen. He could but hope he wouldn't be charged for it. He knew that their criminal behaviour was very much a consequence of that dreadful war or the despairing loss of their family. He had some sympathy with that, having suffered some bad issues himself.

Fog was now drifting in from the canal and dusk was already starting to fall as he and Willie stood at the back door of a hotel engaged in selling the chef a load of eggs. When Danny had asked Willie where these had come from, he'd muttered something about a family member keeping hens and it was his job to sell them. He suspected members of the gang had stolen a large number from hen huts belonging to a nearby farmer as they too were selling some to other folk. At first believing what Willie had told him and not wishing to be battered again by him, he'd agreed to help sell these eggs, asking for no further details.

It was as they turned to go that a loud voice called out and he felt a strong hand grab hold of his ear, and that of Willie's too. 'Nah then, let's be having you. What are you doing here?'

To his horror, Danny saw that it was a copper. Some police often felt sorry for young lads not being legally entitled to a place to live, provided with little in the way of food let alone jobs or apprenticeships, which meant they had to devise ways of looking after themselves. Others, however, felt a strong need to do their duty, as this one clearly believed.

'I'm not doing owt wrong. Just visiting me sister who works here,' Danny stated rapidly. 'And this is my mate. He hasn't done nowt either.'

The constable frowned, doubt creasing his face. 'Name please, as well as that of your sister.'

He felt a swirl of alarm bubble within him. Why had he stupidly said this when he'd no idea whether this hotel was the one where his sister worked. He sincerely hoped it wasn't as that would be entirely inappropriate and unfortunate. Yet having no wish to be charged with this stupid crime, Danny politely obeyed, his heart pounding. The kitchen door had firmly slammed shut and the chef vanished, as had the eggs, for which Willie, who was in charge, had appropriately been paid. Would that chef reveal what they were up to if he too was interrogated? And Danny didn't dare to guess how Joanne would react were she to discover what had happened, if this was where she worked. Right now the constable was giving Willie a telling-off, demanding to know exactly what activities he was involved in. 'Are you engaged in some deal with this hotel or simply a visit?'

Willie was looking very flustered and kept squeaking over the pain he was enduring over the clasp of his ear. He did attempt to agree with Danny's comment. 'We just paid a call to sell a few eggs, my family produce, so can we go now?'

Thankfully letting go of both their ears the copper glowered at them, then burst out laughing. 'I suspect you might be involved in summat but since I've no proof I'll let you go.' Set on escaping, they turned to run away. 'Hold on, you do need to show thanks for my generosity.'

Willie slipped him two half crowns then as they both ran away the copper stood roaring with laughter and slipped the money in his pocket.

'At least we escaped thanks to your stupid comment,' Willie said to Danny. 'But bloody expensive, so it'll cost you summat too.'

19

1947

When spring came in early March, Evie suggested she'd like to take her son and daughters on a boat trip on the Manchester Ship Canal. 'Having been built between 1887 and 1894 it follows the course of the River Irwell to finally reach the sea at Liverpool. Would you like that trip?' she asked them. Joanne and Danny eagerly agreed they would. Megan merely gave a shrug and a frown, as she so often did in response to whatever her mother offered to do.

'I prefer walking on a beach, cycling or playing games, not sitting in a damp boat.'

'The sun is shining, always a delight to see, so I reckon you'll enjoy it,' Evie said brightly, aching to see a smile in her young daughter's face.

'Why would I?' she responded sharply.

Danny gave her a wink. 'Because this trip provides the people of Manchester with a treat, as well as a route for the delivery of goods I have to deal with. That's where I mainly work.'

Seeing how her brother's comments had finally persuaded her to join them, Evie sighed. What a problem this lovely young daughter was. At times she would become withdrawn and tense, still sulky and indifferent towards both of her parents. She would look affronted if her father asked her to fetch something for him, not taking into account his difficulty in walking or reaching for things. And though he frequently attempted to gain her interest, striving to improve his mental condition, Megan barely listened to a word he said. Locked in silence and living in a world of her own, she would constantly be absorbed with reading, drawing or doing her homework. On one occasion he asked her to come and sit by him. 'If you've fetched a book from the library, I could read it to you, love,' he said.

'I can read perfectly well.'

'Sorry, 'course you can. Then come and read to me, lass.'

Saying nothing more she gave him a scathing look, not moving an inch.

'Oh, leave her in peace, Donald,' Evie had chuckled, not wishing him to fall into despair. 'Actually it's time for supper, could you set the table, lovey.'

'I'm not employed to do such things, so why would I?' Feeling the need to help her daughter remain calm, Evie had given a bit of a giggle. 'I'm not running a boarding house like your dear aunts although I expect they too asked you to set tables for them.'

She'd jumped to her feet and stalked off upstairs to her room, firmly slamming the door closed, obviously offended by that remark. Evie had given a sigh and Donald a consolatory hug. 'Don't fret, her attitude is a bit dismissive to me too. She'll 'appen come round eventually.'

He'd tried his best to be caring towards Megan but now feeling greatly irritated at receiving no response to anything he said or did, he'd given up making the effort. He'd wrapped himself back in his own personal difficulties and largely ignored his younger daughter, speaking only to his son and Joanne. Nor did Donald show any desire to accompany them on a trip.

Once on-board ship and seeing the many brightly painted barges and the sun shining upon them out of a velvet blue sky, Danny then pointed to a passing boat. 'That's the barge I work on. Quite small but no tug or ship can be too large if they are to manage to negotiate the locks on the Ship Canal. I do enjoy this job and you can often spot me loading timber. Then I unload it once we reach Liverpool or Birkenhead,' he smilingly told them. 'I only get paid a low rate but am hoping that will improve in time.'

'You're doing well, dear boy,' Evie told him and Joanne agreed, thoroughly enjoying this trip with him. Even Megan gave him a smile of appreciation, if still largely ignoring her mother.

'Me and my colleagues also have fun swimming in the summer in the Bridgewater Canal near Trafford Park,' he said with a laugh. 'Being lined with trees it feels very much like a quiet part of the countryside, which I love. So 'appen if this job doesn't work, I'll look for one back in a farm, summat I allus enjoyed doing despite being a young lad at the time.'

'I hope you don't go off to the countryside any time soon,' Evie said, giving him a woeful smile.

''Course I won't, Mam, still a bit too young and quite happy to be here.'

If only her daughters thought that too, in

particular Megan who was the difficult one. Putting this worry out of her mind, she bought them all an ice cream. 'Do let's enjoy this lovely day together.'

★ ★ ★

'Have you had a good day?' Donald asked when she arrived back home in the late afternoon.

She smiled and pecked a kiss on his cheek. 'Marvellous, and the three of them have gone off to the pictures now. I'm so sorry you didn't feel well enough to join us, we had great fun. As it's a Saturday and we have a little peace and quiet, I shall help give you and your lovely hair a wash.'

Since there was no bathroom in this miserable little house she brought in the tin bath that hung outside the kitchen door and filled it with hot water from the grange boiler. He settled into it with a gentle sigh of pleasure. 'I was a slave labourer when captured as a PoW and was never granted such blissful attention.'

'I'm happy to be your slave labourer in future,' Evie said with a grin.

'I was, of course, also interrogated. Not at all a good experience. When I refused to answer they'd lock me in a cell with no warmth in it so that I'd soon be freezing cold. Then after several days of starving they'd come for me in the middle of the night and drag me out to take me to the commander's office and start the interrogation all over again. An absolute nightmare! I kept trying to convince them that I had little informa-tion so why waste their time questioning me.

211

They paid no attention to that so I shut up altogether. Saying nothing ever again.'

Evie felt deeply moved that he was finally sharing his anguish with her. 'Did they hurt you?'

'They engaged in quite a lot of torture and abuse, strapping prisoners up, beating and kicking them and enjoyed leaving us in a crumpled mess to starve. If you searched a waste bin for food you could be shot at or stabbed, so it was a situation you had to put up with. They killed quite a lot of my mates and I often saw their corpses dumped. That's enough, it's not something I have any wish to speak of as it would upset you, love. Me too, since I desperately try to block it out of my mind. Fortunately, I remained sane by keeping my mind fixed on you and our childer.'

'Oh, my darling, what a lovely thought. And you're doing so well now in becoming closer to them again. Now I'm going to give you a scrub.'

'That's good to hear.' Reaching up, he gave Evie a kiss, the touch of his mouth upon hers filling her with joy.

No longer the rich dark brown hair it had been before the war, being now grey and fusty, she gave it a good wash with glycerine shampoo. She then gently rubbed his neck and shoulders, arms, legs and feet and other tender parts of his body with a sponge of carbolic soap. 'Hopefully, this will make you feel better.'

'I know another way that might,' he said, as she sat him back on his chair and rubbed him dry with a towel. Holding her close he gave her a kiss. Later, he took her up to bed and made love

212

to her, as they had done on a few blissful occasions since Christmas. He seemed to be making something of a recovery, bless him.

* * *

It was one Sunday a week later that Danny suggested Megan could come for a walk with him by the canal. 'I know you've lost your sporting teams and not managed to be assigned to any yet in this mixed school, so I wondered if you'd like to have a go at fishing. I always enjoy doing a bit of that.'

'Not sure that I'd be any good at it but I'm happy to join you and watch you do some fishing,' she happily agreed.

They walked down Castle Street and crossed the bridge over the Rochdale Canal that enters the Basin, a rumble of trains thundering across the railway arches overhead, till they reached the Bridgewater Canal towpath.

'How these canals stink,' Megan said, giving a grimace. 'Do you still like working on them, Danny, as you told us?'

'I do,' he laughed. 'We transport cotton to Blackburn, Liverpool and other places, and take coal to various factories linked to the canal basin, often having to break the ice on the surface of the water when we go along in the winter. Not easy. There is less cotton and coal to transport than there used to be since the mills are no longer fully operational. We can but hope they'll recover.'

'There's no proof they will, from what I've

heard about Mam's complaints,' she said.

'True, obviously the reason she lost her job in the mill and now has to work for Harold Mullins. The thought of that fills me with horror.' Avoiding going into further detail regarding his low opinion of Harold Mullins, they walked along the towpath and Danny pointed out how the canal basin was crowded with tugs, barges and narrow boats. Once they'd reached a quieter spot he said, 'Right, this is generally a good place for a spot of fishing. Do you want to have a go?'

She watched as he demonstrated how to fling out his fishing rod. The lack of interest in her eyes caused him to hesitate, torn between feeling the need to catch a good selection of fish for their tea, or spending a suitable amount of time teaching her. 'I could start you off and give you some tips,' he said, showing a degree of generosity.

Megan laughed. 'No thanks. If you're so good at this why don't you concentrate on fishing? I very much doubt I'd be any good at it.'

She sat quietly watching him for some time. Danny liked to see her happily smiling at what a peaceful task this was, obviously not something that appealed to her but she'd welcomed this trip out with him, as she so often did.

After a while she said, 'I feel in need of a bit of exercise, having sat still for so long. I'll take a little walk further along the towpath, to look for some flowers.'

'Don't go too far,' he instructed her.

'I won't, bossy brother,' she teasingly told him, wrinkling her nose in a fun scowl.

Giving a grin, he watched her walk off. Megan was a delight but obviously felt badly in need of the good life she used to enjoy. What a struggle she was having to settle into this new world. He missed the countryside a little himself and she missed those landladies and her school in Blackpool. Joanne had told him that she missed the sea. At least he enjoyed working on the canal here. It was a short time later, having managed to catch three good-sized fish that he heard Megan loudly shout.

'*Danny!*' she screamed.

Blimey, was she in danger of falling into the canal? He instantly jumped to his feet and ran along the towpath round the bend that had blocked him from seeing exactly how far she'd walked. He was appalled when he saw her kneeling on the ground and Willie Mullins standing beside her. He couldn't quite be certain what he was up to but it was obviously not appropriate and filling his sister with panic. He could see how she was trying to push him away. Desperate to rescue her, Danny pelted along the path at a furious speed.

Reaching her, he yelled at Willie, 'Take your filthy hands off my sister, you bastard!'

'Why, I'm just trying to help pick her up since she's fallen,' he said.

Landing him a smack across his shoulders with the fishing rod, Danny watched with pleasure as, waving his arms in a panic, Willie fell backwards into the canal.

'He won't sink will he?' Megan asked, giving a shiver.

Gathering her in his arms, Danny instantly gave her a cuddle. 'No, as you can see he's wisely swimming away. He knocked me in the canal once for no good reason, so he deserved to suffer the same bleedin' mess for pestering you.' Taking his sister's hand, he gave it a gentle squeeze and took her to sit with him on a nearby bench. 'Are you sure you're all right, Megan? I deeply feel the need to understand and support you. Tell me what he did. Was he touching you?' he asked delicately.

She gave a nod even though tears rolled down her cheeks. As she quietly began to speak, Danny had to lower his head to listen, a fury developing within him as he heard what she had to say.

'I was idly picking flowers from the bank beside the towpath when I heard a voice say, 'Hey there, gorgeous!' Looking up I saw that young man. He seemed familiar and I realized who he was, having seen him at that Christmas party. I felt swamped with a sudden attack of panic. Turning to run I found the way back down the towpath blocked by him, standing with his legs astride and his hands in his pockets. I gave a gasp, wondering why he was not letting me pass. I feared he might be planning to touch or kiss me, a terrifying prospect that made me sway with fear.'

'Oh, I'm sure it did.'

'When he saw the panic in my eyes he just laughed, telling me I was growing into a most attractive girl but was a bit shy and far too quiet. He asked if I felt the need for him to give me a cuddle to cheer me up. I firmly told him not to

216

touch me and backed away. The dread of what he might do pounded in my heart. I thought how stupid of me to take a walk on my own. Giving another spurt of laughter, he took a step towards me and, reaching out his hand, he slid it over my cheek, down my neck and looked as if he would go on to caress my breasts. That's when I jumped away, screamed, and shouted for you, Danny. I then fell down on my knees.'

'Good Lord, what a flamin' bastard he is.'

Megan gave a shiver. 'His eyes were filled with such an odd expression I thought I was about to go through what I did back in the past, or worse,' she whimpered.

'Oh my God! Are you saying that something similar happened to you in Keswick at the start of the war? I didn't know that, although was aware something had upset you, which is why you were moved.' Joanne had sent him a note saying they had to go, not explaining the full details. Could it have been Willie, the lad who'd created problems for him too? Megan's silence about the past seemed to indicate that she had no wish to speak of whatever it was that had upset her. Now he needed to know. 'Tell me what he did to you back then, love.'

She took a breath. 'Being young at the time I can't entirely recall all the details. Just as well, as I've no wish to remember or speak of it, having blocked it out of my head.'

'You can tell me, Megan, being your brother.'

Giving her head a shake, she said, 'Not right now. Can we go home, please?'

''Course we can. Do you want me to tell Mam

about what happened to you just now?'

'No, please don't. I could be fussing over nothing important and I've no wish for her to view me as stupid and shy.'

'You most definitely aren't.'

'Besides, doesn't our mother work for that lad's father? If I were to tell her what happened she'd be sorely tempted to complain to her boss about his son, which could lose her the job.'

Danny felt a glow of rage spark within him at the possibility this dreadful abuse could damage his mother too. How he hated that bastard and sorely longed for his mother to be free of him. 'I'll say nowt to Mam just now, but we could tell Joanne. She surely deserves to know, being most caring of you.'

Megan gave a little smile. 'Maybe. Joanne has had boyfriend problems and needs time to settle down and build a new life for herself too. Let's keep quiet until it feels appropriate to speak of it. I'm all right and recovering from that fumble he made on me.'

'All right, and I'll do what I can to warn that bugger never to come near you again. He certainly has no right to touch or fondle you, which I'll make very clear to him!'

'I think it would have been much safer if I'd stayed in Blackpool.'

'You could be right about that.'

★ ★ ★

It was not a discussion that went down well, the pair of them still not having achieved a close

218

friendship even though Danny did love playing cricket and footie with his gang and had saved him that time from being arrested for stealing eggs. They'd begun the evening by playing a game of football but having socked him with the heavy ball he'd booted at him, they now stood inches apart, a fury darkening both their faces. Danny clenched his fists, making the effort not to thump Willie, which could involve himself in another fight, possibly with the rest of the gang too.

'I didn't do anything dreadful, only being friendly. You'd no bloody right to chuck me in the canal just because I was teasing that pretty little girl. What's wrong with that? It was just a bit of fun,' Willie protested.

'I have every right to protect her since she's my young sister and only twelve years old, not old enough for such attention. Nor does she like you or any other nasty lad wishing to fondle her. So if you ever flamin' well touch her again I'll mek sure you sink next time.'

'I could chuck you out of our gang for mekin' that threat,' Willie roared.

Pausing, Danny gave him a sour smirk. 'And I could report you to the police if you ever attempted to pester her again. Got that?' Then, turning to his mates he calmly asked, 'I'm quite friendly with you lads, do you want me to leave this gang because of this complaint or not?'

Some remained safely silent being a little nervous of their leader; others agreed that Danny should stay. One said, 'I wouldn't want my little sister to be kissed by a lad older than her either,

219

and we do like having you as a member of our footie team, so why would we?'

'Quite,' Danny said, and calmly folding his arms met Willie's furious glare with a grin. 'You've been a right pain in the ass for my sister, so keep well away from her in future.'

'You don't know owt and making this threat will do you no good at all.'

220

20

The following Sunday afternoon when Joanne visited her family she was happy to take a walk with her brother and sister. There was a small patch of blue sky and a ray of sunshine lighting a prettily painted barge as they walked down by the canal, which brought a resonance of happiness to her heart. Pausing to gaze out over the Giant's Basin, a great curving overflow sluice that takes surplus water from the canal down into the river Medlock, she watched Danny put his arm around Megan's hunched shoulder, meeting her troubled gaze with a comforting smile. Then leaning against the wall he quietly told Joanne what Willie had done to Megan.

She listened to him in stunned horror. 'Oh no, not again.'

Giving a jerk, Danny gritted his teeth in fury. 'Are you saying he was the one who did something to her before? I remember being charged with . . . ' He stopped speaking, as if still wishing to keep this issue private.

Joanne gave him a pitying look. 'What were you charged with back then, Danny?'

Giving a glower he paused to take a breath then finally said, 'I was accused of having assaulted some girl or other, as well as nicking fruit and veg from that farm. I was given no details or names and furiously insisted that I was innocent of both charges. Ignoring my defence, I was sent to that bloomin' camp. As was Willie Mullins. Was it him what hurt you back then, Megan?'

Joanne put her arm around her sister to give her a comforting hug. 'I do know a little more than Danny but not a great deal, since you've had no wish to speak of the specific details. Do you think you can manage to tell us about it now, sweetheart?'

Taking a deep breath, Megan began to slowly speak. 'Being only a small kid just turned seven years old when we were living in Keswick in 1941, I agree that I've never wished to speak of it. But seeing that lad start to touch me by the canal the other day, what happened back then came shooting into my mind. A cold terror seeped through my veins. I'm so grateful that you saved me, Danny.'

'Thank God I did. You may not remember but Willie Mullins was billeted in Keswick too, around twelve years old at the time and a real jerk. What did he do to you when you were nobbut a young kid?'

Seeing the distress in her face and tears flooding her eyes, Joanne said, 'I think it's time for you to tell us whatever you can remember about that issue, lovey. I agree with Danny that he needs to know in case it was Willie who touched you back then as well as now, since he's had problems with him too.'

'Let's find somewhere private,' Danny said, and took them down to the old lock on the River Irwell. There was no movement of boats or barges, the river quite silent on this Sunday when there was little work taking place, the trees looked brightly rich with scarlet berries. They settled on the bench as if they were in a secret world of their own.

After some moments, Megan began to tell her story. 'I was happily exploring the woodland by the lake late one afternoon. It was one of those quiet, still days in autumn, the leaves like a palette of russet and the sky very cloudy and dark. Joanne was chatting to the steamboat manager so didn't notice when a man suddenly leaped out from behind one of the trees and squeezed my bottom. A bit like that Wing Commander Ramsbotham did, as you recall.'

'Oh, what a dreadful man he was too,' Joanne said. 'No wonder you were furious with him.'

'Being so young I felt frozen with shock. Then, standing under the tree, he slipped his hand inside his coat, looking as if he was holding something and quietly whispered to me, asking if he could show me something. Not able to see exactly who he was or what he was doing, being clothed in a coat and hat in the dark damp of that woodland, I just gave a blink and stepped back. He came closer, his hand making strange jerking movements. That's when I saw what he was holding and fell to my knees in horror, losing all strength in myself. I felt the urge to run away but couldn't move an inch, my knees glued to the ground. Screwing my eyes tight shut, I desperately wanted to shut out the awful sight of it. The sound of his grunting rattled in my ears, making me feel sick. A flurry of terror hammered up through my throat and I gave a scream.'

223

'Oh, my God, what a nasty bugger that lad is,' Danny stoutly declared. 'How dare he show himself in such a dreadful way to a little girl. He should be locked up for that.'

'Hearing her scream that's when I realized something terrible was happening to her, as you did the other day,' Joanne said. 'I ran like hell to find her shaking with fright as she lay huddled on the ground. Had I seen that stupid lad, I too would have been sorely tempted to thump him or toss him in the lake. The offender had, of course, run off before I arrived, so to be honest it could have been anyone, a perfect stranger. We've no proof that it was this Willie. She was in a state of hysteria and a flood of tears so could only tell me briefly what had happened. I remember you crying and saying that you wanted to go home, Megan. It was then I decided that, having endured problems where we were previously billeted, moving on again would be the right thing to do.

'We went immediately to see the billeting officer. I strongly made the point we were not happy there and seeing the distress Megan was in he did catch my drift, insisting I give him more details. I was obliged to roughly explain what she'd suffered but couldn't give specific details or name who was guilty of that, not having seen exactly what happened to her or the man responsible. You were unable to explain or say a word, weren't you, Megan, being so young and in a state of frozen terror. He kindly arranged for our swift departure.'

'Was that the officer who delivered your note?

You sent me one saying you were leaving but didn't go into any details as to why.'

'Sorry about that, but, as I say, I couldn't. The officer simply gave me a stamp so that I could post it to you. He was a most helpful man who ultimately had us transported to Blackpool, far away from the anguish Megan had suffered. I did write to you later, to say where we were living.'

Danny gave a sigh. 'Sadly, within days I was moved to that camp charged with being a problem evacuee who'd nicked fruit and veg, as well as this issue. Whether that accusation came from that billeting officer or the farmer's wife, I've no idea. She was adamant that I had to leave. I believe it must have come from Willie, as that bloody lad was also evacuated to the camp and very much into weird behaviour, which he still is. We had a terrible row when I blamed him at the time and he claimed his innocence, sounding very full of himself. He proved to be a real nightmare towards me throughout the war. We were never decent friends ever again as a result of that problem. I believed he could well have been guilty.'

'I can well understand that. He was totally weird back then and just as bad today, in spite of having grown up. Maybe his brain and common sense were seriously damaged by the loss of his mother. Who knows? I'm so sorry you were charged, Danny. How ridiculous that was. I feel a strong desire to go and give him a good telling-off or complain to Harold Mullins about his bloomin' son,' Joanne said, cuddling her young sister close in her arms.

225

'No, don't do that, sis,' Megan cried. 'That could make things worse.'

Danny hastily agreed. 'You might be right. We mustn't say a word or it could not only risk more danger for our Megan, but also create a problem for Mam since she hasn't yet found another job. Let's just keep quiet and protect our sister. That's what I tried to do by belting Willie Mullins, being her brother. And later *I* gave that stupid lad a good telling-off, making sure he'd never pester her again. He raged at me but I did receive support from his mates, so reckon I made the point.'

'Let's be confident that you're right about that and she will be safe,' Joanne agreed, giving him a smile. 'Hopefully, you won't suffer either.'

Danny gave a snort of disdain. 'If I have worse problems with him as a result, like the time he attempted to drop me off a cliff I was climbing, I'll skin him alive. Right now we need to make a pact to keep our eyes and brains alert to what-ever Willie Mullins might do, in order to protect our sister.'

'I don't wish to set eyes on him ever again,' Megan said, giving a shudder.

And giving each other a warm hug, they shook hands to make a pact on this decision.

★ ★ ★

'Did you enjoy your walk with Danny and Megan? Where did you go?' Evie asked when Joanne returned.

'We had a lovely stroll along the towpaths of

226

the Rochdale and Bridgewater Canals.'

'And had a good chat?'

'Of course, nothing important just having a laugh and sharing our experiences. Danny told us more about his job, how he helps the barge owner to work the locks. There are apparently nine along what they call the Castlefield Flight, and the last lock on the Rochdale Canal was once owned by the Duke of Bridgewater. He does seem to know quite a lot about the history of these canals.'

'And has Megan cheered up?'

Joanne smiled. 'A little. Danny and Megan have now gone on a cycle ride, as she so likes to do.' Then, jumping to her feet, Joanne offered to put the kettle on and make them a cup of tea, Donald being out with Davie at the local pub.

'He's always most caring of her, never agreeable for her to go any place on her own.' What a caring boy he is, Evie thought. Her lovely young daughter was much more friendly with her brother, never sharply disagreeing with him as she frequently did with her. She wondered why Joanne made little mention of the bad experiences they must have suffered during the war, which was possibly what caused Megan to be in such a mess. Evie had still learned little of her children's evacuation problems, even from Danny. At least Donald had now spoken a little of his own anguish and was slowly recovering, but how could she persuade Megan to calm down? 'I should 'appen have come with you for some exercise this morning, instead of spending my time busily knitting. I am a bit obsessed with this work,' she said, feeling a little guilty.

'That's good for you. What is it you're making, Mam?'

As Joanne came to sit beside her, Evie showed her what she was stitching. 'I'm knitting a lace scarf with one ply soft white wool. You thread the stitches on to double pointed needles. Put the needle purlwise into the first stitch on the front needle and pull the yarn through, then do the same on the back needle.' She went on to demonstrate and explain what more was involved in this task, showing the pattern she'd designed. 'I'm really enjoying it. Do you want to have a go?'

'Not sure I'd be any good at this, Mam, but I'll give it a try,' Joanne said. She valiantly attempted to follow her instructions to slip the stitch off the knitting needle when required, then put the needle into the next stitch and pull the yarn through. Some of their chatting and laughter came about when what she was doing went badly wrong, and then Joanne spoke of the joy, triumph and family happiness they'd enjoyed back in the past. Evie found it delightful that her daughter loved to dwell on the fun they'd had together when she was young, rather than the misfortunes of today's world.

Joanne gave a grimace. 'I do have different priorities from other people. Throughout the war I always left folk who didn't appeal to us, entirely the right decision to make in my humble opinion, in spite of the problems it created by separating us, Mam. Do consider how remaining working for your employer could badly affect you too.'

Evie gave her a shrewd look. 'You are making a valid point and, as you see, I am planning to do some work for myself, which I hope will result in earning me enough to eventually resign from that horrible job.' A part of Evie wondered if she was too old to start a business of her own, now being in her forties, and did she even have the time and energy? She could but hope so.

'Do you have a plan how that will come about?'

'Once I've created a number of lace scarves, shawls, tray cloths, curtains and garments to sell I intend to make an enquiry at Campfield Market to see if I can rent a stall. I love crocheting too, so could make some trims that can be attached to pillowcases or tablecloths.'

'That could possibly work well,' Joanne agreed. 'You are quite talented at such tasks. Unfortunately, there's still a depression on, Mam, so it might not be easy to make a lot of money at first but will surely get better once the economy of the country improves. If it doesn't work could an alternative be for you to attempt to get your job back at the mill? Wouldn't Mr Eccles, the mill owner, be keen to employ you again?'

Evie gave a chuckle. 'Sadly he wouldn't, love, the mill being in the process of closing down. Yes, it does have some machines that would be excellent for lacemaking and have never been used much throughout the war. The mill concentrated on making parachutes, mosquito nets and camouflage netting, which were useful for the troops but didn't make the mill a great

229

deal of money. Lace for fashion purposes lost attention, which will hopefully recover. I wish I had the money to buy one of those machines. Wouldn't that be grand, then I could start my own business.'

'Why don't you? That might cost more than even I've offered to supply you with. You could always speak to your bank manager and ask for a loan.'

'By heck, that's a fascinating idea. I might give that a go one day. Right now I'll stick to working by hand. I might buy myself a spinning wheel then I could create my own yarn, twisting and winding it on the spindle to make sure it's as fine and light as I like it to be with not too much tension in it.'

'That would be brilliant. I do admire your plan, Mam, and would be happy to help any way I can, even if it's just selling on the market stall for you, since I'm not too good at this job,' she laughed, still struggling to knit correctly. 'What a gifted lady you are. But it might be useful to have a word with the mill owner and ask what it would cost were you to buy one of those machines.'

'Eeh, I'll 'appen try that, love.'

★ ★ ★

A day or two later when Joanne went to pick up Megan from school, watching tribes of girls and boys come charging out, she saw no sign of her sister. When they'd all vanished, her heart began to pound in agony. She hurried into the school and looked everywhere for her. Seeing no sign of Megan, she found her teacher and asked where she was. She was stunned to hear that she hadn't attended school at all that day.

'We assumed she was ill,' said her teacher, giving a worried frown. 'Are you saying she isn't?'

Now guessing where Megan had gone, Joanne was not at all surprised. Giving a shake of her head, she said, 'She isn't at all unwell but I think I know where she could have gone. Back to Blackpool where we both lived as evacuees.'

'Do let me know if she's all right,' the teacher called, as she watched Joanne hurry away.

What if she was wrong about this and something dreadful had happened to her, such as being assaulted again by that Willie? The thought he might have kidnapped Megan was too dreadful to contemplate, causing a nag of anxiety to rattle through her. Rushing to the local post office she bought some paper and an envelope and quickly wrote a letter to the landladies in Blackpool, asking if Megan was safely there at Jubilee House.

Dear Aunties,
I was alarmed to find Megan has disappeared, and very worried about her decision to leave without telling us. I suspect she is with you lovely ladies whom she adores. If she is, please take care of her and ask her to write to me, then I'll come out to see her as soon as I can. We're desperate to know she's all right.
Much love, Joanne.

Quickly posting the letter Joanne, steadfastly hurried home.

Her poor mother looked utterly stricken when she heard that Megan had not attended school that day and was now missing. 'Why would she leave when we were getting on a little better? I admit she would sometimes fall into a sulk and be a bit dismissive on occasions of some request or suggestion I made. I once asked her to set the table for lunch and she tartly told me she wasn't employed by me so why would she do such things. I confess I gave a bit of a chuckle at that comment, pointing out I wasn't running a boarding house, which didn't go down well either. I can but hope she is safely with those landladies and not in any danger. Thank you for writing to them and do please let me know as soon you have word.'

'I will, Mam, don't worry. It was a silly thing for Megan to go off without telling us. I'm quite cross with her, but assuming that's where she's gone I'm sure she'll be perfectly safe.'

21

Evie heard a knock on the door and was shocked to find a policeman standing there. He coolly informed her that her son had been arrested for shoplifting.

'*What?*' She met his strong gaze with panic in her own. 'Where is he?'

'He's at the police station being questioned. We reckoned you'd wish to come and support him.'

Grabbing her coat, she hastily agreed, seriously aware that many lads were guilty of theft and looting during the war, their lack of parental control often blamed for this. They'd been given heavy fines or a short sentence while others could suffer a beating with a birch rod on their back or shoulders, a punishment often handed out by the courts. A most worrying prospect that some of this might happen to Danny.

At the police station, the desk sergeant was taking a few particulars in a desultory way. Stepping forward, Evie gave her son a good telling-off. 'Speak up and tell him what you can. Why the hell would you do such a stupid thing?'

'Not guilty,' he firmly announced.

Hearing the desk sergeant give a snort of disbelief, Evie turned to him with a frown. 'What proof have you got that he's guilty? I appreciate many young lads have been stupidly involved in

233

petty crimes throughout the war, often when shops were damaged or air raids were taking place. Or even stealing a bit of food if they were hungry. I don't believe my son has done any such dreadful things, so he could be innocent.'

'He was seen hanging around at Woolies by an assistant who then noticed the disappearance of several watches, which were found in his pocket. That's a most serious theft.'

Staring in stunned shock at Danny, Evie saw how he quickly hung his head down. If this was true he could be jailed for years. Valiantly attempting to protect him, she said, 'Presumably these watches can be returned to Woolies, since they've been found. I'll happily pay a fine if that would help and make damn sure my stupid son never does such a dreadful thing ever again.' Noticing the disapproving expression on the policeman's face, she realized this was not at all a sensible suggestion to make.

'I'm afraid that decision will be up to the local magistrate, not to you, dear lady. This lad will be called upon to appear at court on Monday morning. You can now take him home and give him another good telling-off.'

Filled with dismay as she knew how severe courts could be, once outside Evie actually gave her beloved son's hand a sharp smack. 'Why on earth would you do such a dreadful thing, you stupid lad?'

'I've said that I did nowt. Please believe me, Mam. It were other members of the gang, not me. I was appalled by what I saw 'em doing, although you were right to say why some lads did daft things like pinching biscuits, being poverty-stricken and hungry. I've seen 'em do that but why they nicked these watches, I've no idea. When that assistant approached, one of that gang must have shoved them watches in my pocket. I didn't realize that until they'd all disappeared and I was searched.'

Evie gave a groan. 'So why didn't you tell that to the police?'

A bleakness penetrated his face. 'Because I fear what that gang might do to me if I told the police what they were up to.'

'Oh, love, I can sympathize with that. Why did you become involved with them, and who do you think was guilty of this crime, as well as shoving those watches in your pocket in order to put the blame on you? You can tell me and I promise I won't mention it to the police but will try to find some other way to save you.'

Now he was looking very sheepish. 'I reckon it were Willie Mullins. He's been a pain in the ass for years. I thought we'd at last made friends again and joining my mates in his gang would put some fun in my life. I've regretted that decision ever since, as it was obviously a bad mistake even though I am still friendly with the other lads.'

'Oh, my goodness!' Gazing at him in stunned dismay, it came to Evie that she would have to speak to Harold and explain that *her* son had been put into this dreadful mess by *his*. Heaven help her, that would not be easy. Would this save Danny or so infuriate that dreadful man that her own life could be ruined too?

When Joanne dashed over later that morning to inform her mother that Megan was indeed in Blackpool with those landladies, she was disappointed to find her absent, only her father sitting by the fire with a gloomy expression on his tired face.

'Are you not feeling well, Dad?' she asked, an anxiety curling within her.

'I'm not doing too badly, at least sleeping better. The trouble is we now have a more serious problem.' She was shocked when he told her that Danny had been charged with shoplifting, his face glowering in fury. After making him a mug of tea, she settled on the sofa to listen as he went on to explain how Evie had been called to attend the police station, his son having been arrested.

'Oh no! I can't believe he would do such a thing.' Joanne gave his hand a squeeze, expressing her hope that Danny would hopefully prove his innocence and would soon be released. Not being in a happy frame of mind she felt a strong desire to reveal who she suspected might have charged him with this crime. She'd always felt close to her father. Why would she not? If she was right and Harold Mullins's nasty son had wrongly charged Danny with theft yet again, as he had done in the past, it could create even worse problems for her brother, being sent to jail rather than that camp for problem evacuees.

As for her mother, it could be bad for her too if Harold Mullins found his son accused of both these catastrophes upon their family. He could take his revenge by sacking Mam and throwing her out of this house, making them all homeless. And whether it would be right or wrong to reveal what her sister had suffered early in the war, as well as more recently, was hard to decide. She too had felt in danger. Thankfully, Megan had written a letter in which she'd said:

This is where I can happily live and be safe. I assumed you'd object to my leaving but I've no wish to risk that nasty lad ever choosing to touch me again. I shall miss my family but please don't tell Mam and Dad the real reason why I came back here, just say that I prefer this school. I no longer have the courage to stay in Manchester since I don't trust him one bit.

Escaping might have been a sensible solution for her. Thank heaven she was now safe. As both Danny and Megan had insisted, Joanne knew she must remain silent and not speak of this problem. Having no wish for their mother to lose her job until she'd established a business for herself, she must agree with this decision. What a mess it would be if she learned the truth. Nor could she tell her father either.

Stifling a sigh, feeling a mix of relief and despair at the situation her beloved sister was in, she briefly assured him that Megan had safely returned to the landladies whom she thought of as her aunts in Blackpool. 'I've received a letter from her saying she's delighted to be back at the school she used to attend, having felt a certain homesickness for it and her friends, and those dear ladies, of course.'

'By heck, that's a relief to know,' he murmured.

'I have written back, indicating that I'm on my way over to see her. I'll be off first thing tomorrow, Dad, to speak to her and check she's all right and ask what took it into her head to dash off like this. I really think she should try harder to settle here and be more friendly with you both, a point I'll most certainly make. I'll also inform her teacher at the school here, who was concerned about her absence.'

'I'll tell your mam where she is but she will be disappointed and upset at losing Megan again. We'll both miss her, although right now we're more concerned about our son.'

'I appreciate that Mam must be seriously distressed but has other problems too. Do let me know if I can help.'

Saying goodbye and kissing him on his pale hollow cheek, Joanne urged her father not to worry, reminding him that her mother was a strong woman good at battling for her kids. 'I'm sure she'll do her best to save Danny.'

She then cycled away back to her loft at the hotel near Victoria Station, tears running down her cheeks as she feared the worst could happen to her brother.

★ ★ ★

Later, returning from the police station, Evie sat by the fire in the kitchen her mind whirling round in sheer panic as she briefly explained to

238

Donald what had happened and how she felt desperate to save Danny from jail. 'Why on earth would our son agree to join this gang, being aware of what a problem that Willie Mullins could be? It sounds as if that lad's now in charge of a gang of criminal youths. Did Danny join them because he was bored or feels he's been neglected by us, his loving parents who haven't seen him for years?'

'He is in a bit of a muddle and I have tried to sort him out and give him proper instructions on what he should do with his life,' Donald said, looking cross.

'Why did you feel the need to do that? He's so happy to be back home and loves that job I found for him working on the canal barges. Oh dear, maybe your constant harassment of him was the reason he went in search of a bit of fun and sport, which has landed him in a right mess. Danny doesn't like you being too strict and controlling, love. I fully understand why that overcomes you at times because of this sense of despondency you're suffering from, but you need to calm down and stop fretting.'

'Don't say that, Evie. I am trying to shut off the pain in my life and recover from those issues, which is not proving to be easy. I thought I was getting a lot better.'

'So you are, darling, but you do sometimes fall into a grim mood.'

'I know, much as I try not to. We've also lost Megan again. Joanne popped in to say that she's gone to visit those landladies she sees as her aunts.'

'I guessed that could be the case,' Evie said with a sigh. 'I'll mek us a cuppa then we'll have a chat about what I could possibly do to sort this problem of Danny's out, as well as collect Megan yet again,' she said. After giving him a kiss, she jumped up to put the kettle on the stove.

Catching hold of her hand, he pulled her back down and gently explained how Joanne had heard their young daughter fully intended to remain in Blackpool. 'It seems she misses her favourite school and prefers to live with those landladies.'

Evie's face went pale with dismay. 'Oh no, why would she decide to do that when I thought she was gradually settling in here? What a mess this war has made upon our family.'

'Let's sort out Danny's problem first, love,' he said, gently patting her cheek.

'Aye, you're right. Surely shoplifting isn't too bad a crime, not with kids dipping their greedy fingers into displays at Woolies, naively failing to consider the consequences.'

'Stealing those watches is a much more serious issue.'

'Don't say that, love.'

As they sat drinking their tea, they kept on talking and striving to find a solution to both these issues, losing their son and daughter for very different reasons. 'Willie apparently created problems for Danny before this one and whatever that cocky lad did clearly distressed him. I believe he must have once badly affected a mountain climb Danny was involved in, judging

240

by the way he's turned against that sport. He certainly has no wish to speak of such details other than with derision, so it must have been pretty scary.'

'I can sympathize with that, having a similar reaction towards pain and fear in this bloody war. Mebbe Harold Mullins's son dislikes the fact his father gave you a job rather than him.'

'Goodness, I hadn't thought of that. I suppose you could be right there. According to Danny, that lad hasn't yet found one, even though he's now eighteen years old.'

'You have admitted that Mullins is not an easy man and, as I've suggested before, it would probably be wise for you to stop working for him.'

Evie firmly shook her head. 'I wish I could. As you know, I have failed to find other employment and started working for myself. But I'm not yet earning anything from that so we badly need the income I get from him. And if I left that job we'd be thrown out of this house. Considering there are no others available to rent, even though some are starting to be built, we cannot take that risk. In particular, I feel I should try hard to care and accommodate our children. I'm sure Joanne will do her best to persuade Megan to come back home. I know you aren't fit enough to find employment but you mustn't worry. I can cope.'

'Do as I say, wife, and leave this job,' he snapped, giving her a furious glare, something he repeatedly did whenever she didn't agree with him. 'I have a small pension from the Army, so that'll do for us.'

'Sadly that's not enough for us to live on. I do

241

feel the need to do my bit and yes, I will speak to Harold Mullins but I can't risk messing up our lives even more. There has always been a shortage of decent housing in Manchester, not least before the war. Now, because half of this city was bombed in the Blitz, it'll take a load o' dosh to rebuild the necessary number of houses. It certainly won't be done with any speed.'

'Don't be bloomin' negative.'

Weary that Donald was again becoming argumentative, she felt anxious not to upset him or risk putting him into a flaring temper. Evie gave him another little kiss then washed up the cups and suggested they went off to bed. 'I'll give this issue more thought and do what I can to get Harold Mullins's help. Let's not worry about it right now. We need some sleep.'

The only possible way she could think of to help Danny escape this charge was to tackle Harold on the subject. Would he be aware of his son's bad behaviour and be prepared to do the right thing to help save her own lad? She could but hope so.

★ ★ ★

The train journey from Manchester Piccadilly to Blackpool now only taking about an hour and a half, Joanne was seated with Megan the following afternoon in Stanley Park quite close to the lake. Megan had a sulky expression on her face, as if dreading what she was about to be told, showing no sign of her usual dimpled smile. 'I'll like to know what possessed you to dash off

242

without telling a soul,' Joanne asked quietly.

'It seemed the right thing to do,' Megan sternly remarked. 'It was my decision, not anyone else's.'

'Charming, so that's your attitude to your entire family, is it? You intend to be entirely dismissive of me and Danny, as well as Mam and Dad?'

Giving a heavy sigh, she said, 'The truth is that living in that place was not only boring but pretty scary, making me feel dull, awkward and unsure of my safety. In particular, I hated that mixed school, packed with horrible lads. That house is a mess too, though thanks to Danny I was no longer stuck in that bed with my mother. But I strongly felt the need to return to the house and school that I like best. What's wrong with that?'

'I can understand your difficulty in settling there due to what you sadly experienced, even in that mixed school considering your poor attitude towards lads. Your mother is dreadfully upset not only because she has no notion of the reason why you ran away, but you dashed off without saying a word, unprepared to discuss the issues that were bothering you. Not at all a pleasant thing to do. Most scary for us not to be told where you were going.'

'Oh, that would have been far too difficult.'

'Nor do I approve of the way you were still a little unfriendly and uncaring towards her and Dad.'

'I did sometimes feel a bit withdrawn and tense, but what was the point in hanging around when I wasn't convinced either of my parents cared a toss about me, let alone loved me?'

'She's your mother and absolutely adores you. Why wouldn't she be thrilled to have you and all of us back home? It was quite heartbreaking for her when she had to see us off on that train at the start of the war. I know we've had problems but so has she, worrying where we were and if our dad was still alive, let alone struggling to look after herself with bombing constantly taking place and losing friends and her home. Dad's problems, having been a PoW, are something we have to live with. He is working hard to find faith in himself and his future, let alone prove his love for you. So show him some sympathy and consideration too.'

A shimmer of guilt was now flickering in her sister's eyes and a frown creasing her young face. 'I hadn't thought about any of that. The thing is, I do feel much safer and happier here, Joanne, even though I badly miss you. I still wish to stay in Blackpool.'

Joanne stifled a sigh. 'I do appreciate that the high school you are attending here is a good one, but if you've no wish to return then maybe you could consider spending school holidays back in Castlefield with Mam and Dad. Will you give that possibility due consideration? And please do attempt to be kinder and more loving towards them. Some children no longer have any parents left, as a result of that blasted war. You should appreciate being more fortunate and having a family who loves you dearly.'

Looking most contrite, Megan gave a little nod. 'I will, I promise.'

244

22

'Are you implying that you'll do nowt to help?' Evie demanded of Harold, sounding desperately upset and irritated. Tackling him on the subject was not proving to be at all easy. She had told him that despite his innocence she feared Danny could end up in jail, thanks to his son's stupid gang, and begged for his assistance. He absolutely refused. They were seated in the Dog and Duck, his favourite pub where he liked to go whenever she asked to speak to him. 'This could be a bad decision on your part, taking into account I could charge your son for landing mine in trouble.'

Harold burst out laughing, claiming he felt an enormous sympathy for Willie who probably had a few debts too, considering his equal passion for gambling. 'Your son shouldn't have been such an idiot as to hang around in Woolies. He should have scarpered off with the rest of his mates. Maybe I'll give my lad a job once I'm certain he could be properly trained, now that I'm working entirely for myself in my own business, the mill having closed. I would then have to sack you, which would be a shame,' he commented sharply.

'You can't be serious,' Evie said, a slight tremor in her tone of voice. 'Why would you do that?'

Harold gave a snort of disgust. 'Most bosses

do not tolerate insubordination from their workers. Nor do I. Few women are free to do as they please these days. If they have families and husbands to feed, they shouldn't risk offending the man in charge of their income. Women employees need to remain respectful and obedient. I reckon you ought to acquire the habit of being more polite and tolerant of my decisions.'

What rubbish he spoke. Why on earth would women tolerate being so badly treated? Because of the work they'd done during the war in place of men, women had become hardened and independent, which now didn't always go down well. They were expected to concentrate on caring for a family and home, so what was wrong with her doing that? 'It's Danny I'm concerned about, not myself. I thought I'd made that clear.'

'Aye, but were I to offer to help with this issue, it would cost you summat by way of thanks. If you agree with that it may well lead me into paradise.'

'I've no idea what you're talking about.'

He chuckled, taking another slurp of his beer. 'You know that I've allus admired you as a fancy lady, so if you agree to accommodate my desire for us to have sex, I'll make sure your lad will be let off.'

Evie stared at him in stunned disbelief. What a voracious and appalling man he was, a fact she'd been aware of for some time as he constantly attempted to control her. Her tendency to appear reasonably smart whenever she went out and about meant she'd dressed herself in a burgundy pleated frock with Bakelite buttons.

Now Evie deeply wished she hadn't bothered to do that. The last thing she wanted was to give the impression she was endeavouring to charm Mullins into making such a dreadful proposition.

Admittedly, she and her darling husband enjoyed lovemaking only on rare occasions, no doubt because of the mental problems he had as a consequence of being a PoW during the war. Having to change bedrooms to accommodate their daughter hadn't helped. But now they again happily shared a bed their relationship was much better. There were, however, many nights when he would give her a gentle kiss or stroke her cheek, then sadly admit he couldn't gather the necessary virility to demonstrate his love for her. Evie lived in hope once he fully recovered their situation would improve. She certainly had no desire to have sex with any other man. If this obscene salacious Mullins imagined he could force her to willingly embark on copulation with him, he was behaving like a self-opinionated cuckoo. 'Don't be ridiculous. I'm a happily married woman so why would I ever allow you to do such a thing?' she staunchly remarked.

'Why would you not?' he asked calmly. 'It's what we chaps are entitled to.'

Much to her dismay, he reached over to slide his hand over her face, neck and breasts, then, reaching under the table, fondled her thighs, sliding his fingers up dangerously close to her private parts. After frantically pulling herself free of his touch, Evie furiously slapped him across his face, recalling how Joanne had slapped his son, Willie, when he kissed her after that dance.

What a dreadful father and son they were.

Unmoved by this attack, he again burst out laughing. 'We could have great fun, you and me.'

Firmly stabbing her blunt-tipped thumb upon her chest Evie met his amused gaze with a light of battle in her eyes. '*I'm* not stupid, so don't ever imagine I'll permit anyone to take advantage of me. Certainly not you. I dread to believe what you're expecting of me.'

His thin lips twisted in disdain. 'If you don't agree to oblige me with this requirement I have of you, not only will you lose your job and that house you're renting off me, your son could end up in jail for months or mebbe years. I'll certainly mek sure my lad is safe and yours will have to pay the price for your obstinacy. 'Course, I could allus persuade your beautiful daughter to accommodate me instead.'

Horror echoed through her at the sound of these dreadful threats, her anger and courage swiftly collapsing. How could she ever allow this sickening man to assault Joanne, let alone herself? Far too dreadful to contemplate. And how could she risk ruining the life of her beloved son? She fell silent for some minutes, a cold petrified mix of fear and fury descending within her. Evie felt herself shaking with desperation, questioning herself how she could manage to escape this demand. Surely she'd find some way of avoiding him.

'The question is, do you want to spare your lad from jail?' he asked smoothly.

Danny being incarcerated was the last thing she'd wish to happen. Hadn't he suffered enough during the war, not least because of this dratted man's son always putting the blame for his ill behaviour upon him? 'It would break my heart to see his freedom destroyed.'

'Quite,' Harold said, giving her a cynical smile. 'I reckon you'll find it worth your while to allow me a little pleasure in return for my assistance with this problem.'

Fearful of what might happen to Danny and Joanne too, if she didn't agree to this man's demand, Evie sat in stunned dismay at the table, her brain furiously striving to find another solution. She'd tried to convince the police her boy was innocent but they weren't prepared to listen. Danny could suffer badly if she refused to allow Harold to do what he required of her. A numbness crept over her as she valiantly attempted to shut out concern for herself, concentrating entirely on her beloved children. Taking a deep breath, she said, 'Assuming I agree to whatever you demand of me, how will you settle this problem?'

'I'll speak to the constable at the police station.'

'When?'

'As soon as you've done what I require.'

She gave a firm shake of her head. 'No, you must deal with this issue first.'

'Right, we'll go now then shall we, my car being quite close by in the street?'

As he issued this order, giving a searing smile, Evie rose slowly to her feet, put on her coat and followed him out to his car, her heart pounding. Seated in the passenger seat beside him, she felt a sense of dread echo through her as he drove off

249

at speed. Had she made a disastrous decision, or could she find some way to escape this problem? Right now she must do battle for her son, so only time would tell.

Anxious for him to succeed in cancelling Danny's charge, Evie determinedly accompanied Harold into the police station and carefully listened to what he had to say to the desk sergeant. He largely blamed the rest of the lads in the gang who had cleverly run off, claiming Danny and Willie were both innocent but a bit messed up having been evacuees. Nothing of what he said appeared to convince this policeman in charge, any more than what Evie herself had attempted to say in her son's defence. But then Harold leaned forward to whisper something in his ear, making a comment that she couldn't hear.

A flurry of surprise and agreement flickered in the police sergeant's face. 'That's good to know, sir. We'll drop this charge then, but make sure those two lads don't involve themselves with that crime gang ever again.'

'We will indeed,' Harold said, giving a smirk of satisfaction.

As they left, Evie demanded to know what it was he'd said that had brought about this success. Giving a chuckle, he happily told her. 'That copper is a client of mine, so I generously offered to cancel his debts if he let both of our lads off the hook, which he happily agreed to do. Now this mess has been settled we'll take a nice quiet drive and have a bit of fun, eh?'

She felt a soar of a relief that Danny was at last free of this charge but terror again resonated through her as she desperately strived to think of a way to escape this demand. 'Not right now. I need to speak to my son and tell him he's free.'

'You'll do what I say and when,' Harold snarled.

Glancing around in panic, wondering if she should just run away, Evie suddenly saw Donald approaching and her heart leaped with joy. Hurrying over to him, she gave her husband a kiss. 'Hello, love. Are you off to the pub for your usual pint of beer?'

''Course I am. You can come and join me if you like and tell me what you've managed to achieve for our Danny. Joanne convinced me that you'd succeed. Do hope that's true.'

'I definitely have some good news,' she said, then, turning to meet Harold's glowering frown, she calmly thanked him for his help and, slipping her arm in her husband's, walked away. But deep within her was the fear that not having allowed Harold to do what he claimed she must in return for his assistance, how could she be certain he would never attempt to assault her, or Joanne? And he could allow his dratted son to put Danny in difficulties again. She must somehow make sure she kept them and herself safe.

★ ★ ★

Joanne was thrilled to hear that the charge against Danny had thankfully been dropped when she called in to see her parents on Monday afternoon. 'What a relief that is. I'm sure you must have won this battle with the police. Well

251

done, for what you achieved,' she said, giving her mother a warm hug and a kiss. She appeared oddly silent, despite having resolved Danny's issue. She was, of course, fully occupied with her lacemaking. No doubt desperately worrying about her young daughter too, let alone her sick husband. What a dreadful mess she was in as a consequence of that blasted war. It made Joanne wonder if this was the moment she should risk explaining how Megan had suffered too, stating what that man's dreadful son had done to her lovely sister, not simply on one occasion. Steadfastly she said nothing on the subject, not wishing to create further problems for her mother. Joanne wondered if she'd sought assistance from Willie's father, probably not an easy experience.

To her surprise she heard her father mutter that as well as the police she'd also spoken to her employer, Harold Mullins, who was furious over the charge she made upon his son but did manage to persuade the police to drop it.

'Oh dear, how did he manage that, Mam?' Joanne asked.

As if attempting not to give any details in answer to this question, Evie said, 'Danny is free, that's all that matters. I am hoping to resign from this job soon so have again spoken to the local authority at the city hall on Albert Square, asking if they can find us a house as we're in danger of losing this one.'

'Did he threaten you with that?' Donald shouted sharply. 'He can't chuck us out even if you do resign, as I reckon you should since I can go on paying the rent out of my war pension. I'll

252

tell him that, next time I see him in the Dog and Duck.'

'No need for you to do that, darling,' Evie tactfully pointed out. 'I'm sure the local council will find us somewhere to move to.'

'Stuff and nonsense!'

'They promised they would, dear, don't panic. I also approached the manager at Campfield Market and he has agreed I can occupy a stall out on the street, the inside market being full. I've booked it for six weeks to give it a try.'

'Oh, that would be great! What a brave and determined lady you are,' Joanne said.

'She is indeed,' her father agreed, a sparkle of admiration and a flicker of tears in his dark eyes.

'When do you reckon you'll manage to start working for yourself, Mam?'

'Fairly soon, having no wish to remain with Mullins. Since I now have a number of products, I intend to start this Saturday. As you can get that day off I'd like you to join me, lovey, as I'd greatly welcome your assistance.'

'I will be delighted to help. Now where is Danny?' she asked.

'Out fishing, of course, in his favourite spot by the canal.'

Going at once to speak to him, Joanne settled on the towpath beside him watching the narrow boats with their brightly painted bows drift to and fro. She asked if he was feeling better now that he was free and he quietly assured her that he was. 'The farm work taught me the value of the weather and season, animals, the demand and right way to supply food so why would I

253

steal summat? I've never done that. Willie had no bloomin' right to accuse me of anything. I'm an honest lad. Yes, his bossiness towards me did make me feel miserable at times over being away from home and my family, having no one to support or protect me. Sadly, not even you, Joanne, after we'd both been moved on, although I know you battled for us siblings to remain together. I confess that being an evacuee has made me a more confident and independent person.'

'There is a degree of logic to that, but feeling separated from our family can be a bit depressing. I felt sorry about that and, as you know, Megan too was in a mess. You are now much stronger in spirit, as well as good at fishing,' she said with a chuckle, watching him pull a fish out of the water and drop it in his jar. 'I'm so hopeful you'll deal better with life in future.'

'Oh, aye, I certainly will. I hope Megan will too.'

'Don't have anything more to do with that stupid Willie Mullins. He needs to grow up and learn to behave better, so steer clear of him until he does. I'm planning to go and see Megan again soon and will try once more to persuade her to come back home to join us, though I'm not convinced she will.'

Pulling his face, he gave his head a shake. 'I very much doubt you'll succeed with that, but give her my love and best wishes. Tell her I'll come to see her too, as soon as I can get a bit of time off work.'

★ ★ ★

When they arrived together at Campfield Market early on Saturday morning, Joanne saw many lorries fetching cabbages and leeks, peas and carrots from farms in Cheshire and Lancashire, as well as slabs of wet fish, mackerel, cod and salmon from other places. Stalls that lined the pavement from Tonman Street to Deansgate were packed by various holders selling shoes and boots, socks and clothes, freshly baked pies and cakes, kettles, crockery and many other household goods. The one that Evie had been granted was little more than a trestle table at the far end of the street, upon which she laid out various lace scarves, collars, shawls, tray cloths and ribbons as well as crocheted items.

The old Victorian, iron-framed market building was soon crowded with people, as it always was on a Saturday. The wind was blowing but the sun shining so hopefully it wouldn't rain. There was a small-sheeted cover over this stall, which would surely protect these lovely products Evie had made from being damaged, if that were to happen.

'Look at these beautiful patterns,' her mother called out, holding up a scarf. A woman paused to examine them and to their joy showed an interest in buying one, offering a slightly lower price than the one Evie had named. Happily agreeing, a deal was struck.

'Good for you. You weren't too disappointed with her offer, were you, Mam?'

Giving a wink, she said, 'Nay, love, always ask a bit more than we expect to get.'

Joanne carefully took note of her instructions

on what price to ask for each item, and the lowest they'd accept.

Campfield had once been a thriving market but now it looked a little derelict with bombed-out buildings and warehouses close by. Children played in the rubble and people hurried by with their collars turned up against the wind, avoiding viewing the desolation all around. Joanne noticed that not far away was a man on crutches selling matches, clearly having been damaged in the war. Many wounded men were having great difficulty in finding work so this was quite a common activity, no doubt the only way for some to make an income. She went over to buy a packet of matches off him. She didn't smoke but Donald did, and of course her mother needed matches to keep the range fire burning.

'Bless you,' he said, and as Joanne happily told him how she was helping her mother earn a crust of an income, he wished Evie best wishes too.

The market at first remained quiet with few sales, but once people had bought the food and essentials they required, interest in these lace items grew, as well as the desire for a warm and pretty scarf. As the day wore on, sales improved tremendously. By the end of the afternoon, Evie was bursting with happiness for the success they'd achieved.

'As I've bought us some lovely meat and potato pies, it's time for us to go home and enjoy a good meal. Then I must get on with knitting more,' she announced.

'Well done, Mam. I'll come and join you on this market stall any time,' Joanne said, giving her a hug.

256

23

Joanne was delighted when she was granted a week's holiday to join her sister who had a week off school, it being Easter. Her wages provided the necessary funds and she wrote to tell Aunt Annie when she'd like to arrive and was duly welcomed and told she could share her sister's room, as she used to do.

When Joanne arrived at Central Station she hurried straight to Jubilee House just a few streets away. It felt good to view the sea. Dozens of tourists were enjoying a walk on the beach or a tram tour along the promenade and children a ride on the donkeys. Some would no doubt be having fun on the Pleasure Beach, Madame Tussauds or climbing up Blackpool Tower. She looked forward to enjoying some of this herself over the coming week. Best of all, it was a joy to see her sister come running out of Jubilee House the moment she saw her walking down the street, and leap into her arms. Joanne happily hugged her then found herself wiping her sister's tears away when she began to cry.

'Oh, I'm so pleased to see you, sis.'

'Me too, lovey.'

Later, as they walked arm in arm in Stanley Park, the aerodrome now closed so it was much quieter and with plenty of sports taking place including netball and tennis, which Megan loved to watch or take part in, Joanne quietly listened to her explanation.

'I have grown a bit fond of Mam and do miss her. I miss you even more, so it wasn't an easy decision to make. I just felt the instinct to run away, to escape that dreadful lad and be safe.'

'I can fully understand that feeling, darling,' Joanne said, pointing out how she and her mother both missed her but tactfully avoided sounding cross, having no wish to fall out or upset her. After giving her Danny's good wishes, she told her a little of what he'd been through recently, thanks to problems from Willie Mullins yet again. 'I really feel the need to give that lad a good telling-off and make sure he leaves us all in peace in future. Amazingly, Mam persuaded his father to help convince the police of Danny's innocence and the charge was dropped.'

'Thank goodness for that. Can we now have some fun?'

'Why not!'

Joanne revelled in having a wonderful week's holiday with her young sister, enjoying all the fun and entertainment which Blackpool was expert at providing, as well as swimming in the sea and lazing on the beach. They attended shows on the North Pier as well as the Winter Gardens, the Tower Ballroom and the Grand Theatre, listening to bands playing favourite songs of Joanne's including 'We'll Meet Again', 'Always in My Heart' a song written by Glenn Miller, and heard George Formby, who lived close by, singing 'Aunty Maggie's Remedy' and 'When I'm Cleaning Windows'. What fun he was, such a star and a great comedian, actor and singer, who'd happily entertained the troops throughout the war. There were many more stars playing including Frank Randle, Jimmy Clitheroe, a young man who looked very like a boy, and Tessie O'Shea who worked most summers here in Blackpool. Joanne and Megan always managed to find cheap seats near the back and would happily join in the singing whenever allowed. What a treat that was.

There were no troops now staying at Jubilee House but it was fully occupied by many Lancashire folk also enjoying a week's holiday. Whenever Megan was happily playing some game with her friends, Joanne found herself spending a little time with Bernie. He had never intruded upon the visits they made together but on this occasion suggested they take one of their regular walks along the beach or pier.

'Are you still interested in finding shells?' he asked, and she laughingly shook her head.

'Where on earth would I put them? Certainly not in the loft bedroom where I live, not at all as large or attractive as the one you created, just simple servants' quarters,' she laughed. 'So no thanks, please don't find me any more shells.'

Grinning, he too gave a chuckle. 'So what are your plans for the future?' he asked and Joanne told him how she quite enjoyed working at this hotel as well as assisting her mother who'd taken on a stall at Campfield Market. 'That was fun and she's good at producing these lacy products, although whether I could ever knit, sew or crochet as well as she does is most doubtful. So

259

how are you doing? What are your future plans?'

'Difficult to decide. My aunts have decided they've no intention of retiring for some time yet. They're feeling perfectly capable of continuing to work through their fifties and sixties, having recovered from the exhaustion they went through during the war. Nor have they any wish to disturb Megan by sending her to a different school. But what I will choose to do is a bit of a puzzle. I've enjoyed updating and improving parts of the house and learned a great deal by doing those jobs, such as putting new bathrooms in. I still enjoy helping with the cooking so who knows what I'll decide.'

He looked so confused and puzzled that Joanne felt a surge of sympathy and concern rattle through her. She believed she'd done entirely the right thing by refusing his offer of marriage, so what on earth was troubling her? He was a fine young man but she was not in love with him, Joanne stoutly reminded herself. She had no emotion for him at all, had she? Although when he took her on the roller coaster on Pleasure Beach, his arm firmly tucked around her shoulder holding her close to make her feel safe, she was amazed by the delight that sparked within her at their closeness, or perhaps simply a sense of relief. Despite it having been built in the thirties and operational throughout the war she'd always carefully avoided it, feeling something of a coward. Now she felt an excitement glow within her at the fun she enjoyed sharing on this scary roller coaster with Bernie.

What an accommodating young man he was,

as his aunts kept telling her.

She found herself looking forward to receiving an invitation for them to attend a dance together in the Tower Ballroom, as had happened many times before. When no offer came forth, she couldn't resist going with Megan, who loved dancing too, and they were on holiday. It was as they laughingly enjoyed a dance together that Joanne saw Bernie dancing cheek to cheek with a pretty young girl. Something inside her pounded with surprise and a flicker of disappointment. Obviously this was the reason he'd not been interested in taking her dancing. 'Gosh, I wonder who she is?' Megan whispered, also catching sight of him.

'No idea, have you?'

'Nope, but he surely has the right to find himself another girlfriend, you having dumped him.'

'And no doubt he wishes to keep this date private. I think we'd better disappear.' Feeling slightly guilty at having no wish to be introduced to this girl or interfere in his new relationship, Joanne grabbed her sister's arm and they quickly slipped away. Yet she felt oddly jealous seeing him with a new girlfriend and a deep sense of regret that despite them having enjoyed some fun time together this week, he had not invited her to dance with him.

★   ★   ★

Evie deeply regretted not being able to accompany Joanne, greatly missing her young

261

daughter but unable to take a week off, let alone leave her husband. She did hope to pop over one day to see Megan and was delighted when she received a letter from the landladies inviting her to call whenever she wished.

'Will you come with me?' she asked Donald, who gave a sad shake of his head.

'No thanks, I'd love to see Megan but the prospect of travelling by train and walking around an unknown and busy town just fills me with horror. I allus feel the need to stay quietly at home as my legs can't walk far and, as you know, I tend to get into something of a state if I go somewhere I know nowt about.'

Giving him a hug and kiss, she promised to ask Cathie to look after him on the day she went, saying she'd probably go at the end of the week so that she could come home with Joanne.

When the time came for her to leave she chose to wear her burgundy floral dress with a neat navy blue jacket and brimmed hat, wishing to appear smart. The moment she arrived at the Central Station in Blackpool she found Joanne and Megan had come to meet her and felt delighted when her young daughter gave her a warm hug and a kiss, at last displaying a fondness for her. Oh, but how she regretted that Megan was happily living with these landladies and not with her. Not at all easy to come to terms with.

'I'm hoping I can persuade you to come home, darling,' she said softly.

'Sorry, Mam, I've nothing against you, honest, but this is where I happily live with my aunts and enjoy going to school.'

'I'm sure these lovely landladies will be delighted to meet you and explain how things are,' Joanne quickly assured her, linking her arm. 'Now we'll walk along the promenade to meet them.'

When they reached Jubilee House and Evie saw the ladies her daughters thought of as aunts, she was again pleased to see how lively and pleasant they looked. Both sisters were dark haired with spectacles over their bright brown eyes, dressed in most sensible long tweed skirts and pretty white silk blouses neatly tied at the collar with a bow. They politely shook her hand, welcoming her into their private parlour where they had set out tea and cakes in florally designed crockery on a polished table beside the window. Noticing this was covered with a white lace tablecloth she was most impressed.

'How beautiful this is,' Evie said, giving it a gentle stroke with her fingers. 'I've been involved in creating textiles of this nature for years, apart from during the war when we spent most of our time making parachutes. Now I'm starting to sell tablecloths like this as well as other lace products.'

'How wonderful to hear that,' Annie said. 'Do sit down and tell us more.'

Evie happily did so, saying how she created such items by hand. Smiling, she thanked Sadie as she handed tea and cakes to her. Her two daughters came to sit beside her, listening as they chatted about this subject for some time. Annie showed her other domestic lace cloths they had, which had apparently been in their family for years, and Evie spoke of her own mother's skill at this task.

Eventually, Joanne got up and started to collect the empty cups and plates to place them on a tray. 'I shall leave you in peace to chat with our aunts, Mam. Megan will come with me to help wash these up.'

Watching as the girls dutifully departed to allow her some privacy, Evie felt she'd at last been granted the opportunity to discuss what had haunted her for some time. 'I would like to thank you both for caring for my darling daughters. I do hope that hasn't been a nightmare for you, Misses Fairhurst.'

'Not at all,' Annie gently stated.

'We've loved having them here,' Sadie warmly told her. 'And do call us by our first names, dear lady. And may I call you Evelyn?'

'Of course, although generally I prefer Evie,' she said with a smile. 'You must have been shocked though when Megan recently turned up again.'

Annie gave a shake of her head. 'We were a little surprised but the dear girl felt very much in need of returning to the school she's familiar with and the sports she enjoys with her friends. The changes in her life have caused her some confusion, I believe. But we certainly have no objection to her staying here with us as we're most fond of her.'

Sadie gave Evie a gentle smile. 'We are indeed, and appreciate that Megan wishes to stay here during term-time. We do fully understand that you'll miss her. She has stated that she'll miss you and her siblings too so will be happy to return home for each school holiday and half term. How would you feel about that?'

This was a compromise that Evie found slightly painful but realized she must accept. Aware how her girls had developed a strong sense of self-determination over the years of their evacuation, this was a practical decision made by Megan. And to her surprise she did feel a warm admiration for these delightful ladies who were clearly content for Megan to remain under their care, at least for a part of each year. The prospect of having Megan return home to Manchester for weeks at a time filled her with delight and relief. Much better than nothing. 'That would be perfectly acceptable. Spending holidays with my younger daughter is something I would greatly look forward to.'

'Of course you would, dear lady. She could, of course, also visit you for the odd weekend, if she wished,' Annie added.

'That would be good too,' Evie agreed, making it clear that she would contribute a reasonable sum for Megan's accommodation and care. The two ladies attempted to convince her that wasn't at all necessary but ultimately felt obliged to accept this offer, Evie being her mother. An agreement between them duly accomplished, Evie happily spent the rest of the day being shown around Blackpool by her young daughter.

★　★　★

Having enjoyed a wonderful week's holiday Joanne said goodbye to the lovely landladies and

Bernie, as well as her sister, saying how she looked forward to seeing Megan again soon when she came home for the summer holidays. She then caught the train with her mother and for a while they sat in silence, each obsessed with their personal thoughts and concerns.

'I'm so glad you came today. I did feel it was vital that you accepted Megan's decision and not depress yourself with regret. She is growing more fond of you and looking forward to spending the summer with you, Mam. But staying here during term-time works well for her, having lived here so long.'

'Aye, 'course it does. What about you, lovey, do you miss Blackpool too, not to mention that lovely young man, Bernie, you spent time with?'

Surprised to find herself blushing, Joanne gave a wry smile. 'He's a pleasant young man and we always had a sort of friendship but he only offered to marry me because I'd made a stupid mistake.' She at last went on to briefly explain what she'd feared had happened to her, seeing a look of shock reverberate in her mother's face.

Then a flash of sympathy appeared in her mother's eyes. 'Who was he, this fella?'

'A GI I got to know. He charmed, kissed and caressed me for weeks, then did whatever he fancied before vanishing out of my life. I stupidly believed that he loved me, which he clearly didn't, not having heard from him since. You must swear to me that you won't ever mention this to a soul, Mam, certainly not Dad.' She went on to briefly explain how the doctor had examined her and insisted she was still a virgin.

266

'I can but hope he was right and at least I was not pregnant.'

'Thank God for that.'

'That's when I cancelled Bernie's offer of marriage to protect me. I was ashamed of being so naive, innocent and stupid. If only I hadn't been,' she said, managing a tremulous smile. 'I feel decimated and unable to trust any man ever again. A few of my work colleagues have shown a little interest in me, but I feel none for them. I doubt I'll find anyone to love ever again.' Tears filled her eyes, misery yawning like a black pit inside her.

Her mother had fallen silent, as if struggling to find appropriate words, then, grasping her daughter's hand, she gave it a sympathetic squeeze. 'You can understand why I never wanted to lose you. Sending my children away as evacuees seemed the right way to keep you safe during that blasted war. But aware that I would no longer be around to protect my girls and son as you grew up was not at all easy to live with. I wish I had been, love.'

'I wish you had too, Mam, but such was the reality of war. Now I have no faith in myself, considering I was a piece of shabby rubbish.'

'No you weren't, love. *You* did nothing wrong. That GI was the culprit, not you. Many men of all nationalities were polite and well behaved throughout the war. Others created havoc, obsessed with satisfaction for themselves, possibly because they feared death. Block this issue out of your head and concentrate on building yourself a good life, then this low opinion of

267

yourself will pass, given time.'

'Thanks, Mam, what a treasure you are. I will follow your advice as well as learn more about knitting and sewing,' she assured her, causing them both to laugh, happily aware they were growing ever closer.

It was as they turned to walk down the maze of small yards and lanes leading off Wood Street towards their house, that they saw Danny come tearing towards them. When he reached them he stopped running and stood panting for breath, his eyes stretched wide in devastation as he said that when he'd arrived home he'd found his father dangling from the ceiling. 'He's hanged himself, Mam.'

24

Joanne found her father's funeral most distressing, not at all what she'd expected to happen. She remembered the happy years she'd spent with him when she was young. He'd taught her how to ride the bicycle he bought her, and would often sit with her on his lap singing her songs or telling stories that made her laugh. She'd missed him so much and had been delighted to find him safely home again at the end of the war.

Rain sheeted down from grey clouds, a typical April shower, as they stood huddled beneath their umbrellas in the cemetery. Joanne put her arm around her mother and could feel Evie shaking as she quietly wept. Megan, having been brought by Bernie to Manchester on the train, was tucked close beside her mother too, holding her other arm. Joanne felt a great appreciation and sense of comfort for Bernie's kind support, such a caring lad. His closeness felt so appealing. Danny was standing beside them looking ashen pale, not surprising considering he was the one who found his father hanging from the ceiling light in the living-kitchen, the chair he'd stood on having been kicked away. Cathie and Brenda were also attending the funeral, as well as Davie and a few more of Donald's old friends plus members of the RAF, all too aware of what he'd suffered as a pilot in the war and as a PoW.

Now he was gone for ever. Why on earth

269

would he commit suicide when he'd been making a good recovery?

Barely having listened to the prayers the vicar was reading, she now heard him saying: 'We now commit his body to the ground; earth to earth, ashes to ashes, dust to dust: in the sure and certain hope of the resurrection to eternal life.' Tears flooded her eyes as she watched her father's coffin deposited into the cold dark earth. How would they face life without him?

Cathie, Brenda, various stalwart members of the RAF and a few neighbours joined them for the wake, gathering together in the living-kitchen where they were provided with the tea and sandwiches Joanne had prepared, surprisingly with Bernie's assistance. Curtains were drawn and photos of Donald displayed on the dresser. Memories of him were shared and much consolation and sympathy offered to his family. Once everyone had politely departed, the three of them, and Bernie, sat with her mother at the table, a degree of silence permeating through them.

'Admittedly Donald was still a bit authoritative as a result of that trauma he suffered,' Evie remarked woefully. 'Sometimes treating his son and daughters as if they were young kids, even though they'd grown much older and are far more independent, having become accustomed to coping with their own problems and decisions in life.'

Joanne smiled. 'We could sympathize with that fatherly feeling in him. I remember Danny describing a conversation he'd had with him

270

about the effect of the war and how he'd said very little.'

Looking devastated by his loss, her brother gave a nod. 'He did speak of the day his crew had died when their plane had been shot down, then said; 'I struggled to get my legs out of my seat, pulled up the pack of my parachute while doing my utmost to stop the aircraft from falling out of the sky. By the time we jumped we were too close to the earth to genuinely survive.' It was then that he'd been caught by the enemy but made no mention of that. He instantly changed the subject and bossed me into doing more work. At other times he's been quite attentive and sympathetic of our problems, if still extremely silent about the anguish he'd experienced as a PoW.'

Joanne could understand the damaging effect this must have had upon Donald. 'Oh, but why did he choose to depart?'

'God knows,' Danny groaned. 'I doubt I'll ever get over what I saw he'd done that day. It was so terrifying I felt I'd failed him in some way, that I should have been around to protect him.'

Wiping the tears from her eyes, Evie put her arms around her son. 'You were most caring of him. I know your dad hasn't been easy to live with recently, having mental issues, but he would not have revealed the anguish he'd suffered if he hadn't felt a closeness with you, love. Possibly he killed himself because he couldn't get over the fact he'd lost his mates, in addition to having been captured and tortured, and maybe again fell into a severe depression, as he tended to do at times. Who knows what he endured as a prisoner of war. It's tragic and most odd that he lost all hope for himself in life when we genuinely believed he was improving. And he did love me so much, as well as his children.'

'He did indeed, and had sorely missed us. How tragic that he'd finally lost the courage to remain alive, despite his ill health being slowly on the mend. Poor man!' Joanne shuddered, the pain in her chest filling her entire body with despair.

Getting to his feet, Bernie gave a little cough and politely informed them that he was now off to find himself a room for the night.

'No need for that,' Joanne quickly told him. 'We do appreciate you accompanying Megan here, which made sure she had a safe journey. The hotel where I work has kindly offered a room for you at a low rate, so I've booked it for you.'

'Oh, thanks, that's good to know.' He quietly sat down again, giving her a smile.

Turning to her mother, Joanne gently patted her hand. 'I'll stay with you tonight, Mam, or longer if you wish.'

'No need, love. I have Megan and Danny here and I know you'll be working first thing in the morning although — '

She was interrupted by Megan. 'I can't stay here tomorrow, Mam. I have to get back to school. But I'll see you in July, when the term is over.'

'I've got the necessary tickets so I'll be taking her back,' Bernie politely informed her.

272

A bleakness came into Evie's face as she attempted to politely smile. 'Oh, I hadn't thought about that. I dare say you're right, Megan, and will look forward to seeing you again soon, darling. And you too, Joanne. I always enjoy seeing you when you visit or come to stay, particularly when you help with my stall on your Saturday off. Although I think I'll give it a miss this week, as well as the job I do for Mullins. I'm not feeling capable of working right now.' Tears again filled her eyes, rolling untouched down her cheeks.

Joanne gave her mother a warm hug as she gently wiped them away. 'A good idea. I can fully understand your need for a break and time to relax. Do allow yourself time to deal with your grief. Then you'll need to press on with life and perhaps plan a new future.'

'If that man you work for is anything like his son I reckon you should resign and work for yourself,' Megan stated firmly, sticking up her pert chin as she tightened her mouth.

'She is making a valid point,' Joanne agreed softly, clearly realizing her sister had no wish to say too much. 'Have you decided whether you'll resign?'

'I was definitely in the process of making such a decision. Right now I'm too locked in grief, but will hopefully come to a conclusion once I get my brain working again and feel ready to return to work, if only for myself. Oh, but why did Donald leave me?' And covering her face with her hands, she began to sob again.

The following day, Joanne joined her sister and Bernie, walking with them to Victoria

Station. 'Here's some money, lovey, so go and buy yourself a book to read on the journey and some sweeties.' As her sister scuttled off to WHSmith she put out her hand to give Bernie's a shake. 'Goodbye and thanks for your help. She's nearly thirteen now but still in need of care, and does trust you.'

'That's good to hear, although she does tell me off if I don't obey her instructions.'

Joanne laughed. 'I know that feeling. She's a very determined and self-opinionated girl. Do let me know when the school closes and she'll be free to return home and spend some valuable time with our mam. I'll come to collect her if you like, as you will probably be busily occupied with your own work, aware that in the summer holidays Blackpool is packed with tourists.'

'Not sure whether the school closes the first or second week in July. I'll make sure she writes to give you that information once she investigates that. I may well bring her if I feel the urge to visit Manchester or wish to see you again. If you're not against that. I assume we can at least be friends?'

Taking a short pause, Joanne lowered her eyes and gave a little nod. 'Of course.' Strangely, a part of her wished they could be more than that.

Moments later, the train came puffing in, sending a shaft of smoke everywhere. Megan gave her a hug and a kiss, promising to write to her every week and looked forward to seeing her soon. Bernie helped her sister safely on-board then Joanne stepped back to wave as she watched the train chug out. A part of her wished she too could have gone with Megan and Bernie, and yet how could she bear to leave her mother, now that she was largely alone?

* * *

In the days following, deeply grieving for the loss of her beloved husband, Evie found herself sitting doing nothing, rarely eating or sleeping, her mind locked up in the happy years they'd spent together. They used to regularly go to dance halls, their favourites being the Ritz and the Palais de Danse on Rochdale Road. They'd also loved walking in Platt Fields and Philips Park. And once they were married they'd frequently made love and revelled in caring for their children. The effect of losing Donald seemed to have destroyed her ability to contemplate how to live, let alone reorganize her future. Facing life without him felt utterly devastating.

Oh, and how she missed her daughters too. Joanne was now local and called in to see her most days, being aware of the grief she was suffering. Megan was far away back in Blackpool where she was at least happy and would be home again soon. When Joanne had been sexually fondled by that GI, she'd believed that was because he'd been in love with her, as she'd loved him. Maybe he had been quite fond of her and thankfully didn't actually seduce her. How she prayed she never would be.

Harold Mullins's threat was entirely terrifying. He'd never been faithful to his wife; always keen to explore other women. Evie certainly had no intention of allowing that ever to happen to her. Thank God Donald had appeared and innocently succeeded in helping her to escape him the day he'd threatened to seduce her, if only by buying her a shandy in the pub. If he hadn't, she'd have found some way to escape that bastard. Evie was still filled with a sickening fear over what Mullins had threatened to do, dreading he might attempt it again. She could but hope he would now have the respect to leave her in peace, having lost her husband.

Valiantly attempting to block the pain out of her head and free herself from him, she resorted to fully occupying herself with lacemaking. Some of it was scalloped, embroidered, floral and quite delicate bridal lace veils. Thanks to her sales on Campfield Market her income was gradually improving, although not yet sufficient to live on. Evie firmly decided that once it reached a sensible level, she would gladly resign from this illegal betting job she was involved in.

She still felt desperately in need of the money she earned from this work she did for that dreadful man, not least because she still had children to pay for one way or another. Joanne was becoming responsible for herself but Danny earned very little, being still young, and she of course had volunteered to pay those landladies for their care of Megan. Would she be entitled to some of her husband's pension? Evie wasn't even certain about that. Having still failed to find a new job, flat or house, she had no choice but to continue working for Mullins, at least for a little while longer.

One evening when she again delivered the usual small sums of repaid debts she'd collected from his betting clients, he instructed her to step into his house. This was not something she had any wish to do so quietly refused. 'Sorry, but I have to go and cook supper for my son. I've handed you the money and list of people who paid.'

'I wish to discuss something of importance with you,' he said. Evie felt deeply disturbed when he took hold of her arm and led her inside. Directing her to sit in a chair by the fire, he handed her a glass of port then poured himself a glass of whisky. 'My sympathy for the loss of your husband,' he said. He raised his glass in respect then took a long sip of his whisky. 'You must be feeling a bit lonely. Whenever tha feel in need of a little company you're free to come and join me at the Dog and Duck any evening, or for a meal here if you want. May I get you summat now?'

'No thank you,' she firmly remarked. Not taking a sip of the port she set it down on the small table beside her. 'As I said, I must go to cook supper for my son. What is it that you wished to say to me?'

'That I find you most eye-catching and attractive, dear lady. And no doubt you're feeling a bit lonely.' With a roguish glimmer of desire in his eyes he reached over, pulled her into his arms and strongly kissed her, pushing his tongue into her mouth. Evie felt her throat choke with horror, the acrid taste of whisky creating a sense of bile within her. As she struggled to free herself she felt his hand thump her face then clamp hold of her breasts.

'Get off me!' she screamed.

When he at last lifted his head up to take a breath, she attempted to fiercely shove him away and slap his face. Ignoring her effort to protect herself, he kept on kissing and fondling her. Evie desperately fought him, realizing that however hard she tried it was proving to be extremely difficult. He possessed an insatiable sexual appetite, which put her in serious danger. There was no one around to hear her shout, or come running to save her. His hand was now roaming up her bare thigh. Dear God, how could she defend herself? Reaching out her arm, she found a large lump of coal in the bucket by the fire. She grabbed it and slammed him hard on his head. Giving a yell, he fell backwards onto the rug.

After jumping to her feet, Evie ran like hell out of the house.

When she arrived home no one was around to see how distressed and upset she was, her house being empty of her entire family. Even Danny hadn't come home from work yet, or else her sixteen-year-old son was off playing footie or some other sport with his mates. Looking in the mirror, she saw that her face bore a bruise on the cheek where he'd thumped her. Tears flooded in her brown eyes as she gazed at Donald's empty chair where he would usually be contentedly reading the evening paper and smoking his favourite cigarettes. He did used to sometimes complain if she was late home and felt in need of food. Were her darling husband still around he would surely be showing great care for her. How would she cope with the problems of life without him? A dreadful prospect.

Going upstairs to the sink in the small closet she scrubbed herself clean all over: her thighs, breasts, face and all parts of her as well as her hair. Harold had grabbed a lock of it, his dark eyes gleaming with desire as he'd pulled her to him to push open her mouth with his fat tongue. The decision to resign and escape his employment was now paramount in her head. Nothing on earth would ever persuade her to work for that bastard ever again.

★ ★ ★

When Joanne called in an hour later, she was shocked to see the sorry state her mother was in, her face pale and bruised as she sat weeping in a chair by the fire. 'What on earth has happened? Have you had an accident, Mam?'

'Not sure I should tell you.'

'Yes, you must.' After pouring her a glass of water to drink, Joanne wiped her mother's eyes and sat beside her to give her a cuddle. 'Go on, I'm listening.'

Evie briefly told her what she'd gone through today and how she'd had to fight and bash him before managing to escape. Then she went on to mention how Mullins had demanded sex in return for what he'd done to save Danny.

'Oh, my God! Thank goodness you managed to protect yourself and escape. What a dreadful father and son the Mullinses are. It's entirely

279

wrong that they have this flaw within them to abuse and assault women and girls.' It was then that Joanne finally told her mother what Megan too had suffered years ago and more recently down by the canal when Danny had thankfully saved her. 'She'd blocked it out of her head for years but we all agree who it was who created this havoc for her, that stupid lad who again attempted to fondle her. What a nightmare they are.'

Evie looked deeply shocked and alarmed. 'Thank you for telling me this whole sorry tale she suffered. I did suspect something had happened to upset Megan.'

'It was indeed a dreadful disaster for my young sister. I protected her by moving her away, thankfully to Blackpool where these lovely ladies accepted us. Having been threatened a second time that's partly the real reason she's moved back now, in order to remain safe. Danny spoke to that dreadful lad, ordering him never to touch his sister ever again. There's nothing more we can do about it. We must simply live with the reality of what happened, not having any genuine proof. Please don't mention to Megan and Danny what I've told you; I've no wish to upset them. I confess the three of us made a pact not to tell you, Mam. We were anxious not to risk you losing your job and home by complaining to Harold Mullins about what his son did to her, which could put you in an even greater mess. But hearing what he did to you, I decided you deserved to be told. I'm hoping you will now resign, Mam. Do tell me what you intend to do.'

Evie took a furious deep breath. 'That lad is a nasty piece of work. I'm relieved to think Megan is safely settled back in Blackpool. She will be home soon for the summer when we must keep a careful watch over her.'

'We must indeed.'

'And yes, I do intend to stop working for that bastard, then will make a strong effort to build up my own business.'

25

Evie rewrote a letter of resignation to Harold Mullins a dozen times before reducing it to a simple statement, taking out all the rants and complaints she'd felt the need to state. Best to mention nothing of these resentments she felt towards her employer and his son, and simply ensure she was merely stating how she now wished to work for herself. Once it was done she asked Danny if he'd push it through Harold's letterbox for her.

'I've at last come to the decision to leave this job and work for myself,' she said, making no mention of the true reason. Were her son to be aware of the attack Mullins had made upon her that could insight him to seek justice, which would result in danger for him too.

''Course, Mam, no problem,' he agreed, and took it off with him the very next morning to deliver it on his way to the tug where he worked on the canal.

Receiving no response to her resignation or any apology for what he did to her, she was filled with a sickening fear that Harold Mullins might attempt to assault her again, praying that would never happen. Whenever Evie went out to do a little shopping, she kept a close eye on whether he was following her. It was one morning as she was trotting along Wood Street that she was horrified to see him approach and noticed elements of a bruise on his forehead, most of it no doubt being under his hair which was where she'd hit him with that thick piece of coal.

'Ah, there you are. You've not delivered any of those paid debts people owe me for some days. Why is that?'

'You know damn well, Harold, that I've resigned. My son delivered it to your door the other day. How can you pretend not to understand the reason I did that?'

'I assume your reason was very stupid. You're a most difficult and obstinate woman if still quite attractive.' He gently rubbed his hand over his sore head then gave a smirk of laughter. 'You may have asked your son to deliver that resignation but I'm not convinced he did. Can't recall spotting it at all. Young Danny would be aware that you couldn't survive without the income you earn from me and probably feared losing the home he lives in. However, now that you've lost your husband and I daresay most of his pension, I'd be happy to accommodate you. Would you care to move in and live with me? That would be gradely, as we make a good team in many ways.'

'Never! Nor have I any wish to work for you ever again in my entire life. As I explained when I resigned. Having lost my darling husband and children, who are mainly accommodated elsewhere, I no longer feel any need for a large income so wish to be free to work for myself.'

'I reckon you will come back to work for me, once you've got over your loss. Otherwise you'd need to keep your entire family out of my way,' he sourly snapped and marched away.

What did he mean by that? Evie wondered, feeling a nugget of fear escalate within her. Taking a sigh, she strived to convince herself that she'd safely made her point and didn't for a moment believe his tale that Danny hadn't delivered her resignation. Most definitely a lie. Apart from caring for her son, her two daughters were living in places Mullins wasn't aware of. But would *she* be safely free of him? God help her if she wasn't.

When she told Danny she'd again been pestered by Mullins to remain in that debt-collecting job, he assured her that he had indeed delivered her resignation. 'Don't worry, Mam, you've made the right decision.'

She had indeed, and how she loved making lace and knitting by hand. In the weeks following Donald's death, Evie concentrated on working hard for herself. Keeping her mind occupied with this helped her to cope with her bleak sense of loss. It came to her that no matter how hard she worked, often till quite late each night no longer being tied up in caring for her darling husband, it took some time for her to create a scarf or a tray cloth to sell. That was because she'd frequently lapse into tears or fall into silent grief. She was determined not to worry if her income was low, although it was slowly improving now that she was regularly running a market stall on Campfield Market. Concentrating on resolving how she could earn more money, she began to spend time thinking what could be done to produce more goods to sell. Recalling the conversation she'd had with

Joanne, it was then that an idea came to her.

Determined to remain free from the demands Mullins had made upon her by earning herself a decent income, she called to see Mr Eccles, the one-time owner of the mill. Now that it had closed she quickly explained her future plan and asked if he'd any of those looms left that she could use for creating lace, were she able to find the appropriate money to purchase them. 'I would need to rent somewhere to work on them, were you to have one or two available,' she explained politely.

This old man sounded fascinated and greatly admiring of her plan, apologizing for dismissing her and many other women who'd been good workers. 'The mill having been partly bombed during the war and the textile industry in something of a mess, it was no longer in profit. I too was in a sorry state over the loss of family members and lost interest in carrying on working, no longer being young. I did what I could for a while, many men having been in need of employment, but eventually decided it was time for me to retire. I paid them a modest sum each when I dismissed them. I still haven't got around to selling the mill, very much doubt I'll ever succeed in that, the country also in a desperate state. However, you'd be welcome to rent one of my outdoor buildings if you like, Mrs Talbert,' he offered, much to her delight.

'What a kind man you are,' she said. 'That would be wonderful.'

He named a reasonable cost for the machines and rental of an outbuilding, which Evie gratefully accepted. She then went to call and see her bank manager to discuss the plan and details she'd agreed with the previous mill owner, requesting a modest loan to cover these costs. He listened most carefully and, to her great relief, made a good offer. It would seem she could now make a strong move forward.

★ ★ ★

Meeting up with her two friends, Enid Wilson and Lizzie Parkin, who'd also lost their jobs at the end of the war, as well as her niece, Evie explained the details of her small business plan, expressing a request to know if they'd like to work for her. They instantly agreed, as they too were well experienced at textile work.

'By heck, I'd love to work for you, still being unemployed,' Enid stated.

'Me too,' Lizzie Parkin agreed, 'being currently employed in a part-time job and earning very little money.'

Evie warmly thanked them all, beginning to feel a strong optimism for her future. How delighted she was to reach a happy agreement with these three good women workers.

'I'd be happy to knit or create lace material by hand at home, being mainly tied up with caring for Heather,' Cathie said. 'Now happily married, I reckon I'm pregnant, so could have a baby of my own soon.'

'Oh, congratulations. That's a thrill to hear,' Evie said, giving her a hug, as did Enid and Lizzie.

'I can't say I'm an expert at this sort of assignment but I've always enjoyed knitting and sewing. As you know, my mother Rona worked in a cotton mill all her life, so I learned a great deal from her. I used to work in the tyre factory down by the docks, then having lost that job after the war worked instead in a Christmas card factory with Brenda. My friend is now happily occupied in a biscuit company but this would be much more attractive for me. I really fancy it.'

'It'll take a little time for me to arrange it but meanwhile I'll provide you with the necessary material so that you can all start by hand-knitting socks or a fine lace shawl. Then once I have the machines delivered and set up, Enid and Lizzie can make a start working on them with me and you can decide what you wish to create.'

'That's great to know,' Lizzie said with a grin.

Promising to keep them informed, Evie hurried home. Settling at the kitchen table she wrote a list of jobs that needed to be done: renting and cleaning whichever of those outbuildings appeared appropriate; checking two or three of the necessary looms before having them moved over. She must then buy yarn and wool of various colours, including plenty of white for the lace; and a selection of buttons. She would also copy out the patterns she'd designed and bought. How wonderful to be free of that dreadful job and now to be facing a business of her own that would be entirely fascinating.

★   ★   ★

It was as Danny walked along Castle Quay towards the canal the next day that he found himself struck and knocked over. Assuming it was Willie again starting a fight he whipped round to jump to his feet ready to hit him back, only to find himself astonished to discover that it was actually that lad's father, Harold Mullins. He tactfully dropped his fist but gave a glower of fury. 'Why the hell did you do that?'

'Tell your mother that she must keep on working for me otherwise you'll lose your job too,' he snarled.

'What the hangment are ye talking about? Why would she keep working for yer when she's clearly fed up wi' a job involved in illegal betting? Being an independent and quite talented lady, Mam has decided to work for herself. I delivered her letter of resignation to you so you've no right to expect her to return, or threaten to ruin my job either.'

Stepping forward, Mullins almost spat in Danny's face, very much stinking of whisky. 'Your mother owes me thanks for how I saved you from jail. So if she doesn't carry on collecting the debts she's recently failed to get, let alone show her appreciation for my assistance, I'll make the point to your employer what a thief you are and mek damn sure you lose your job too.'

Danny felt a blast of fear rattle in his chest, stunned by this remark. Watching Mullins walk away with a smirk in his twisted mouth and a gleam of triumph in his bloodshot eyes, Danny came to an instant decision. Not for the world would he attempt to persuade his mother to continue working for this bastard. Mebbe he should leave the area were he to carry out this threat. Not a pleasant thought but possibly the only sensible thing to do. Where to go and what to do was very much the question. Not easy to decide. He could but hope the pressure to leave wouldn't occur, he thought as he went to bed.

It was around dawn that he heard a hammering on the door. Danny went to answer it then gave a shout, 'Mam, we're being ordered to leave this house.'

Running downstairs in her dressing gown, Evie looked appalled to find two men tossing her precious belongings out into the street. It was indeed a shock and desperately infuriating. Faced with being moved out was something of a disaster. Where on earth could they live now?

★ ★ ★

Leaving Danny in charge of their belongings piled in a heap on the pavement with the troubling threat of rain very much prevalent, Evie hurried to the town hall in Albert Square, determined to reveal her problem and hope they could find a new home for her. She had contacted the local authority on several occasions and they'd promised to let her know as soon as they found one. As she hurried along Deansgate, she kept glancing behind her, feeling the strange sensation she could hear someone following her. Could it be Harold Mullins? She dreaded that prospect.

On reaching the town hall, she sat in a queue

for an hour or more but to her relief was finally called to receive attention. Carefully giving details of how she'd been banished from her home, now working for herself instead of the person who owned it, she tactfully made no mention of his attempt to assault her. Evie had no wish to risk worse problems if Mullins found her making such a charge. All she needed to do was carefully avoid him in future.

The conversation began with questions about the size of her family and how many rooms she'd require. Evie explained that her husband had recently died, her son was now home and although her daughters were living elsewhere as a consequence of being evacuees during the war, they too did visit her on occasions. 'I'm not in an easy situation but do care deeply for my family and feel the need to accommodate them.'

'So sorry to hear these troubles you have been through, Mrs Talbert. We do have something to offer,' the kind lady involved in dealing with this difficult social problem warmly assured her. She went on to explain how Manchester was still struggling to find enough money to build new homes but had apparently spent a fortune on providing hundreds of prefabs. 'These were not cheap to build but there is one available for you to rent, as you certainly have no need to buy one. Admittedly they have no foundations and are rather small but well equipped with fitted cupboards, a bathroom, wash boiler, electricity, gas cooker and generally a small garden.'

'Oh, that would be wonderful, thank you so much. Where is it, exactly?'

The lady carefully showed her a map of them in Heaton Park.

Depression struck her, it being not at all where she wished to live. 'Oh, but that's a few miles away from Castlefield where my son works and me too. Have you anything nearer?'

Searching again through her papers, she said, 'Maybe a room in a lodging house on Byrom Street. You must appreciate that houses are still in very short supply. Ah, there's a two-bedroom flat over a shop on Ivy Street. Would that do for you?'

'Oh, that would be fine for now,' she said, and watched in relief as the lady wrote down details of the address.

It was on her way out that she saw Mullins standing in the square close to the memorial statue of Prince Albert, obviously having followed her as she suspected. What a nightmare he was! Stepping back into the town hall in the hope he hadn't seen her, she asked if there was another exit and was thankfully shown one.

Evie quickly reached the butcher's shop on Ivy Street and politely spoke to the owner, asking if the flat above was still available. He agreed that it was and, taking her back out on to the street, unlocked the side door and led her up the stairs.

It was small and neat with only a gas fire and basic furniture in the living room, had a tiny kitchen, a bathroom, which was surely a good thing, plus two bedrooms. One possessed twin beds and the other a single being much smaller, which would suit Danny perfectly well. When Megan came to stay for her school holiday, she could occupy the twin bed next to her. If both girls came at once she'd have to ask Danny if he'd sleep on the sofa. This flat wasn't perfect but they were badly in need of a place to live so she mustn't make too much fuss about it. Learning of the modest rent he required, Evie gladly accepted that and they shook hands. She then readily handed over a week's rent in advance.

'We do wish to move in right away, having lost where we're living now. Is that all right?'

''Course it is, Mrs Talbert. You're most welcome.'

It took her no time at all to find Davie who readily agreed to help her move, as he did before. He was utterly shocked to find all their belongings had been tossed into the street. After picking them up, he brought everything in his Ford van and carried them up the stairs to the flat, expressing his sympathy for her situation and wishing her good luck in this accommodation she'd managed to find. Nor did Davie charge her a penny. Instead, he went and bought her and Danny some fish and chips, as well as himself, and they sat happily eating together in the kitchen.

'Sorry you were forced to move just because you'd decided to resign from that job with Mullins and work for yourself, having lost your hubby. I miss Donald too; what a good friend he was. I just can't understand why he chose to commit suicide when he was gradually getting so much better.'

'He was trying so hard to deal with those

mental issues, so I don't understand that either,' Evie said, feeling a slur of anguish yet again. 'Now I have to build a new life for myself.'

'Good for you. Mullins is not someone I'd ever miss either, even if he fell off a perch like a stupid parrot.'

Evie gave a chuckle, carefully saying nothing about the real reason she'd decided to move. Wisely, neither did Danny mention his, merely exchanging a silent blink with her. She then thanked Davie for his help, insisting on giving him enough to buy himself a pint of beer and a packet of fags.

'Cheerio, dear lady, and if you need any more assistance wi' summat just let me know.' And off he went, whistling happily.

Evie spent the rest of the day tidying, cleaning, unpacking and sorting clothes, crockery, bed-linen and other goods she'd steadfastly insisted upon putting safely in bags when those men had started tossing their belongings out into the street. A part of her felt quite pleased she'd found this flat. It was fairly small and basic but nothing like as bad as that horrible messy house they'd rented from Mullins. And the owner was much more kind and friendly. Evie felt very much in a position to build herself a new life. Surely that was a good thing.

26

Joanne was surprised and rather thrilled when Bernie called in at the hotel one morning to see her. Agreeing to meet up with him later for a coffee in a small café on St Ann's Square she was relieved to hear that Megan was doing well at the high school and greatly looking forward to spending the summer with her and their mother.

'Your sister was concerned about how you're coping on your own here, so I obeyed what she asked of me and came to see how you were getting along.'

Joanne gave a chuckle. 'She can be quite bossy, in a nice sort of way as we are very close. Thank goodness she's well. Seeing you here put me in a panic that Megan might have some problem or other because she's lost her dad.'

'She doesn't appear to be greatly grieving for the loss of her father, saying she was no longer very familiar with him. I daresay you are, however.'

Joanne gave a nod. 'I am indeed. Losing Dad was dreadful. Why he committed suicide is beyond belief. I thought he was becoming so much braver and more normal in his attitude to life. At least he will now be with his crew. I also call most days to see how Mam is, as she's obviously swamped in grief. She has left that job she's been working in for years and is now bravely attempting to engage herself with knitting and sewing in order to keep her mind calm and build a new future for herself. I can but hope that works for her. So how are you doing?' she asked, feeling an odd sort of concern for him too.

A grin appeared in his square, friendly face. 'Cooking is so far my best accomplishment but as you know my aunts have no longer any urge to retire. I've learned a great deal more in recent years, adding a couple of bathrooms as well as that extra bedroom in the loft at Jubilee House. I've therefore decided to work for myself and maybe become a plumber and odd job worker. What do you think of that?'

'Eminently amazing,' she declared. 'I'm sure you'll do well with that in Blackpool, supporting lots of other landladies.'

'Actually, I've found myself a flat to rent here in Manchester, a city I rather like the look of. It's not exactly what I had in mind but worth a try in the circumstances. Nor will I instantly make a load of dosh but fortunately my parents did leave me some money to support me, which will help. I trust you're not against my moving here.'

'Oh, of course not.' Joanne felt startled to hear this; a mix of pleasure and nervous unease cascading through her at the prospect of him living close by. But why would she not welcome his presence? They'd been friends in a way for years in spite of her amused view of him when he was young, always thinking Bernie Flynn to be rather humdrum and boring. She'd certainly never looked upon him as a possible love of her life. And because of what she'd been through, she'd reached a point of feeling the need to keep well away from him and all other men; aware he was clearly avoiding her too, as his aunts had pointed out. Were their friendship to grow closer, she doubted that would be a good thing. Not a relationship she'd ever wished to experience, or did she?

As if reading her mind, he said, 'I believe it's quite acceptable to continue our friendship but I assure you that's all it will ever be. Nothing more.'

Obviously it had been foolish of her to imagine something special might develop between them. He was making it abundantly clear that never would occur. And he did have a new girlfriend, so why had he chosen to come here? As he said, claiming he loved this city. Joanne firmly reminded herself that if she regretted his lack of interest in her it was probably only because she was wrapped up in grief, having lost her father as well as missing her sister. She was also still feeling a little lonely, having reached a stage where she sorely felt in need for more love in her life. Not something she should ever expect to achieve with Bernie Flynn. What a mix-up she was in. Flushed with an odd sense of disappointment but giving him a dazzling smile, she said, 'That's good to hear, although you need to appreciate there is no beach for us to walk on or collect shells, or a sea around here for the fishing and swimming we used to do, only canals.'

He gave a chuckle. 'That's fine, we could perhaps take a boat ride on occasions instead.'

'I suppose we could. I do take trips on the Manchester Ship Canal sometimes with Danny,

Megan and Mam, which can be great fun.'

'That sounds good. And I certainly won't ever pester you for a date. I fully intend to concentrate on building my business, although we could meet up like this for the odd coffee or a walk by the canal now and then, couldn't we?'

'Why not?'

Joanne met his blank gaze, feeling an odd flicker of disillusionment that there was no sign of the exquisite admiration he used to show in his grey eyes. Wasn't she fully aware that Bernie never had truly loved her? He'd merely offered that proposal because he was a most caring lad, bearing in mind the situation she'd believed herself to be in. Now a hardworking twenty-one-year-old he was evidently creating a new life for himself, attracted by this busy city but making it very apparent he had no wish to be too close with her. He was a friend and that was all he ever would be. Trying not to look at his long, fit legs or recall how he'd charmingly danced with her so much better than that dreadful Willie Mullins, Joanne warned herself to accept reality. Oh, but how she regretted seeing him dance cheek to cheek with that pretty girl. She'd almost felt jealous.

★ ★ ★

Happily settled in the flat, Evie fully occupied herself with lace knitting. She still often found herself weeping at night in bed, making it difficult for her to sleep. When she awoke each morning the emptiness beside her would bring back the memory of her loss and she'd weep again. Steadfastly working was surely the only way to block out the agony she felt and remain healthy and sane. Concentrating on this task, she found that wool finely spun by hand was ideal for knitting lace garments as she worked on creating an evening stole, which was already looking beautiful. This morning, calling to see Cathie, Evie delivered the necessary fine white wool, design plans and equipment she needed to also work by hand. Her niece was delighted to see her and happily made Evie a cup of coffee while being carefully instructed on how to set about this job she'd gladly agreed to do.

'I'm suggesting you start by making a scarf. It needs to be fine and delicate, beautiful and imaginative. If this pattern doesn't work for you, do let me know and I'll come to help.'

'I'm sure it'll be fine. I'm so looking forward to doing this,' Cathie said, smiling as her aunt gave Heather a loving cuddle.

'How are you feeling, love?'

'Fine,' she said with a smile. 'Four months pregnant now so feeling much better. What about you? Considering the anguish you've had to go through losing Uncle Donald and with your darling daughters no longer around much, I don't know how you're managing to cope all on your own.'

'By keeping busy and looking forward to a time my girls will be happy to visit me or return home, as Megan will do when her summer holiday comes. Danny, of course, is still around, thank goodness.' She carefully shut out the fear that her son too might move on, recently having reminded her how he'd enjoyed living in the country rather than here in this badly damaged city. What a nightmare that evacuation had proved to be, not at all what she'd hoped for. But then that dratted war had gone on far longer than they'd expected and her young children were now rapidly growing up.

Evie next went to busily arrange moving the looms she'd bought into the rented outbuilding granted to her. Davie and his mate helped with that too. These machines were quite old but perfectly clean. Much to her interest Evie had discovered that the post-war knitting industry was recruiting thousands of men and women, hoping to make it as successful as it was before the war. Quite a good prospect, considering the shortage of labour. She too was determined to build herself a good business of a similar nature. People were tired of the mess and rationing created by the war, feeling eager to buy them-selves pretty clothes, scarves and for some a lovely wedding veil. She checked these looms were working properly and made some improve-ments on them if they weren't. Once they were well set up, she brought in Enid and Lizzie, the friends who were eager to work for her.

'I've brought this wool, being appropriately light and silky, yarn, cotton and copies of various patterns I've either bought or designed for you to consider. You could do Fair Isle style knitting if you prefer, which is very popular. You're free to make whatever suits you. Gloves, socks, scarves, collars, vests, jumpers or lace garments, your choice.'

'That's most generous of you, Evie,' Lizzie told her. 'We'll enjoy making those decisions as well as happily working with you.'

'Aye, we will,' Enid agreed.

'I'm sure you're aware that some of these designs are quite complex and the length of thread involved in a machine could be quite long, going on for ever,' Evie said, as they began to investigate the looms. 'So take care what you initially decide and remember these machines will require cleaning at the end of each and every week. And any silk lace material you produce has to be thoroughly washed before we can put it up for sale.'

'Don't worry, Evie, we'll cope with all that's involved, once we've made up our minds what to produce. I'm very good at making hairnets,' Lizzie said with a chuckle. 'I reckon we'll start by making something small and simple, 'appen gloves and socks or mebbe a toy teddy bear. We'll then move on to more glamorous garments. Looking forward to that.'

Evie laughed. 'Sounds good. A wide variety of products would be an excellent idea. I love anything made of lace but living here in the north many people feel in desperate need of wearing warm jumpers. They also like looking smart and beautiful in whatever items of clothing they buy, so I reckon we should try to create and sell a fair selection. At first I'll be selling them at Campfield Market but as we increase our number of products I'll look into other places too.'

'Excellent idea. We'll look into that too if you like.'

They carried on chatting and testing out the looms for some time before finally Evie decided it was time to pack up and go home. Handing over keys to each of them, she walked away with a sense of achievement and satisfaction in her heart. The decisions and support of her friends were proving to be exceptionally reliable and good, giving her a new purpose in life. Surely a good thing considering her daughters and son were rapidly growing up and developing their own lives.

★ ★ ★

Joanne found it surprisingly agreeable to have Bernie living close by. Occasionally they would take a walk together but never went to the pictures, theatres or dancing. Nor did he ever invite her out for a date. He was kind and they enjoyed a little time together. Blocking the past out of her head she almost forgot how much of a friend he'd become to her. Then it oddly occurred to her how she would miss him, were he ever to become seriously involved with that girl, whoever she was. It was a question she suddenly felt the desire to ask as they strolled along the canal towpath. 'I see you're now happily settled here in Manchester. Have you found yourself a girlfriend?'

'I might have,' he said, sounding more provocative than she expected. 'What would you feel about that? Would it please you?'

She shrugged her shoulders, feeling a strange sense of dismay growing within her. Joanne remembered how she'd once longed to stroke the fluffy locks of his hair and felt her fingers itching as if they wished to do that now. Gone was the hesitant, foolish young girl she'd been during the war and in her place was one surely far more strong, sensible and confident of her own abilities. It was a good feeling but Joanne was astonished to find herself beginning to feel attracted to Bernie, even though he showed no interest in her at all. 'I've no idea. Not my business. Just asked what came into my head.'

'Are you teasing me?'

'No, of course not. Simply curious to know how you're settling here.' She tactfully made no mention of seeing him dancing with that pretty girl.

'Maybe I'm rather cautious of involving myself with anyone right now, having been let down by you in the past. I remember you accusing me of not loving you, and coldly informing me that you didn't care for me either when you cancelled our wedding. That hurt and I've no wish to repeat that anguish. I came here since I quite liked this city. Do you expect me to stick around and wait for ever for you to change your mind? Sorry, can't do that. It would be a complete waste of time. You made it very clear you would never be interested in me.'

Joanne flushed, feeling embarrassed and concerned by this dismissive remark while appreciating he was possibly making a valid point. She hadn't at all believed in his feelings for her, so why would they ever be attracted to each other? Had her emotion changed, or was she simply in a state of depression? Swallowing the hard lump that came into her throat, she said, 'I admit that back then I wasn't thinking clearly, far too obsessed with my alleged situation. When I discovered that wasn't a problem, I remember feeling deeply relieved but also embarrassed by the mess I'd made of my life and yours. Please don't bring that issue up ever again. Best to forget what happened and look at life afresh. And as you clearly explained, we'll never be anything but mere friends. A fact I must accept.'

'You're right, I'll never mention it again,' he agreed. 'Maybe I should return to Blackpool, where I've enjoyed a better life.' It was then that she saw him walk away, not at all what she'd wanted him to do.

Had she been entirely wrong to ask Bernie about his girlfriend, of whom he'd given no details? Joanne felt wracked with guilt for having offended him, let alone how dismissive she'd behaved towards him in the past, being totally wrapped up in herself. How young and foolish and a stupid dreamer she'd been to become obsessed with that GI who had only been interested in having sex with girls, there being a war on. She'd been devastated when Teddy had left, paying no attention to Bernie and considering him to be of no interest to her.

Now Joanne felt her life was in a state of confusion, not as engrossed with her occupation at this hotel as she'd originally been, feeling no interest at all in the young men who kept on asking her out for a date. Even Andy the chef had amazingly asked her out again, having broken his relationship with Shirley, a request she'd stoutly refused. It was Bernie she wished to go on a date with. The thought of him going back to live in Blackpool made Joanne feel a longing to return too. Working at Jubilee House had been much more fun and she'd love to be closer to her darling sister, as well as Bernie. Seeing him with that girl had filled her with a realization that she ached for his attention, feeling a longing to take her place in his arms. She could hardly resist this handsome young man who was proving to be most enticing. Her feelings for him had grown so much deeper, the thought of losing Bernie filled her with dread. Now that she realized she'd probably loved him for some time Joanne felt she'd ruined their relationship as he was no longer at all interested in her.

27

Summer 1947

Once Megan's school closed for the summer, Joanne had gone to collect her sister and bring her home to the flat to live with their mother and Danny, thanks to her agreement with this suggestion. She'd so enjoyed seeing quite a lot of her over the summer months and would happily continue to do so until the new term started in September, which would be upon them soon. What she would do after that was undecided.

This afternoon Mam planned to take them on the number two bus to visit Heaton Park, looking forward to a pleasant walk. There used to be Air Force trainees stationed there during the war. Now it was simply a beautiful park and Joanne was itching to see the lake, orangery and gardens, something she'd regularly enjoyed seeing in Stanley Park.

When they arrived, she was amazed to find her mother taking them to a section of Heaton Park filled with prefabs.

'I was offered one of these and do wonder if it would be worth trying,' she said, pointing out what they each possessed and expressing an admiration of their gardens, many of them well cared for and quite attractive.

'I thought you were happily settled in that flat, Mam?' Joanne said.

'It's fine for now but not really big enough for my family. I know you two girls are currently living elsewhere, I just hope that won't go on for ever.'

Catching a glimmer of alarm in her younger sister's eyes Joanne felt a degree of sympathy for both Megan and her mother. 'I admit that our lives are in a bit of a turmoil, but such is reality. I can't say I'm carried away with working at this hotel. It's large and well run but you don't generally find much opportunity to become friendly with the guests. They tend to come and go rather quickly being mainly businessmen rather than tourists staying for a week or more. Not certain how long I'll remain there or what I plan to do with my life in future.'

'Decisions are not easy to make in today's world, our lovely country being in debt and still battling to recover from the war, not to mention all the poor men involved in it,' her mother agreed, giving a sigh. 'And finding a home is not easy either.'

'These prefabs do look lovely and would surely suit you to live in one, Mam. Although I'm afraid they wouldn't work for me.'

'Nor me,' Megan said.

Taking hold of each of their hands, Evie gave them a little kiss. 'I love both you girls and you're quite right. I have to accept that you're pretty grown-up now and very much in charge of organizing your own lives. At least you are safe and survived the war by being evacuated, so why would I complain about how that has given you a strong sense of freedom? I'm not convinced

Danny intends to stay around here much longer either. He seems a bit restless or harassed at the moment for some reason.'

Joanne gave a troubled frown. 'Have you asked what's bothering him?'

Her mother shook her head. 'Daren't do that as I've no wish to upset him or sound as if I agree for him to return to the countryside he keeps speaking of.'

This time when Joanne met Megan's sharp glance she fell silent, something in her sister's expression warning her to say nothing more on this subject. Could that Willie Mullins be creating more problems for Danny?

They enjoyed a lovely walk around the boating lake, bowling green, temple and gardens. What a treat it was. They then took an afternoon tea and went on to the Gaumont Cinema to see James Stewart in *It's a Wonderful Life*. They came out happily smiling as it had proved to be such a fun day together. Joanne gave her mother a hug as they caught the bus to take them back to Castlefield, promising to see her soon. Then, hugging Megan, she found her sister whisper that she'd ask Danny what was worrying him. Giving a nod, Joanne softly responded, 'Do let me know what you find out, lovey.' Then she stood giving them a wave as the bus drove away.

★ ★ ★

Danny found the conversation Megan had with him not at all easy, then finally felt obliged to admit that Harold Mullins had threatened him with another charge of theft. She looked utterly shocked and cross. 'How dare he accuse you of that when it was clearly his son Willie who was involved in that crime, not you? What a dreadful man he is.'

'He is indeed. Nowt but a nightmare, as is his bossy son. Don't worry, I intend to have a word with Willie and ask his opinion on how to deal with this issue.'

'You'll be lucky to get anywhere with him either. Willie is an even worse person, as I know only too well. Do take care or he could hammer you again.'

'You could be right there, chuck. I will attempt to remain calm and make sure I protect myself. But I need to do what I can to stop the Mullinses harassing us.'

Willie gave a snort, a weird glimmer of satisfaction on his face when he heard Danny complain about the threats his father had made upon him. 'Doesn't surprise me in the least. Naturally he had no wish for me to be charged.'

The pair of them were sitting by the canal each nursing a bottle of beer that Willie had managed to buy from the Dog and Duck, appearing older than his eighteen years. Danny gave a scowl. 'Not surprised about that, him being very self-obsessed, a right pain in the ass. I feel flummoxed over how to deal with this problem, which I've been worrying about for some time and is now getting worse. He refused to believe a word I said when I explained I was innocent of that charge of theft, as you well know.'

'Not that I trust him as far as I could throw him either. Can't say we get on well but I felt the need to protect myself, so why would I not accept any charge against you too?'

'Because you'd no wish to be nicked?'

'Aye, I almost was nicked over that stupid shoplifting. If it happens again the police sergeant has warned me I'd be in danger of going down for three months or more.'

'Damaging our friendship over the years has done you no good at all, Willie.'

'I reckon you're right about that. It was 'appen not a sensible way of dealing with my problems. I do need to get a grip on life and stop being so madly depressed.'

Danny felt a little surprised by this comment, indicating a change in his attitude, very nearly an apology. 'Thankfully, on that occasion Mam supported me and won my freedom. Now he's threatening to inform my employer that I'm a thief and I will lose my job if I can't persuade Mam to go back working for him. Why would I do that when she too is sick of him and wishes to be free to work for herself?'

Willie gave an odd little frown. 'He is a nightmare. I know she resigned but he won't even grant me a bloody job, so not sure how to recommend what you could do to sort this problem out. He entirely controls his business as a bookie and spends most of his time out and about collecting the debts owed him. I daresay he gets fed up wi' doing all of that himself, never liking to be too busy but won't let go of his superiority. When he returns home he gulps down whatever food I've left keeping warm for him then goes off to the pub. He doesn't cook, clean, wash up or keep anything tidy, ordering me to do those jobs. Not that he's ever impressed by my effort, never satisfied with owt I do for him, so 'appen he fancies having your mam around to look after him instead.'

Danny was instantly filled with horror, realizing there was more to this problem than he'd at first thought. 'What a dreadful prospect. You're saying this barney is due to the fact he demands the need for a woman's care and attention, in particular my mam? That's shocking! What I'm asking is for you to warn your dad to leave her in peace. That's what she deserves, having lost her spouse, as he sadly lost his.'

Willie gave a snort. 'He felt no grief for the loss of my mum, so how could I tell him to do that? He's never interested in a word I say.'

'Right, so force him to listen to you about this problem and tell your dad that I'll skin him alive and roast him over a pit if he harasses me or my mam ever again.'

'Don't talk daft. I agree the way you keep tabs on your family is most impressive and fairly daunting but it pays to hold yer fire, Danny. Dad would find it quite pleasant to have an attractive woman like your mam take care of him in his old age. He definitely feels the need for one who panders to his every whim and whom he can have fun with.'

'Because he's a nasty piece of work. Just tell him to find himself another woman. Not my

310

mother.' And Danny stoutly walked away, having strongly made the point.

★ ★ ★

Bernie called again at the hotel one day and surprised her by inviting her to go out for a date with him. Hardly able to believe her good fortune, Joanne was thrilled and gladly agreed. Or was this invitation just a way of saying goodbye before he returned to Blackpool? Not an endearing prospect.

She chose to wear a low-necked green satin dress that Aunt Sadie had once made for her birthday and noticed how his pale pink lips curved upwards into an endearing smile when they met up. 'You look lovely.'

'Thank you,' she said, feeling a rosy flush colour her cheeks.

He took her to a smart restaurant on Albert Square, one that appeared rather grand and expensive. She carefully studied the menu, looking for something inexpensive but Bernie selected roast chicken and a glass of white wine each, followed by a chocolate sponge. Surely there was nothing wrong in savouring such a treat, considering how pleased she was to be with him. And perhaps he was happy to provide it because she'd accepted this date, or else this could just be a way of saying goodbye if he was about to head back to Blackpool. What a worry that was. As they sat eating this delicious meal they happily listened to a young man playing a piano and singing: 'A String of Pearls'; 'Happy

Days Are Here Again'; and 'All the Nice Girls
Love a Sailor'.

'Unfortunately I'm not a sailor,' Bernie said
with a chuckle.

Joanne laughed at that too. 'Just as well since
you weren't old enough to join up in the war.
Thank goodness for that.'

'I was a bit of an idiot in the Home Guard,
despite doing my best to work hard delivering
posters and letters as well as making a note of
things I saw happening. I even had a go at
keeping rabbits for the pot. Most of the chaps
were old, some friendly and pleased with my
efforts, while others were quite bossy towards me
and other youngsters.'

'That's something you have to accept when
you're young, but it was good of you to assist
them. The chefs and bosses at the hotel are at
times equally domineering and judgmental of
me, not accustomed to working in a restaurant
as posh as this one.' The chef, who'd pestered
her for another date and she'd steadfastly
declined, had not been at all friendly since,
generally most disparaging towards her. 'No
matter what their poor opinion of me when I
don't accept their invitation to go some place,
I'm determined to hold on to my rights, just as
Megan determinedly hangs on to hers, bless her.'

'She does indeed, being a determined little
madam,' he agreed, and they both laughed. 'I'm
sure your mother holds on to hers too.'

Bernie's gaze collided with hers, which felt
quite stirring. He was fun and very intoxicating,
the enticing warmth of his close friendship

running through her like fire. His sculpted mouth curled into an entrancing smile and she ached to taste it and stroke his soft cheeks. Instead, Joanne quickly moved on to say how her mother had been dispatched out of her home but had fortunately found herself a small flat. 'I do worry about the grief and work she's involving herself in and go to see her whenever I can.'

'I know the feeling,' he said. 'Your mother's a lovely lady, if she generally works far too hard.'

'She says that's the best way for her to keep sane. And, of course, wishes to support us, her children, which is surely a good cause even though only Danny lives with her now, we girls largely living elsewhere.'

'I appreciate that the fact you were evacuated must have created problems for your family relationship but at least you were spared the horrors of war as well as the trauma of being bombed here in Manchester. How old were you when this war started? You must have been quite young.'

'I certainly was, just eleven years old, but in charge of my siblings. Best not to go on about that.' Her childhood and wartime problems were not something Joanne had any wish to speak of, bearing in mind the mess she'd made of her life back in the past. 'You too were young and spared the horrors of war, but we're both now grown-up.'

'We are indeed.'

Once they'd finished the meal he walked her leisurely back to the hotel, not linking her arm, save for when they crossed the road. They were so irresistibly close that she felt the urge to reach up and kiss him, perhaps as an excuse to thank him for the generosity he'd once shown towards her. Definitely not an issue she should ever mention. She considered herself most fortunate to have received that generous offer Bernie had made to marry her, claiming to be her best friend and quite fond of her, willing to help maintain her reputation. And he was deeply offended when she'd cancelled his offer. Reminding herself she'd not believed herself to be in love with him back then, Joanne felt she really shouldn't object to his lack of interest in her now. It did feel slightly daunting though, her feelings for him having changed completely. Oh, and a part of her lived in hope that he would not announce he was about to leave.

'I suppose you'll be going off to Blackpool soon, to meet up with that girlfriend I saw you dancing with, cheek to cheek, at the Tower Ballroom.'

He stopped walking to look at her in surprise. 'Did you really? She's not my girlfriend. Never was. It was just how she fancied dancing with me. Why didn't you come over to say hello, then we could have had a dance too?'

'I didn't feel I had that right, having frequently pushed you away,' she softly told him, making no mention of how a part of her felt a strong desire for him. But finding his closeness irresistible, she twinkled her gaze provocatively up at him. 'Now I do love spending time with you.'

'That's good to hear.'

After giving her a smile, he kissed the tip of

314

her nose, which quite stunned her. Could that be a glimmer of affection on his face? Such a possibility brought excitement into her heart. Feeling her breathing quicken, Joanne tilted up her chin, arched her neck and enticingly slanted a teasing glance up at him. 'You are now an important part of my life, so can I please have another kiss?'

He pulled her close and kissed her with passion.

When he paused to take a breath, she softly murmured, 'Not certain what you feel about me, Bernie, but I reckon I do love you. A sensation that's been developing within me for some time. If you still don't care a jot for me, then feel free to walk away. If I end up in tears don't blame yourself, just accept that it was stupid of me from the start to be dismissive of our so-called friendship.'

'You're not stupid, darling, just beautiful and I love you too. Always have.' It was then that he again gathered her tightly in his arms and kissed her with even greater passion. 'I think we're very much a couple. Secretly always have been.'

Joanne's senses skittered with the thrill of his touch and this comment. What a joy that was, and how wonderful that she'd felt willing to take this risk, having no wish to contemplate life without him. 'Oh, I do hope we are,' she said, snuggling into his arms as he kissed her yet again.

'You are very much an important part of my life too, and always will be, darling.'

When they finally arrived back at the hotel,

Joanne was shocked to find her mother waiting for her, her face ashen. Running over to Joanne, she began to cry. 'To my horror, love, I've found that Megan has gone missing again. God knows why!'

28

'Where the hell do you reckon she's gone? Did she tell you?' Evie cried. 'I'm aware Megan is very independent, Joanne, so assume she could have returned to Blackpool, although why she didn't say she wanted to leave is a bit of a worry. Has she become fed up with me yet again?'

'I don't believe she would do that, Mam, but confess I'm equally concerned,' Joanne said, giving a puzzled frown. 'She didn't mention to me either that she wished to leave here. It's only a couple of weeks before her school opens in early September so if she feels the urge to go back and prepare for that, why didn't she say so? Most odd. Have you had a disagreement with her about something?'

'Not that I'm aware of, although there are times she says very little, being very wrapped up in herself. Although nothing like as silent as she used to be. I thought we were growing quite close.'

'Of course you are. She's most fond of you now. When did you realize she'd gone?'

'At suppertime. She visited the library this afternoon for another book, but didn't return in time for supper. Concerned that she was late I went over to find her and fetch her home, assuming she'd got caught up in reading and forgotten the time. To my horror I found the library was closed and she was nowhere around.

317

She couldn't be locked up in there, could she?'

'Oh, my goodness, I suppose that's a possibility, if they didn't notice her stuck in some corner reading. Although I agree she might have taken the whim to return to Blackpool.' Giving her mother a hug, Joanne promised to catch a train first thing in the morning to check that's where she was and why.

Bernie gently patted her shoulder. 'No need to do that. I fortunately fitted my aunt's boarding house with a telephone before I left. It took a bit of an argy-bargy to persuade them to allow me to do that but I pointed out that not only could I then regularly keep in touch by ringing them, it would help them to receive more residents. So it's fixed.'

'Oh, that's wonderful. Well done!'

'Come on, let's find a telephone box and give them a ring.'

To her dismay Joanne discovered that Megan had not yet arrived. She tactfully pointed out that her sister was very likely on her way. Aunt Annie was greatly surprised to hear that Megan would soon be returning, not having told them. 'Night is almost upon us so a train may not be available. She could be stuck on some platform or other. I promise to keep a watch out for her and suggest you ring again first thing in the morning, or later tonight if you like,' Annie said, which they readily agreed to do.

Joanne and Bernie then hurried over to Victoria Station, searching the platforms and waiting rooms but sadly found no sign of her. 'You do sometimes have to change trains, so she could be stuck at another station, Wigan, Preston or wherever as Aunt Annie suggested. She could have fallen asleep and got lost some place. I'll hang around here and catch the first train I can to check out those possible stations and various platforms. Don't worry, I'm sure we'll find her,' Bernie said, giving Joanne a comforting hug. 'I'll ring you at the hotel when I do.'

'Thank you so much. I'll keep looking for her here, and check the library.'

Not having received a much-needed call from him, the next morning Joanne rang Aunt Annie again. She was greatly disturbed to hear Megan still hadn't arrived, the two landladies' response increasingly concerned. Joanne explained how they were still desperately looking for her and that Bernie was checking various stations and might arrive soon. Promising to ring again, she handed over the hotel number in case they received any news.

Joanne then rushed to the flat, finding her mother restlessly walking round and round in an obvious state of anguish and looking utterly exhausted, as was she too, having suffered a mainly sleepless night. 'So far we've failed to find Megan anywhere,' she sadly informed her, going on to explain how and where they'd searched and the response from the dear landladies.

'Then I'll go off to the library to see if she was indeed so busy reading in a corner that she found herself locked in,' Evie said, pulling on her coat.

'Good idea. I'll investigate the various parks where she loved to play games, in case she had

319

an accident there, and I'll again ring the aunts.'

'You search for her too, Danny,' Evie called as she dashed off.

Turning to Joanne, Danny said, 'Actually, I'll go and speak to Willie. The last time I spoke to him was when I tried to get his help to stop his father from insisting that Mam continue working for him. He said the reason was probably because he felt in sore need of freely employing a woman to do domestic jobs in the house, provide him with good food and take care of him. Since Mam obviously refused that, mebbe his father is attempting to persuade Megan to work for him instead.'

'What a terrifying thought,' Joanne said. 'Are you suggesting that Mam and I should tackle Harold Mullins and see if that's what he's up to?'

'No, don't you do that. Mam has gone off to the library, which might be the solution. You can check if those landladies have any news yet, as well as visit those parks for the reason you mentioned. I'll speak to Willie again to see what he knows and ask for his help. Then we'll decide what to do next.'

Sharing a nod of agreement and a deeply anxious gaze, they each set off in search of Megan.

★ ★ ★

'What would I know?' Willie tartly remarked. 'As I said, I don't get on well with my father. He largely ignores me, just treating me like a servant

320

to do all the chores Mum used to do.'

'Has he taken our Megan to mek her do such work? That's what's worrying me,' Danny snapped.

Willie shook his head. 'I haven't seen her around, although I do understand why you're anxious about that possibility. I'm sorry to hear that she's missing, being a pretty little girl.'

'You're almost as bad as him, 'appen worse, considering what you did to my young sister. It's time to grow up and get over such nonsense and the nasty things you did.'

'Stop accusing me of such rubbish,' he roared. 'I do regret what I jokingly did when I saw her by the canal that day, probably as a result of the mess my family was in during the war. My mum having been tragically killed did leave me in a state of mental anguish.'

Knowing he'd heard his mother tell him this, Danny couldn't really see why Willie was mentioning it right now, but felt he must be a little sympathetic. 'I'm sorry to hear that. I assume she was bombed wherever she lived or worked?'

'No, she wasn't. She drowned when the barge we used to live in crashed into a bridge. Dad was always quite mocking and would tell me off whenever I showed a gloomy response over the loss of my lovely mum, claiming I should put her out of my mind and concentrate on the future. He doesn't miss her, as I told you, the pair of them never having got on terribly well. Absolutely wrong in my humble opinion. How can I ever get over losing her? As a consequence, I do suffer the odd nightmare and have had some depression and psycho problems.'

Danny felt slightly surprised by all that he'd just heard and the anguish still glittering in this lad's eyes. 'I can understand that. You've sadly done loads of stupid mad things over the years, to me as well as to my younger sister.'

An echo of guilt flickered in his eyes. 'I know, that's partly because I've allus felt a bit jealous of you and your family, being much closer than mine. Sorry about that. But as I said when we had that previous conversation, I'm not as guilty as my dad.'

'According to my mother he was a difficult man to work for, mainly because he's involved in betting, which is illegal, and allus horrible to her when she didn't deliver sufficient of the money owed him. Not at all as bad as your nasty tricks. I've certainly been told of what you did to my younger sister back in Keswick when she was just a young lass.'

'What the bleedin' hell are you talking about?' Willie snarled. 'You and I did have problems back then and I admit to being responsible for that thieving of fruit and veg, still being in a savage mess because of the tragedy I'd suffered and not wishing to be nicked. But I never saw or touched Megan back then, not as I stupidly did by way of a joke when I saw her by the canal, and do apologize for that.'

'Oh aye, and you did touch her by the lake in Keswick, grabbed her bum then displayed a part of yourself.'

Willie fell into a stunned silence for some minutes, then sternly remarked, 'I never did.

322

That could have been my dad. He came to visit me on the odd occasion when I was living there.'

'*What?*' Danny stared at him aghast. 'Are you suggesting your father is a pervert, not you?'

'I am. Like I say, I've never done owt as bad as he does. I did once suspect he fancied your sister Joanne, so I followed her on occasions to check she was safe.'

'I never knew that. We allus assumed *you* were the problem. Why would it be him?'

'Because he's an idiot and, as you've pointed out, something of a pervert. I did see him once attempt to fondle your mother when he was talking to her in the Dog and Duck about that shoplifting you were charged with. I was sneaking a look through the window, reckoning I might be charged too but fortunately wasn't. He obviously fancied her.'

'Good Lord, what a nightmare if what you've said about his attack on Megan in the past is true. So if he has taken control of my sister again, she could be in serious danger. Where the hell do you reckon she might be?'

'Not sure I can answer that. I could take you to have a look in our house, just in case she's there, then I'll mebbe come up with other possibilities. We could give it a go. I certainly feel willing to be your mate and help.'

Danny met his open-eyed gaze with an element of surprise in his own, then seeing Willie put out his hand he readily shook it. 'Right, I'm desperate to find her so show me whatever you can and I'll see if I can start to trust you.'

Evie found no sign of Megan in the library. Speaking to the librarian she was told that they did know her quite well since she frequently came to read there, but hadn't seen her for some days. Evie desperately explained how her daughter had supposedly set off to come to the library then gone missing. 'If she wasn't here then she may have returned to Blackpool, where she'd once been evacuated.' Feeling the need to express her fears she went on to say how she dreaded the prospect that Harold Mullins, her former employer, might have kidnapped her daughter as a punishment for abandoning her job. 'Sorry, to bother you with all of this, but that's what I must go and investigate.'

'Ah, I can see that's a possibility since he's a difficult man who tragically lost his wife. I have details of her death, were you interested to read it,' the librarian said. And going over to a section of the bookshelves containing old newspapers, handed her one. Evie read what she showed her in stunned dismay, remembering her dear friend Jane, then she slammed it shut, thanked this kind lady and dashed off.

'Have you found her?' Evie yelled when she bounced into the flat finding Joanne waiting impatiently for her.

Her daughter shook her head. 'I've looked everywhere but found no sign, and again rang the landladies and spoke to Aunt Sadie this time. She said Aunt Annie is out searching for her too.'

'Oh, my goodness, what a mess she could be

in. Would you believe what I've just learned from the librarian?' As she started to speak of what she'd been shown in that old newspaper, the door opened and Danny and Willie came dashing in. She quickly stopped talking to run over with an appeal in her eyes for good news, only to find Danny sadly shake his head.

'We've searched Mullins's house, thanks to Willie here, and found no sign of her. I take it you two haven't either, so where do we look next?'

'Heaven help us, I've no idea,' Joanne said, filled with despair.

'Hasn't Bernie gone looking for her too? Have you heard from him?'

Joanne shook her head. 'Not yet, he's probably busy checking Wigan and Preston.'

'So why hasn't he rung you? Could it be that he's run off with her?'

'*What?*' This suggestion filled Joanne with alarm. Bernie and Megan were good friends and her sister was quite fond of him. But bearing in mind how he treated her like a young sister, and how close he'd come to herself yesterday evening, why would she consider such a possibility? It was a sensation she instantly banished from her mind. 'Don't talk nonsense. He would never do that. Bernie fully respects her and fears Megan may have fallen asleep and missed getting off the train at the right place. He is busily searching for her at various stations.'

'Let's hope you're right but what if you don't hear from him soon? How can you prove he's not the guilty one?'

'Because he's a kind and caring friend.' Joanne felt most grateful when her mother put her arm about her and assured her son that she believed Bernie to be a most pleasant young man who would never do such a dreadful thing. It was then that she heard Willie give a little cough. Looking into his pale face she was shocked by the guilt she saw enveloping it.

'Are you the one who ran off with her?' Evie asked.

Taking a deep breath, he gave a firm shake of his head. 'No, I'm as innocent as hopefully that Bernie fellow is. But feel there's more I should tell you, Mrs Talbert. I heard what you started to say about my mum when we walked in. I should perhaps inform you that I saw her drown. She'd been having a row with Dad about a woman he'd been having an affair with. In fury, he knocked her off our barge. She fell backwards into the canal and when she screamed, not being much of a swimmer, he made no attempt to save her, just spun the steering wheel round and smashed the boat into her.'

'Oh, my God, what a dreadful story.'

'And now I'm thinking that with my father's liking for women and young girls, and the fact that he is no doubt the one who assaulted Megan back in the past, it could mean he has taken her away some place.'

'The prospect of her being assaulted by Mullins, as I was, is too dreadful to contemplate,' Evie said, looking frozen in horror. 'Or could she too be killed as she would never allow him to assault her?'

'Heaven help her, where could she be? We must find her.'

'As he still owns a barge, that's where she could be,' Willie said. 'Come on, I'll take you there now.'

The expression on her mother's face showed her desperate wish to believe that Willie was entirely wrong and Megan would come home soon or else had safely arrived in Blackpool. Joanne leaped to her feet, eager to join Danny and Willie in this search. Insisting her mother stayed home in case Megan did turn up, she instructed her to call the police if they were not back soon. Then the three of them hurried off in search of her beloved sister.

29

Joanne couldn't help thinking what a worrying suggestion Danny had made implying Megan might have run off with Bernie some place. Why would he do that and surely she could trust him? Whether she could trust this young lad, Willie, was very much open to question. Could he be the guilty party or was his accusation of his father absolutely correct? What a terrifying horror to think Harold Mullins might have kidnapped and assaulted her. Was that possible and where on earth could Megan be? What a nightmare this was. Whatever she'd suffered from Teddy, that GI, was nothing by comparison to what her dear sister could be facing now.

They ran between smoke-blackened warehouses and tumbledown sheds, stepping over the criss-crossed railway lines that linked the various wharfs. Fog from the canal rolled around the lamplights as they hurried along the street. The darkness of the alleyways around the canal basin filled Joanne with nervousness and she found herself taking in gulps of cool evening air, but the sour stink of the canal did her no good at all. She was also alarmed to hear the squeaking of rats as they scuttled under the bridge, and to see sections of the black swirling canal water glinting in the light from a pale moon. The possibility Megan might be dumped in the canal, as that man's wife had been, was too terrifying to contemplate.

'Here it is,' Willie said, reaching a barge hooked up to the towpath. 'I'll go in first, and you follow me when I give you a shout.'

It was a long narrow boat, painted green at the prow, a row of four windows down each side and the stern with a steering wheel at the back, the roof trimmed with blue. Joanne itched to go in with him but hid with Danny beneath a nearby tree quite close to the barge, carefully listening for him to call. They waited for some long moments, hearing nothing.

'What if Willie's been lying to us and it's him who's locked Megan up and is now going to hurt her?' Joanne eventually whispered.

Danny glanced at her in dismay. 'Lord, I hadn't thought of that. I've never trusted him either so why would I do that now? Come on, let's go.'

'Quietly, right?' Joanne said.

They crept over and climbed onto the prow. Leaning close to the door, they attempted to listen to whatever was going on inside. She could hear some harsh mumbling, sounding as if Willie was engaged in a row with his father, but couldn't quite get a grip on what was being said. 'I haven't heard him call out for us, have you? Can you hear what they're saying?' she whispered to Danny.

'I heard his father say, 'don't you boss me, lad, I'll do what I wish.' The thing is, how can we trust either of them?' They heard a loud bang and glanced at each other in shock. The conversation went silent after that, save for a weird sound of scraping and clattering.

'There could be a problem so we're going in now,' Joanne snapped and, pushing open the door, stepped into the cabin.

She saw Willie lying on the floor, looking unconscious, Harold Mullins apparently in the process of dragging him through the far door. Looking up, he stared at them in shock. 'What the bleedin' hell are you doing here?'

'We're searching for my missing sister,' Joanne firmly stated. 'Do you know where she is? Willie did suggest we should call here to search for her.'

'And what have you done to your son?' Danny asked.

'He fell, so that's his fault. And why would I know where your sister is? Nowt to do wi' me.'

'Oh, I think it is,' Joanne sternly remarked. 'Willie suggested you might have kidnapped her as a punishment for my mother's refusal to keep on working for you. Why would she wish to do that when you're an absolute bastard, constantly harassing and threatening her with assault? If that's the case, hand her over right now. If we don't take her home soon, Mam will call the police.'

He snorted. 'She'd never have the courage to do that.'

It was then they heard a loud whistling out on the towpath.

'Ah, I reckon they might have arrived already. Well done, Mam,' Danny said.

Turning on his heel, Mullins shoved him aside and dashed out of the door. Seconds later they saw him charging off along the towpath being pursued by the police. Having fortunately come round, Willie struggled to his feet, looking a bit dazed, then took them along to a tiny cabin at the far end of the barge. 'I saw Dad heading for this cabin when I arrived and I challenged him, asking if this was where Megan was locked up. We had a row then he yanked me away, gave me a thump and knocked me over. I felt a tumult of fear that he might chuck me in the canal, as he had done with my mum, and was so glad to see you two arrive.'

'How do we get in that cabin if it's locked?' Danny quickly asked.

'I know where the keys are kept,' Willie said and rushing to a board grabbed the necessary.

Unlocking the cabin door, they found Megan tied up with rope and a scarf stuffed in her mouth, looking entirely unconscious. Danny swiftly unfastened her and Joanne gathered her close in her arms to gently wake her. Seeing her sister's pale blue eyes flood with tears when she saw them, Joanne gave her a soft kiss. 'Don't cry, lovey, you're quite safe now.'

A policewoman came hurrying in with two ambulance men and Megan was lifted onto a stretcher and taken to hospital, Joanne and Danny accompanying her. Willie too was taken with them, having been hit over the head. What a relief Joanne now felt in her heart, although still an anxiety that Megan could have been harmed by that dreadful man.

★ ★ ★

It was the following morning, having recovered and come round, that Megan revealed to this kind policewoman how Harold Mullins had grabbed her when he saw her walking to the library the previous afternoon. 'He told me that my mother had fallen ill and he must take me to her, so I got into his car, believing what he said. Instead of taking me home or to a hospital where I assumed she'd be, he took me down to the Rochdale Canal and shoved me into that barge. I was terrified. It came to me then that it was not Willie who'd attacked me back in the war but his father, something I hadn't been aware of.'

Evie held her daughter close, riveted with fear. 'Joanne did recently explain to me what you'd suffered, even though she'd no conviction of who it might have been. What has Mullins done to you now, love? I hope nothing too dreadful.'

'Probably because I was screaming, kicking and fighting him like mad, doing everything I could to keep him off me, he became irritated and tied me to that bed, ordering me to calm down. He said that he'd be back to see me later in the day, as I was a pretty girl he adored and would bring me some food. I felt sick and lay weeping for hours, dreading he would again attempt to assault me. By the time he returned towards evening I was starving hungry, had wet the bed and was in a dreadful state. He untied me, gave me a dish of soup and pushed his thing out at me, as he had done all those years ago. This time, instead of falling on my knees I threw the soup back at him and kicked him, which made him scream. Then he smacked my face hard and tied me up again as I passed out. Am I safe or did he indeed assault me?'

'I've spoken to the doctor who has thankfully assured me that you were not raped,' Joanne said, giving her a smile. 'Listening to what you did to Mullins, he's probably in a sorry state himself, after you kicked him. Good for you. You did the right thing to protect yourself. He then found his son had arrived to challenge him. Thanks to Willie, who guessed where you might be, we were able to rescue you, lovey,' Joanne said.

'And I called the police the moment they left,' Evie said, giving a grin. 'In spite of the terror you've been through, darling girl, you are now safe. What a dreadful man Mullins is.'

'We are aware of that,' the policewoman agreed, telling them that Mullins had been arrested and charged with the murder of his wife as well as this kidnap and attempted assault, as a result of what they'd heard from his son, Willie.

It was then that a freezing cold reverberated through Evie as a terrible thought entered her head. 'Did Harold Mullins by any chance also kill my husband? I found it hard to understand why Donald would commit suicide when he was recovering well and clearly still adored me and his entire family, in spite of the mental issues he'd suffered as an ex-PoW. So what if he didn't?'

This was a shock now shared by the policewoman. Carefully listening to Evie's story, she gave a promise to fully investigate this possibility too and went off to speak to her colleagues. Some time later they were informed that Harold Mullins had been charged with that too.

★ ★ ★

Bernie arrived at the family's flat late that afternoon, Joanne having rung the landladies to inform them Megan had been found. He was delighted to see she was safe and well and gave her and Joanne a hug. He then listened in dismay to what she'd gone through and how Willie had fortunately helped them to discover where she'd been hidden.

Giving Bernie a sly grin, Danny said, 'Actually, we did wonder whether you'd been the one to run off with her, since you'd disappeared.'

'*What*? I was searching for her too, spent hours getting on and off trains to explore various stations and platforms. Feeling very much in despair and getting nowhere, I went back to Jubilee House and found my aunts were also looking to see if she was with any of her friends or hiding in the school. I too helped search various parts of Blackpool. What a nightmare it was.'

'So why didn't you ring me?' Joanne asked quietly.

'I did, love. I rang the hotel a couple of times, although not early yesterday morning when I was stuck on a train. They told me you weren't there but they'd give you a message when you returned.'

'Oh dear, I only popped back once to see if you'd rung, being fully engaged in searching for her too, but no one told me that you had. Maybe the person who took your call just put a note in my room and I was so preoccupied I didn't think to go up there. Sorry about that. I did ring Aunt Annie at one point and she told me where she believed you were. Nor did I have time to return again to the hotel once we headed for that barge.'

'I would never hurt Megan, Danny. I've always looked upon her as a little sister, having known her since she was quite young.'

'Don't fret about that, he was just in a bit of a mix-up trying to decide where she was and I stoutly defended you,' Joanne told him, giving him a kiss on his cheek, her adoring gaze riveted upon him.

'Aye, I don't reckon I was too serious about making that charge,' Danny said. 'Just feeling in a panic. I apologize. I've been accused of wrong things too. Harold Mullins, on the other hand, has escaped being charged for years over the horrors and deaths he's been responsible for. He ruined his wife and son's life and now Mam's and ours. What a piece of muck he is.'

Walking her back to the hotel, Bernie kept his arm around Joanne's shoulders and she tucked hers around his waist. As they reached a quiet part by St John's churchyard on Byrom Street, he pulled her closer, stroking his hands over her hair, cheeks and neck. Joanne's senses skittered at the thrill of his touch.

When he slid down on one knee, a smile tugging at his lips, he said, 'Will you please marry me in this lovely church. I do love you, darling.'

Joanne gave a little gasp of excitement. 'Oh, yes please. I love you too.' Locked in more kisses she felt a lighting of passion within her that felt utterly intoxicating. They were indeed a couple in love.

Epilogue

Evie was in a state of joy. It was 1953, the year of the coronation for Elizabeth II. It would be such a delight to see this young Queen crowned and her entire family was coming to meet up for a wonderful get-together and celebration. It would be even more fun than the VE Day at the end of the war when she'd felt desperate for news of her daughters. What a nightmare she'd gone through during and after the war, feeling she'd lost her beloved children. Once having finally found them again she'd struggled to cope with their problems. Her younger daughter in particular had not been easy, very silent and dismissive with little memory of her mother and father, not at first caring a jot about them. It had taken a while before her elder daughter had been prepared to reveal her own problems, as well as her sister's. Such was the reality of being an evacuee in those days.

Now, life had improved enormously. Edmund Hillary and Tenzing Norgay had reached the summit of Everest, the world's highest mountain on 29 May. How wonderful for them to be the first to achieve that. Lancashire was in a much better state and, according to Megan, two local football teams had taken part in the FA Cup Final at Wembley, Blackpool having beaten Bolton, a match her young daughter had naturally gone to watch. As Evie happily cut up loaves of bread and made sandwiches in preparation for this event, her mind played over the improvements that had entered all of their lives.

Joanne had married Bernie early in 1948 at St John's Church in Castlefield and all the family had attended, including those lovely landladies. His Aunt Annie and Aunt Sadie had then chosen to retire, moving out to live in Lytham St Annes. Bernie, her new son-in-law, assisted by his wife Joanne, had taken over Jubilee House in Blackpool, which they brilliantly ran. Evie loved visiting them to stay for a couple of weeks each summer and the odd few days every now and then throughout the year. Now they had three children: four-year-old twin girls, Ellie and Marigold, and a two-year-old little boy named Donald. These treasures were very close to their parents, uncle, cousins and aunts, and in particular to herself as their grandmother. Evie often had them come to stay with her. What a thrill that was.

Megan had continued to live at Jubilee House with Joanne during term-time, joining Evie for every school holiday, which had been a real joy. What fun they'd had together over recent years, visiting places such as Belle Vue as well as their favourite cinemas and theatres, not least various sports, which of course Megan had always taken quite a shine to. Now aged nineteen, Megan was attending Edge Hill college in Ormskirk, working hard and planning to become a teacher.

As for Danny, when he was eighteen, in 1949, he became attracted to the daughter of a local farmer whom he apparently met running a vegetable stall on Campfield Market. The following year they'd become engaged, planning to marry when he turned twenty-one. He was offered a job by her father on the farm in the countryside out on the Pennines not too far from Castlefield, which he loved as he did his fiancée. They were now happily married and had a baby son.

Her niece Cathie now had a daughter of her own; in addition to the lovely adopted Heather she'd taken into her heart, being her mum ever since her sister had died. Her friend Brenda, who lived close to Danny, was also enjoying life having resolved her own problems. What a joy they were too. And what a relief that they'd all finally recovered from the effects of that blasted war.

Poor Willie had taken some time to satisfactorily dispose of his own issues but finally sorted himself and his life out. He closed his father's business, ignoring the debts still owed, and found himself a job in the local rubber factory. Recently he seemed to be settling into a good relationship with a young girl, obviously hoping she would ultimately agree to marry him.

As far as she herself was concerned, Evie thought her life too was in a much better state. As she continued to set out the food she'd prepared, including beef sausages, meat pies and cakes, she gazed around with satisfaction at this delightful small kitchen. She'd thankfully moved out of the flat shortly after Joanne's wedding and happily settled in this lovely prefab with a pretty garden in Heaton Park. She was still fully engaged with lacemaking, by hand as well as working on those looms with her friends in the rented outbuilding by the mill. They were all now earning a good income. And Davie helped by selling products to various shops in addition to assisting her at her stall on Campfield Market.

Losing her husband had been the worst disaster she'd had to deal with. Mullins had finally confessed to killing Donald, wanting rid of him so that he could take control of Evie. How hard she'd had to battle with him to make sure he didn't succeed with that. Eventually she'd forced herself to come to terms with Donald's death, even though she would forever keep him in her heart. And she did have a good friend, Davie, who'd helped her so many times in the past with simple tasks as well as now with her job. Over time he'd started to devote more attention to her, and their relationship had become more interesting and far closer, very much an important part of her life. One of these days they might even decide to marry. He had asked her and Evie was seriously considering this prospect. Right now he was readily arranging chairs in the living room in preparation for this event. What a wonderful family she now had.

Today when they arrived she gave them all a hug and happily cuddled her grandchildren. They were all looking so well dressed, Joanne gorgeous in a pale lemon taffeta dress with a neat bow at the front of her narrow waistline. Megan was wearing a white circular skirt coated with blue flowers; one that Evie herself had made for her. Even all the young men were smartly attired, Davie in particular. It was, of course, a most special day.

They all settled on the chairs in front of the small black-and-white TV to watch the coronation, save for her grandchildren who played around, giggling and rolling about on the rug. It went on for quite a few hours so when it was largely over they went out to enjoy a party, carefully carrying the food she'd prepared.

The street was lined with rows of tables and chairs, packed with their neighbours all engaged in fun and laughter, children running around having a great time. After carrying out their chairs and settling at their table, they happily tucked into the delicious ham sandwiches, salad, meat pies, sausage rolls and cakes she'd made, as well as pots of tea for the ladies and bottles of beer for the young men. Nearby they could see a bonfire roasting hot potatoes and there was even treacle toffee available for the children. Looking around to meet the sparkling glow in the eyes of her darling daughters and son, it came to Evie that her beloved family felt deeply thankful that they'd rediscovered all they'd lost with regard to their relationship during the war. Thanks to the love and support they'd given each other since, they'd finally managed to dismiss all the pain they'd suffered. Peace was at last here to stay and in Evie's heart.

We do hope that you have enjoyed reading this large print book.

Did you know that all of our titles are available for purchase?

We publish a wide range of high quality large print books including:
Romances, Mysteries, Classics
General Fiction
Non Fiction and Westerns

Special interest titles available in large print are:
The Little Oxford Dictionary
Music Book
Song Book
Hymn Book
Service Book

Also available from us courtesy of Oxford University Press:
Young Readers' Dictionary
(large print edition)
Young Readers' Thesaurus
(large print edition)

For further information or a free brochure, please contact us at:
Ulverscroft Large Print Books Ltd.,
The Green, Bradgate Road, Anstey,
Leicester, LE7 7FU, England.
Tel: (00 44) 0116 236 4325
Fax: (00 44) 0116 234 0205

Other titles published by Ulverscroft:

ALWAYS IN MY HEART

Freda Lightfoot

After being held in a camp during the war, Brenda Stuart returns to her late husband's stately home in the Pennines, to be reunited with her young son. A factory-worker's daughter from Manchester, Brenda doesn't belong in such wealthy surroundings — which her father-in-law never lets her forget. Her baby boy is nowhere to be seen. Brenda's only ally is Prue, her beloved sister-in-law who has problems of her own. She has fallen in love with an Italian POW who works on the family estate. Pulling together to work on the land, the two friends try to find happiness, love and Brenda's long lost son.